Breaking Cover

Breaking Cover

F A J J Manasek

First edition
First printing

Other books by author:

Uncommon Value (1995)
Under Cover (1997)
Collecting Old Maps (1998)
Study, Measure, Experiment (with D. Pantalony and R Kremer, 2006)

FOREWARD

Pages vécues? Any intelligent reader may well pose this question. However, the reader should be aware also that it has intentionally been made impossible, for obvious reasons, to reconstruct actual events solely from the dramatization in this book. It would have been irresponsible folly on my part to make the actors more vulnerable than they are already. The events written about are known to but a very few who will no doubt remember and could attest to the overall veracity. To the rest of the readers: take the tales in this book at face value. Then as now, good and evil, kindness and killing, are all embedded in the same matrix and cannot be dissected. They are all shaped by the circumstances of time and place and they often morph back and forth, flitting between sun and shade until they become indistinguishable.

To those of us who remember many parts of the world as they were in that golden age before Eurofication or Americanization this book may bring back memories. If so, let them be memories fond because never again will that world return. I fear had I not transmuted the essences of that world into words they might have been forever lost, and the ghosts from the past that intrude into the now would have been exorcised by the rites of time and the loves, joys, pains, and pleasures recounted here would have dissolved into the miasma of clouded cornea and failing cortex.

Let us bask in the warm recollection of times past and of youth and beauty, of loves and losses, of high adventure and of comrades true and comrades lost. Perhaps it is possible to reach back in time and lift for even a moment some wilt from the fading bloom of youth. Age's ague would ease in awe.

Pristinae virtutis memores

Dial House
Norwich, Vermont
2012

Chapter 1

Friendly sport

Staring intently at a thicket, Blaser, my German Shorthaired Pointer, stood motionless letting us know there was a bird amongst the grass and weeds. I walked slowly toward him, shotgun held low. The cock pheasant exploded from the weeds in a frantic flight away from us. In one unbroken motion I raised my gun, took off the safety, pointed and fired the right barrel. The bird fell and Blaser had the exquisite pleasure of fetching the rooster.

"Nice shot." Red had held his fire since the bird was flying toward my right.

"Thanks." I took the bird from Blaser, gave its neck a good-luck twist and put him into my bag. Red, Blaser, and I continued our slow march down the warm, sunlit Vermont field that sported a mixed crop of corn, sorghum and grass. Great pheasant habitat.

"Word is," said Red, "you're retired."

"Sort of, Red. I'm getting a bit creaky and I rather like chasing birds a bit better than people. Our old group is scattered and I rarely even hear from Lo Ban."

"Any chance we can talk about a job?"

"Oh, sure, why not. I figured something was up when you leave Paris and come all the way to Vermont for just one day's shooting."

Blaser had just gotten a bit birdy again and we stopped talking and concentrated on game. Blaser hadn't gotten on point when a pair of pheasant flushed hard to the left. Red raised his shotgun and in his usual elegant form took both of them —a fine right-left. Both were forty-yard shots and both were clean kills.

"Nice."

"Thanks."

"Well, you might count Paris, but I have been in the States for a week or so. Nice to be back on my farm again." Red's tidy gentleman's farm in Virginia serves as his home when he's in the United States. He even has a nicely¬ maintained grass runway for his airplane.

We were tiptoeing around an issue; that much was clear but the issue itself was not.

"Red, what's this all about? We've worked with each other many times and you wouldn't come this far and then only talk with me in the middle of a Vermont field where the pheasants are doing their best to hide from us. We've shot together many times, Red, and this will look pretty ordinary. Just two friends working a field. But I smelled something big and now I'm convinced."

"Yep. I wanted the shoot for cover. We've done this so many times that it will indeed look pretty ordinary—if anyone's looking."

"Frank, we're getting hammered. Slowly. Two more of my guys were taken out in the past few months. This has been going on for a few years but has gotten worse recently. Everybody's losing people. We can't figure it."

"It's gotta be bad if you're coming here and telling me this. Is it onesies and twosies? Absolutely certain they're all hits or is there something else that can explain it?"

"Absolutely nothing else. At first we thought it was a run of bad luck—an auto accident, salmonella, a hunting accident." Red looked at me carefully. "Even a skydiving accident. But it adds up—there's a creeping erosion and it's demoralizing everyone."

"Big players doing it?"

"Nope. We're convinced it isn't any of the Big Boys. They noticed what's going on and realize full well that pretty soon we're going to have to do something and that means 'doing something' to known agents and the serious governments don't want us to do that. We will do something just because we have to do something. Nobody wins an open war between the coverts. No, we're convinced there's a new game being played and we haven't a clue what it is." Red stopped walking. Even Blaser stopped and looked up at us. "This is goddamn serious and I'm asking you if you'll help."

I whistled to Blaser and we three started working the field again. We didn't say much. We both enjoyed seeing Blaser work the cover.

"Blaser's doing a good job." Red was impressed.

"Thanks. He loves doing this. Say, speaking of dogs, a friend of mine did something funny—he got a new dog and named her 'Taxi'. Sounds very weird when he's in the middle of a cornfield yelling 'Taxi'!"

Red laughed, missing a crossing shot. The left barrel of my Arrizabalaga barked and the bird fell. That was the last bird of the day. The wind picked up a bit and the temperature dropped and we decided to call it quits.

Blaser was tired when we got back to my van and was willing to settle down in his crate and go to sleep. I piled our pheasants next to the crate and slid shut the van's side door. Red and I talked, leaning against the rear of the van in the weakening rays of the late-day sun.

"Red, I haven't any idea about this. Offhand, and I assume you want my gut response, I know absolutely nothing. Haven't heard a thing. But I've been pretty much retired for long enough to lose touch and I no longer get gratuitous signals from the jungle telegraph. There's not even a whisper about this that I can pass on to you. Nada."

"I know, Frank. I wasn't seriously expecting an 'aha!' moment. I was just hoping you would be able to consider taking on some low-level listening. 'Running in background' to use a computer phrase. If you think you might I can fill you in some more. You and your group were always known for the quality of your ears."

"Red, I wish I could just say that I'll spring for it but I can't take on anything alone anymore and have no idea whether or not the Old Group might want to get active again."

The sun was lower and the wind a bit colder.

"I hope I've not disappointed you."

"Let's start driving back and we can talk."

Blaser was still asleep when Red and I got into the van. I started the engine and we drove slowly down the rutted road toward the paved Vermont state highway heading east.

Crossing the Green Mountains is not easy. There are no super-highways or interstates or toll roads. It's all two-lane narrow winding roads with speed limits that range from 50 mph to 25 mph and the changes are sudden. Speed-crazed Massachusetts drivers are interdigitated between hay wagons and huge trailers loaded with logs. All this produces some interesting driving. Interesting but not fast.

I slowed down as we entered Hamish, a small hamlet with a decaying once-white church, some empty stores, a gas station, and a second-hand furniture store. There was also a post office, already closed for the day, and a general store still open. Next to it was a small diner.

"Let's stop—I'm tired, hungry, and still cold. Coffee might be good."

Red agreed and I nosed into the parking lot in front of the diner. A beaten–up red pickup with firewood and a couple bales of hay in the back was next to me and, as we entered the diner, a tan Subaru Forester pulled in next to us.

"You boys like coffee while you're deciding?"

Her name, according to the lapel pin on her greasy blue apron, was Lou.

"Yeah, Lou, that'll be fine. We'll both take leaded."

Red studied the laminated menu overcoated with fingerprints and grease.

Lou brought us our coffee in glass mugs. "Glass mugs. Glass mugs," I thought, "in a freakin' run-down diner." I hate glass mugs. They take the coffee's taste away.

But the coffee was good despite the mugs.

Red and I each ordered a BLT on toasted white with chips and cole slaw. We waited, sipping our coffee.

"This is a tough nut for us," Red mused. "A long time ago I suggested we go ask you for some help on it, but was turned down until now. Frank, we just lost two really good guys. Nothing to go on. It seems as though it'll just keep on happening and we have to do something for the sake of doing something, and that will make matters worse."

"Red, is it just our guys?"

"Mostly ours. Some others, too."

"Common threads?"

Red paused. "I have discretion in what I tell you. Jeezus, Frank, somebody in my biz trusts you. I'm to tell you anything you want to know if you think you'll sign on."

"We both know that whatever you know and whatever I'll learn from you will not be a complete story." I sounded abrupt and Red cocked an eyebrow.

"I can't sign on to this so easy, Red. I can't work alone and I'll need some basic info to even begin to decide if I want to get wet with this one."

"Common thread is that everyone who's disappeared or died has had something to do with Southeast Asia. They're not newbies, been around a long time. Experienced. Two had been retired. Mostly medium-level. Boys and girls."

Our sandwiches arrived and we had our coffee topped off. We ate in silence and I noticed Red studying my face.

"Can't this be a solo job?" Red sounded anxious.

"If I do anything, Red, it won't be solo. I would need to work with one or two others and I don't know if any of them would be interested."

"We're getting long in the tooth. And another thing, Red, this doesn't sound like a quick-in, quick-out kind of thing. It sounds like it could get messy and drag on and on."

"Any dessert, fellas?" Lou was clearing our plates. "More coffee?"

"No thanks, check'll be fine."

I left a few bills on the table and slid out of the booth and caught up with Red at the door.

"Notice the two guys who left just after we did?" asked Red as I started my engine.

"Clothing too new. They were either tourists or two guys who wanted to look like Vermonters and didn't want us to notice them."

I buckled my seat belt. Then, I just sat and stared at the dashboard.

"You OK?"

"Red, I'm tired. We see two guys wearing new clothes and immediately we start watching our backs. I may have burned out. I don't want that anymore. It's a paranoid lifestyle."

The tan Subaru Forester backed out and waited for me to drive off. The Forester followed me, allowing one car to get between us. The intervening car soon turned off but the Forester kept a respectable distance.

"OK. So it's not paranoia. We're made. Now what?"

Red murmured, "Shit!"

"Not the first time. We've both been made before." I felt uneasy despite my cavalier comment.

Red nodded.

It's hard losing a tail on the single-lane winding roads and ours stayed with us for miles. The road swung gently into Lummocks, a tidy village with a 25 mph speed limit and a resident cop that often lurked in a driveway, radar gun at the ready and eager to earn revenue for his town. I was not disappointed. The trooper was in the driveway and as soon as I was beyond his radar I floored it. The tail thought we were making a run for it and the driver tried to keep pace. But he was right in the radar of the Lummocks trooper who was about to meet his quota. The blue lights stopped our tail and we resumed our legal speed.

"Look, Red, let's suppose I think we're able to do this thing and can get some help. What's your time frame?"

"It's as soon as you possibly can."

I wanted to help Red, but wasn't sure I wanted to take on a big job again and this sounded big and serious. I thought about it for the rest of the trip home. We drove on in silence until we reached my house.

"Any conclusions?" Red looked at me expectantly.

"Yeah, and my honest answer is I don't have an answer. I have something serious planned for the next few weeks and when I get back I'll contact Lo Ban. Get his read on it, but frankly, Red, I'm not optimistic about us taking on that job."

I carried the shotguns inside while Red gutted our pheasants. Blaser walked idly about his enclosure, occasionally stretching and yawning.

Red was staying overnight and I was glad for the company. I like the quiet life in Vermont but an occasional visit with a friend from the old days isn't a bad thing. I fed Blaser, who was now lying in front of the fireplace as though asking for a bit of warmth. His idea seemed pretty good and I soon had a modest fire going.

"I just took the breasts on those pheasant and stuck them into the freezer." Red had washed his hands and sat down.

"Thanks for doing that. They'll be appreciated when I get around to do some serious cooking again."

"You need a woman in your life again, Frank."

It took a while for me to answer. "Yeah." I turned to Red. "And you?"

Red stiffened slightly as though about to say something but he didn't and I didn't push the issue. Red's wife, Sylvia, had divorced him about 25 years ago and had died about 5 years ago. Red had raised his two kids.

I got up and fetched a bottle of Johnnie Walker. From the kitchen I called "One cube, right?"

"Right" answered Red.

The Scotch felt good. My legs were tired and I was glad I'd taken Blaser's suggestion and built a fire.

Red and I savored our drinks and let time slide. "I remember when you had those bookcases built." Red nodded toward the two large glass-fronted mahogany bookcases that covered the south wall of the living room. "You must have moved them a dozen times."

I turned and looked at the two cases. Their massive bases and only slightly less massive tops reflected the fire and radiated their own form of warmth. The books within were special to me. My father's Shakespeare, some great nineteenth-century polar exploration and my precious collection of early astronomy books. Each one held special meaning to me and I could recall the exact circumstances by which I had acquired every volume. One shelf contained Percival Lowell's works; not only his Mars works but his lesser-known works on Japan and his privately-issued monograph on the position of the trans-Neptunian planet. I looked at them and smiled.

"Any chance the house is bugged?" Red's cautious comment brought me back to reality.

"None whatsoever. My security systems are good and any intrusion, however innocent is recorded. We've been logged in automatically—even Blaser. I sweep the place regularly, especially the outside. Even after all these years, I sometimes get scared."

"Being scared is good insurance. I'm scared shitless half the time."

"At least it keeps the mind occupied." We both laughed at that.

It was time for a refill and I got Red another cube.

"We've got nothing, Frank. Absolutely nothing."

"Hard to believe. There has to be a scrap or two. An unwiped e-mail, a fax record, something."

"Well, there is something but it might not relate to this issue at all. One of our guys, whose death is listed as a suicide, was found in his London flat. In the corridor we, not the police, found a dry cleaner's ticket. We went to the shop and got ourselves a tweed jacket with no labels. The shop couldn't help—they don't get the names or addresses of people who drop off clothing, figuring they'll come back for their clothes. We traced the fibers and it was very expensive, high-quality tweed. Only a few bespoke shops used it but the rub is that it was almost 20 years old. No records exist any longer of any jacket made with that tweed.

"The second clue, if you can call it that, is a parking receipt found near another 'suicide' of one of our guys. Again, we have no idea if it's related to the death. This time it was here in the States and the receipt was for a parking garage in New Haven, Connecticut. It was old and when we went to the garage we discovered that their cameras pointing to the exits were all dummies. They had so few no-pays that it was cheaper for them not to record traffic. Here again we have no idea if the ticket was related to the death.

"And that's about it."

I didn't answer but sipped my Scotch slowly. The fresh log I had put on the fire was burning and Blaser edged away a bit. He was edgy when it came to sparks.

"So what are some of the possibilities you guys are looking at? What makes you suspect the suicides or even the other deaths? Can't there be a reasonable explanation."

"Yes, each one can be explained. Except that none of the so-called suicides were acting suicidal before their death. Completely out of character. But really, the only thing we have is that they are all our guys and they are all dead."

There had to be something else, but I didn't press Red.

Another log on the fire, another ice cube and another round. It was now dark outside and a light rain was falling.

"On quite another matter, since we're talking shop, Frank, do you remember that guy, Heinrich von Sebum? The guy who preferred to be called 'Carl'?"

"Yeah, he was a freelancer who worked for the sport. Didn't need money. Liked very young women. He worked with us in Laos in the '70s. He's the guy who was fascinated by the mongoose-cobra fights and always argued they were rigged, that the cobra was drugged."

"Yeah, that's the guy. Well, about a year or so ago I was sitting in Russell Square, in London, eating an ice cream cone. It was a pretty day, the roses were blooming and I just decided to have an ice cream cone."

"No apologies or explanations necessary." I smiled. Red had been, in his mind, frivolous.

"Well, I'm about halfway through my ice cream when this guy walks past, turns around, and sits down on my bench. He opens a newspaper and pretends to read.

"'Are you waiting for someone?', he asks me. He's being very careful not to look at me.

"For a while I don't answer and manage to steal a glance at him. I barely recognize him as Carl.

"No, I'm just eating an ice cream cone."

"Good. Meet me in the bar in the Hotel Russell."

"He gets up and leaves. I finish my ice cream and wander off to the Russell. Carl is in the bar, in a corner seat and has his back against the wall.

"I go over. Hello, Carl. Is something wrong?"

"Red, thanks for coming. If you have a minute I'd like to talk with you about something."

"I sit down. Carl orders a whisky and I have mineral water.

"He was gaunt-looking and had a nervous tic. The poor devil was badly frightened. And Carl had never appeared frightened or uneasy before. He was different now."

"Red, I'm not working anymore. I stopped doing freelance and am just trying to live quietly. I have a small flat here in London where I spend some time each year.

"About a year ago I was returning from Paris and took the Channel ferry. I used to like the boat trip and was standing on deck, looking over the rail. Not at anything in particular, just looking."

"Yeah, Carl, I know exactly. I do the same. What happened?"

"Two goons tried to dump me over. They tried to do an alley-oop on me—one on each of my elbows and they tried to lift me up and over the rail.

"I kicked back and fortunately nailed one of the guys in the nuts. He yelped, let go of me, and that gave me the chance to do the same to the other guy. I hurt that bastard pretty badly. I put a thumb right into his eye and I'm certain he'll never use it again. I had eye-stuff all over my thumb. The nut-job hauled him off and they went away —I didn't follow them. I wasn't armed and didn't know how many there might be."

"Did you ever tell anyone about the attack?"

"Red, would you have?

"Anyway, I didn't go on to London but rather went straight to Heathrow and took a flight to Germany and went home to my schloss. I had a colleague—someone I once did some work for—check out my London flat. I was afraid to go there after the ferry incident. The guy I sent disappeared. I've not seen or heard from him since. He's simply gone.

"This is the first time I've been back to London since then and I run into you. Is it a coincidence?"

"Totally. You have my word. I don't mean anything negative, but I haven't thought about you in a long time."

"Good."

"Carl, I cannot tell you anything. Nothing we have in the works involves you. I have no intel for you.

"I paid the tab and left. Since then I've checked up on Carl once in a while and he's still alive.

"Weird, isn't it?"

I didn't answer for a while. Finally, I simply said, "It just makes no sense. It doesn't fit into anything."

"Red, you mentioned that some of your guys died from what appeared to be accidents. Remember Will Farman? He comes to mind only because I knew him well. He telephoned me the day he got diagnosed with pancreatic carcinoma. He was pretty philosophical about it and knew had only a few months to live. He really wanted to make sure I knew where certain of his assets were. A couple of months later he was found dead, shot in his head with a load from his own shotgun. He had gone out grouse hunting that morning, all loaded up on pain meds. He probably knew it was going to be his last hunt.

"Now the relationship between his body and the shotgun was such that it could be argued that he killed himself or that he was shot by someone else.

"He had gone out alone that morning and hadn't even taken a dog with him. That was unusual. Was he going to meet someone? Nobody knows.

"It was no accident. Will never shot at anything by accident and he never missed when he did shoot. So if he shot himself, it was deliberate. We all understood that. He wasn't the sort of guy who would choose to linger and die slowly. But there was the possibility that he had been shot by someone else using his gun and at very close range. I remember getting the call from his wife. Ana was lucid and calm. I suspect she knew what had happened and, in a way, sounded relieved.

"So what are accidents? How much ambiguity is tied to the death of each of your people? Enough to explain it away?"

"Been there, Frank. I also saw the file on Will Farman. It's sealed, but I read it. Will was a very different situation.

"By the way, were his assets taken care of?"

"Distributed according to his wishes. Are you saying something?"

"Just that Will thought that only you and he knew about that stuff. He was wrong. Lots of people knew. After his death it was decided to just ignore the whole thing and that's what we did—ignore it.

"But we are quite positive that our guys are getting bumped off and it has nothing to do with hidden assets or wives."

I was going to say something but let it slide. Will wasn't coming back and it didn't matter.

Neither of us said anything for a while. We were both backing off and we both knew it.

"I heard from little Annie recently. Not really little but I do tease her once in a while. Seems my god-daughter really likes it in Seattle. And how's Sam doing?" Annie and Sam were Red's children, both grown.

"You're right, Annie really likes Seattle and probably won't come back East. Sam? Who knows. He's in D.C. but I hear little from him and he generally ignores me if I try to contact him. Still the same story."

18

"Shit, Red, it's been over 25 years since Sylvia left. And she's been dead how long? And your kid is still angry with you? I know you and he hit a rough patch as he was growing up, but I would have thought that it was over."

"Frank, it goes beyond anything of reason, it used to eat at me and the worst thing is he still won't discuss it. I cannot get through to him. And the strange thing is we were pretty close when he was little."

"Yep, I remember that. He was a neat little kid who really looked up to his Pa."

"I tried asking Annie. She is still very protective of her little brother but I gather she knows the cause. She's just about told me but I can't do anything about it. When Sam was little he visited Sylvia's parents a lot and I encouraged him—I thought it was good and healthy for him to know his grandparents.

"They fucked with his head the same way they had fucked with Sylvia's. Little by little Sam was taught to despise me. They tried the same with Annie, but she was just a tad older and she wouldn't have any of it. She hated those people for what they did.

"And of course, I was too naïve to see what was going on."

"And now Sam continues to dislike you?"

"Profoundly. More so each year. Started out as just a bit snarky and I let it go—I should have explored the reasons but didn't. Hell, I was snarky to my old man, too. I thought Sam was just acting out his independence but I was wrong. It got a bit better once Sylvia died, but he still lets me know how much contempt he has for me at every chance, and then some. I now see him once a year, at best, in some neutral restaurant and try my darndest not to antagonize him, but I sometimes think my sheer existence is all it takes. Rather not see him—it brings back memories that I would rather not have dredged up. But I can't quite do that. I used to try to do nice things for him, arrange surprises, little presents—that sort of thing. Now I no longer even think of doing things like that. Sam is gone, Frank.

"You know, Frank, Sam loved the farm when he was a kid, now he won't go near it. Anything that has to do with me, or us when he was young, is shit to him. Annie loves the farm and loves her memories of it still, but she isn't going to move back. I love the farm but I'm going to sell it in a few years.

"I'm going to retire early, Frank. Move to Manhattan and haunt museums. If I don't disappear."

"Red, not having had any kids, I cannot imagine the anguish. You know, back when Sylvia was divorcing you she spread all that shit around about you. Most just flew by and made her look ridiculous, but some of it must have stuck. That woman really had a hair across her ass and I can well believe her trying to poison your kids' minds. Speak not ill of the dead, Red, but Sylvia blamed you for everything in her life. She kept inviting me to her dinners—she thought I should be flattered, but she was something out of British Comedy's *Keeping Up Appearances*. I finally stopped taking her calls. She was also sort of a John Fowles character and collected people.

"Shit! Thirty years have gone by and that woman still pisses me off, even from her grave. Jeezus.

"And there really isn't anything I can do." Red didn't sound offended. Obviously he had worked this through.

I thought for a bit. "No, I guess not. Annie escaped but Sam got fucked. He threw his father overboard. Ultimately it was his toss."

Red finished the last of his whiskey. He no longer looked perturbed, his momentary anger had left and he was back to level. This must have been an old replay for him. He got up and walked toward the kitchen.

"I'm really not all that hungry, but I could use something to munch on. Mind if I forage?"

"Same here. Why don't I make us some toasted cheese sandwiches?"

"Sounds good."

I cut slabs of extra-sharp Vermont cheddar cheese, put them on bread and slid them into the toaster-oven. We stood in the kitchen leaning up against the counter. We both smiled. We were bullshitting the same way we did decades ago.

"You know, Red, there's a lot of isolated shit that goes on that's unrelated to much of anything else. A year or so ago I heard of a guy who found a small case literally filled with bundles of hundred dollar bills. It was in a rest stop on Interstate 89 going north. He pulls in to spring a leak and he sees this case behind an ornamental boulder. It was partly sticking out from the side of the fake rock. He pops the lid, sees it's full of bills, nonchalantly walks with it to his car and drives off. Didn't even take his leak.

"It had precisely one-point-five million dollars in hundreds. He checks around, watches news stories, reads the police blotter and comes up with nothing. Nobody's been kidnapped, no ransom demands, no armored car heists. Nothing. Just a mil-and-a-half in a small suitcase. The bills were not marked and had random serial numbers.

"Now, it's probably drug money so nobody is going to advertise for it and no doubt some drug dealer or mule is in deep trouble, or deep cement, but nothing public.

"So now this guy has all this cash and he has absolutely no way to launder it. He's gotta be careful because whoever lost the money is no doubt looking for a new high-roller. So all he does with it is take an occasional trip to New York or Montreal and pay for everything with cash. But he's afraid to even do that very often. He's pretty well-off so spending an extra few tens of thousands a year won't be noticeable but there's no way he can move significant amounts of the cash into any of his accounts."

Red thought a bit. "He's screwed. He can't even buy a lot of mid-priced art or antiques and then dump them at auction. He might be able to do that with a hundred grand but not a mill-and-a-half."

We took our cheese sandwiches back into the living room and ate them before the ebbing embers.

"And suppose," I offered, "that Carl knew this guy who found the money and that both of them had had dinner with one of your guys who got killed. Or that one of your guys was in on trying to alley-oop Carl?"

Red snorted. "What a fuckin' mess that would be. We'd never make sense of any of it. And then, there's those guys who tailed us today. That didn't seem to have much point to it at all."

"Sometimes dots aren't meant to be connected. Give me time, Red. Let this percolate and at some point I'll talk with Lo Ban. But I have a bad feeling that there's all sorts of stuff that isn't connected and we'd have the devil of a time sorting through it if we assume connections. Red, there's another thing—I have some personal stuff I need to do first. I'll be out of the country for a while. But I won't forget."

"Good enough." Red knew that was as far as he'd get tonight. And I didn't want to begin worrying about the guys who tailed us. That could come later. "Be sure to bounce it off Lo Ban. He's a pretty sharp guy." Red invoked the name of my long-time friend and colleague for emphasis.

"Carl and the mongoose fights." Red had been silent for a while and had suddenly thought of something. "Carl used to watch the cobra versus mongoose shows put on for tourists." He was laughing now. "Carl had already left Laos but some yahoo Texan flying for Air America managed to bring in a box of rattlesnakes. Convinced the guys running one of the fights to let him put his snake in and he bet a bundle on the rattler. He made a pile of money. The mongoose generally wins over a cobra but the rattler is a pit viper and very fast. The mongoose didn't stand a chance. He did this a few times and then nobody would put their mongoose in the ring with his snakes anymore."

"There's probably a moral in there somewhere." Red didn't answer.

I stayed up for a while after Red had turned in and resurrected a mental picture of a much younger Red, little Annie and still smaller Sam walking with me through the Vermont woods, Annie holding her little brother's hand. I felt a sadness for Red, but an even greater, overwhelming one for Sam who had been made fatherless. And I felt lonely. Blaser's snoring didn't help.

Red got up early the next morning and had made coffee by the time I got downstairs. I fed Blaser, leaving him in his outdoor enclosure, and made us some breakfast.

"I should get going. Thanks for the hospitality and for the day's shooting and the evening's bull-shooting. Let me know if those guys tailing us show up here."

"I'm not too worried. If their bosses are the least bit knowledgeable they'll know I haven't been active in years. It's also no secret where I live and nobody's bothered me here yet. I suspect it was meant more as a signal to you. If so, you've been signaled."

Red smiled. "I hope they noticed our shooting."

He looked up at the sky and the uniform, high layer of clouds that remained after the rain had moved out.

"I'll file IFR from the airport."

We loaded his birds, now nicely frozen, his overnight case, and his shotgun into my van and drove off.

I took Red to the Lebanon, New Hampshire, airport's FBO, where he filed his flight plan for the return to Virginia and paid his tie-down fee. We drove slowly out to the line of tied-down airplanes. Red's was a dowager silver Cessna 180. It looked sleek compared to the tricycle-geared neighbors. I loaded his gear into the baggage compartment.

We shook hands and I stood back.

"Clear!"

I smiled and gave him a thumbs-up, and the engine, catching on the second go-around, soon settled down to a regular rhythm.

A quick wave and Red taxied slowly to the active. A few moments later he began his takeoff roll and I watched as his lights disappeared on his straight-out departure.

Driving home, my first thoughts were that I really didn't want to get involved in Red's problem. After all, our old group hadn't worked a job in a very long time; we were rusty and retired. But then again, Red needed help. Again, that twinge of sadness. And also, I remembered playing with Sam. Fatherless Sam.

When I got back home I grabbed Blaser's towel so I could wipe his paws when I brought him into the house, walked to the back door, and called to him.

There was no answer.

I found Blaser lying on his side, a single shot cleanly through his head.

Chapter 2

Istanbul

The bus going to Istanbul's Taksim Square filled rapidly and I got one of the last seats. I was among the usual sprinkle of American tourists with their freshly laundered jeans, fanny packs, and pant suits, moustached Turkish men and, as befitting the New Turkey, some quite elegant Turkish women in the latest from Paris. The air in the bus was damp and although no one was smoking the odor of tobacco was strong. I struggled to look out but heavy rain on the outside and condensed moisture on the inside blurred the view. I was able to see enough to tell that the building boom continued to fill what used to be vacant space.

My short flight from Athens had been uneventful and I was looking forward to a few days in Istanbul, drinking coffee and raki with old chums. That pleasant thought was still on my mind when the bus pulled into Taksim, and we got off and jostled our ways toward the taxis waiting. I got into a relatively new yellow taxi, identical to dozens of others in the queue. A far cry from the old Packards or Buicks that served this function years ago, before part of the great global wave of prosperity reached these shores. There was a bit of irony, though, and despite the splendid new, modern international airport, new buildings and new taxis, the Turkish currency had depreciated so dramatically that a dollar bought well over a million lira.

"Pera Palas Oteli," I told the driver.

"OK, no problem." The driver's English was another example of the profound changes that had taken place. I was to discover rapidly that English had become almost universal in Istanbul, replacing French or German as the foreign language of choice.

The rain diminished as we continued into the now drizzle that enveloped the city. By the time we pulled up to the Pera Palas, that venerable old hotel on Mesrutiyet Caddesi, the drizzle had stopped and people were walking about, spilling over the narrow sidewalk and nearly filling the street.

"Welcome to the Pera Palas Hotel" greeted me as the doorman opened the taxi door. There was a wonderful feeling of familiarity as I entered the ornate lobby. I seemed to lose years and felt transported back to earlier days. Tired as I was, I noticed that the old hotel seemed brighter and crisper. The place had been painted and the chandeliers and windows cleaned. My old friend had had a face-lift. I stood still a moment, just to survey and to renew my memories of this grand old hotel. I was glad time was being kind to her.

"There is a telephone message for you, sir" announced the check-in clerk as she handed me a folded paper.

Thanking her, I put the paper into my pocket without reading, even though I had no idea from whom the message might be. I was a bit surprised that anyone knew I would be here.

The old mahogany elevator took me up the few flights to my room. It was another pleasant surprise to note that the rooms had been redone recently. The worn carpets replaced with new, and the bedding surprisingly comfortable. However, there remained, as leftovers from the old decor, several overly enlarged reproductions of illustrations from Julia Pardoe's *Beauties of the Bosphorus*. Colored garishly and wearing shabby frames, these prints nonetheless spoke of an Istanbul past that had been replaced in many areas with new, but whose ancestral spirits never disappeared, just layered over to lurk beneath the surface and break through when the present world, or the present iteration, needed a reality check.

Opening the curtains revealed that sunlight was now spilling into the corners of the narrow streets and making the wet city glisten. A mixture of memories swept over me, as it always does whenever I come back to this city. Wonderful memories. The city's sunlit sparkle reminded me of Elizabeth, and her own sparkle that rivaled today's, and that time some 30 years ago, when over a long and languid lunch at Pandeli's we knew, almost without words exchanging, we would spend our lives together. And afterward, walking through the long corridor of the Spice Bazaar holding hands like two teenagers, the old men smiling at us from behind their huge open bags of spices and herbs. Smiling because no doubt our feelings had become transparent and public, or possibly, just because perhaps Elizabeth's golden aura had enveloped us both. And the smiles of the Turks that day added yet another reason why I love this city and its people. Elizabeth. It was she who brought me here this time again, although she has been dead for 30 years.

Glad for the toxieder, coffee, and stainless steel cup in my travel kit, I made myself a cup of instant and stretched out with my stockinged feet up on the old steam radiator. I sipped my coffee while I watched the sunbeams trip along the rooftops and tease away the mist rising to meet them. Ah, yes. It was indeed good to be back.

It was then that I remembered the telephone message the clerk had given me. Giving up my comfortable position, I went to my jacket and retrieved the note from the side pocket.

Swaddled already by one set of memories of an earlier time, memories soft and mellow with edges round, this message cut through them and substituted its own. Memories much harsher and sharp-edged. Memories of a time when our Old Group was still active and struggling against some most difficult situations. The note was quite brief. It was from my long-time colleague and friend, Lo Ban. He was in town and suggested we meet. Oddly, he wanted to meet outdoors. In Taksim Gezi Parki, a pleasant space just north of Taksim Square and in the shadow of the Intercontinental Hotel.

Lo Ban! Here in Istanbul. How he knew I was coming would perhaps remain forever a mystery. I would not ask him. It would be good to see him. Curious, however, that he should want to meet me in the open. I had a nagging thought, a fear perhaps, that it might mean something ominous, but I really didn't want to deal with that possibility just now, when vestiges of the memory of Elizabeth were still caressing my inner spirit.

I looked at my watch. There was plenty of time to make the first of my planned calls and visit my friend Osman Bey before meeting Lo Ban. I rinsed out my coffee cup, left my room, and neglected the grand old elevator. Instead, I walked down the wide, carpeted marble stairs to the lobby and went out into the street, joining the crowd that had appeared seemingly to celebrate the end of the rain, but in reality was not more than the usual choke of people on this busy street.

Going north along Mesrutiyet Caddesi, I turned onto a little street, Kallavi Sokak, which took me to the Isticlal. Isticlal Caddesi is a major pedestrian street, closed to vehicles and lined with shops and generally crowded—as crowded and noisy as London's Oxford Street. Watch the passersby on the Isticlal and you will see a great cross-section of Istanbulis. I joined that ever-present throng and flowed with it. It felt good to be here again; the new Istanbul still had some of the familiar smells, most of the familiar sounds, and the same sense of history yesterday and of reality today, elegance and squalor, and cultures juxtaposed so closely that there was little room for overt conflict. This timeless city was always changing, yet parts of it would never change.

I soon came to the small street I was looking for. Eski Çiçeksi Sokak led me steeply downhill to Kaymakam Resat Bey Sokak, and from there I entered a small alley inconspicuously leading off, and even narrower than, the narrow Resat Bey. This insignificant anastomosis is so well camouflaged that even if one looks for it, one can pass it several times before noticing it. There is nothing in the alley that overtly warrants such concealment and the invisibility of the intersection is surely by accident not design. I left the main foot traffic behind as I slipped down the little alley, slaloming around trash cans, small mounds of rubble and the usual Istanbuli cats.

A hundred yards into the alley is a doorway cut into the stone wall of a building. The doorway is blocked by a coarse wooden door, its iron strap hinges with square headed bolts implying great thickness and giving it the appearance of exceptional strength. A small window near the top is covered by a stout iron grill. No door-knob or latch protrudes and there is no keyhole. The door sports many coats of paint, the latest, a battleship gray, is unsuccessful in holding down the lower layers now blistering through, coming to the surface from the past and joining the today.

I knocked on the door and it was opened quickly. It swung quietly and easily, always a surprise since it appears more massive than well balanced, and it looks as though it ought to creak. Hollywood would have given it a creak.

"Hello, Serhat." The manservant permitted himself a smile. "Is Osman Bey in, please?" I asked in English, my Turkish too rusty to try on the helpful Serhat.

"Yes, He's in the inner room. Come in. I shall tell him you are here. Welcome back to Istanbul."

"Thank you, Serhat." I walked in past the great wooden door that swung shut behind me. It gave a 'thunk' and there was an almost inaudible 'click' as some lock mechanism activated itself. A glance at the door would reveal no visible lock, just a large brass knob. Osman Bey had no problem opening the door, nor did Serhat. However, even after many trips here, I still had no idea how it worked. Osman Bey always let me out personally, but did not ever volunteer to explain his door.

I slipped off my street shoes and slid my feet into a pair of guest slippers. As always, there was a pair large enough for me. It was a good feeling to know, that even after years away, my host remembered. Or had they been here all the time?

Osman Bey, one of the most astute private rare book dealers in Istanbul, was someone I always visited and he usually had several great volumes in my subject areas for sale. Moreover, he was one of the most hospitable people I knew in the trade and a visit to Osman Bey was not only often profitable but always most pleasant. All of us dealers who knew him were very careful about whom we referred to Osman Bey. None of us would ever refer someone without first clearing it with him. We did triage and filtered out the yahoos. Or the possibly dangerous ones.

Osman Bey received me in an inner room, part of an extensive apartment. I had been in much of the apartment and knew that there were other parts I would never see. Now, the door to this inner room was opened by Osman Bey himself. Smiling broadly.

"Welcome back to Istanbul, my friend!"

He squeezed my hand, took my arm and escorted me inside.

Osman Bey is a large, muscular man, whose dark hair belies his age. His deep voice is well-modulated. Fluent in many languages, he generally speaks softly but I can well imagine the sound of his shout. Osman Bey was, as always, dressed well. His jacket was old and its age emphasized its well-enjoyed comfort. The fabric quality justified the obvious expense of the tailoring. We sat down in his inner room and were served with strong Turkish coffee in small silver cups. I remember the first time I had Turkish coffee. It was in the early 1960s and the coffee was served in a small onyx cup. After a sip or two of the pungent liquid I was faced with half a cup of ambiguous sludge, a semi-liquid slurry that had sort of settled to the bottom of the cup. With the consistency of quick-mud it was sufficiently liquid that it seemed reasonable to drink it. And so I did. Only later did I learn. Oh, well. Queen Victoria drank out of a finger bowl.

"Osman Bey, I am sorry, but I must refuse any more. I am at the age when this is about as much coffee I dare drink, however good it is." He smiled, nodded to his servant, and was served another cup.

An inconspicuous door situated between two massive bookcases opened quietly and a portly man entered the room. He shuffled, not from age, but from weight as well as from the undersize carpet slippers he was wearing.

"You know, of course, Rodney Oufle?" He rose as Rodney came into the room.

"Of course." I stood up and shook his hand. Rodney was a long–time antiquarian book dealer and member of the Association of Antiquarian Book sellers who, unlike most of the AAB membership, lived abroad much of the time. I keep running into him in unexpected places. Last time we met was a few years ago when he and I passed, walking in opposite directions on the Janpath in New Delhi; the time before in Alexandria and before that in Cairo. I never knew whether or not these were innocuous, accidental meetings or whether Rodney was, for some reason, following me. Rodney's tastes were a bit extreme for me and his bookdealing always puzzled me. I couldn't figure out if he collected or dealt. His passion was death, and it could always be counted on to supply a few anecdotes.

"Good to see you."

Rodney sat down and poured himself a cup of coffee. Osman Bey did not seem to mind. Rodney then pulled out a small silver cigar case and offered it around. Osman Bey took one of the Schimmelpennincks, Rodney did also, but I declined. "You don't smoke anymore?" asked Rodney.

"Not for some time. I think, though, that when I get to be 75 years old, indeed, if I get to be 75 years old, I shall take it up again."

"My friend, if you make it to 75 I shall personally give you a box of the finest Havanas." Osman Bey smiled. "Unless, of course, you reform before then." He thought the last comment amusing and chortled to himself. I did not understand it.

"By the way," he continued, "Charlotte Lippe is in town. I told her you were coming and she said to say 'hello'."

I tried to keep a poker face. "Haven't seen her in years. She's quite the Ottoman scholar now, isn't she?"

"Indeed. She's working on some manuscripts in the Topkapi archives, and, for now, staying at Bosphorus House. But I've invited her to stay here when she gets tired of that place." He wrinkled his nose at the thought of Bosphorus House.

I was lost in thought for the moment. Charlotte Lippe. Here in Istanbul. Our last meeting, years ago, was a chance encounter in Kyoto and had been a bit awkward. That was the only time I'd seen her since we broke up. Charlotte and I had both been students; Charlotte was a Cliffie and I was living in Vanderbilt Hall on the other side of the Charles. We had been together about a year, but our worlds were separating more and more. One morning, about 3 o'clock, we were finishing breakfast in the Hayes-Bick in Harvard Square when we both sort of knew it was over. We hugged each other outside the Bick and walked apart. Our year had simply vanished and for a long time I felt the void.

"And how is she?"

"Well," answered Osman Bey, and she looks very nice, indeed."

"I heard she's married?"

"No, she's not." I could swear that Osman Bey had a twinkle

in his eye. For some reason he was enjoying my mild discomfort. Rodney was twitching slightly and the heel of his right foot began bouncing up and down. Rodney did this whenever he felt threatened. "But I hear she hasn't changed. Do you want to look her up?"

Osman Bey was even more unfathomable than usual. So Charlotte would be staying with him. How the hell did they know each other that well? And what the hell did he mean by "she hasn't changed"?

"Oh, I don't know if I'll look her up. I'll see how my stay here unfolds. That was all so long ago. But do remember me to her when she moves in." I tried to sound casual but I think I betrayed a slight hint of jealousy at the thought of Charlotte moving in with him. He allowed himself a slight smile. I'm glad I don't play poker with him.

To change the subject I asked, "What brings you here to Istanbul, Rodney? Books?"

Rodney's twitching had stopped and the heel of his foot was no longer bouncing. "Yes and no. I'm researching an old Ottoman form of execution—the hook." Rodney fancied himself a great expert on death and execution. "You know, the method of execution is often dependent upon the reason for the execution. I don't mean the crime of the miscreant, but one must ask the question 'Why execute?' What is the motive of the State? Or for that matter, what is the motive of an individual executing himself? The techniques of suicide are many. And fascinating. Remember that homemade gas chamber I devised?"

I did indeed. Over drinks in the Okura, in Tokyo, Rodney had sketched a small wooden box "easily built by any handyman in his basement" that had a self–latching door and a device that turned on the gas when the door was slammed shut. The door could not be opened from inside and the orifice of the gas pipe opened into a large manifold so that whoever was inside the chamber could not change his mind, either by opening the door or by plugging the gas pipe. And all it took was some hand tools, scrap lumber, and a garden hose.

"Now, take the hook." Rodney continued. "It was sort of like an upside-down question mark with the stem screwed into a horizontal beam. The victim was hog-tied, lifted up over the hook and then lowered so the hook could penetrate his abdomen. He was left there, with the hook working its way through his bowels. If fortunate, the hook would quickly sever his descending aorta. If unfortunate, it would miss the aorta and emerge from his back and he would hang there for days, slowly dying of minor hemorrhage and pain. Why do it this way when it was so much easier to simply drown the victim? Or hang or behead? The garrote works well—it can be quick or slow. The payback has to be great enough to warrant the effort, and the concept of 'payback' is what really interests me."

Osman Bey seemed fascinated by Rodney's exposition. He leaned back on the heavy fabric of the divan and stared intently at Rodney. Osman Bey's inner room was sort of a chamber itself. It had no walls on the street, no windows, and there was no sound from the outside that penetrated its solitude. And presumably there was no sound that escaped the inner room to mingle with the outside noise. And, for a fleeting moment I imagined that, if Osman Bey so wished, one would not be able to leave this chamber.

We listened to Rodney expound on death and executions for some time and the room accumulated the smoke of several more Schimmelpennincks. The smoke hung in a layer midway between the carpeted floor and the wood ceiling that was paneled in an ornate octagon design.

Finally I needed to leave. "I'm sorry, but Lo Ban is in town and I have to meet him shortly."

"Lo Ban in town?" Osman Bey's surprise was genuine. At last here was something he had missed! "He must visit. Bring him with you when you come again."

"I'll do that. I did not know myself that he was in Istanbul until I arrived here. I came in this morning.

"Yes, I know. From Athens," he smiled as he walked me to the door.

I wondered if there was any reason why he should have taken the trouble to find out about my travels. At the time I doubted it was because of Charlotte. And, if he knew about me, why not about Lo Ban? Was Lo Ban too clever or just not on Osman Bey's radar screen?

The great door to the alley swung open. Osman Bey and I shook hands. "Thank you for calling on me. I hope to have the honor of seeing you again before you leave Istanbul."

As I turned away, down the alley. I heard the ominous, faint click as the door locked itself behind me.

Rejoining the throng on the Isticlal, I wandered north to Taksim. I could not shake the thought of Charlotte here in Istanbul— Charlotte, the woman who clung to me and I to her and we two together made love so sweetly that we were convinced we had invented it all by ourselves. Charlotte. Not pretty, certainly not ugly, perhaps even a bit exotic and certainly captivating in a sultry way. Her right eyelid had a slight droop and I learned that when it drooped ever so slightly more it signaled the promise of wonders and joys for us both.

There was still time before I was to meet Lo Ban so I bought a fresh simit from a street vendor and happily ate it while an urchin polished my shoes. He did a splendid job on the toes. They reflected and gleamed as he polished with great dramatic swoops of his rag. The backs of my shoes, not readily visible to me, were, of course, left untouched. And I tipped the lad well beyond his deserve.

I walked around Taksim with the newly polished toes of my shoes gleaming, stood studying the great triumphal arch, and walked a bit more, trying to make myself obvious to anyone who might want to see me, and to try to make the thought of Charlotte disappear. I then headed up to Taksim Gezi Parki, and sat down on a bench that provided an unobstructed view of the near surrounds. Soon, a familiar silhouette appeared, heading toward me.

"Hello, Lo Ban!" I stood up and shook hands with my old comrade. "How splendid to see you! What brings you here?"

Lo Ban sat down next to me. "Well, Manasek, I think it's a very long story. But we do have some catching up to do. Let me brief you on the nasty, then we can play a friendly game of catch-up."

Chapter 3

Lo Ban

Lo Ban and I go back a long time. We first joined forces some decades ago, during the Vietnam War era when we were working together on an anti–biological warfare project at Oxford. During the ensuing years, those times of the cold war, Lo Ban and I took advantage of the global paranoia. We made a natural pair and we were able to assemble a small team. Operating more or less independent of formal government ties, we worked at resolving situations that governments could not handle openly or directly. Our services were much in demand.

I had become a rare book dealer as cover for our operations. Although the decision to use the antiquarian book business as a cover was brilliant I cannot claim credit for it. Being a rare book dealer made travel easier. There was less to explain, since scouring the world for old books seemed, to most people, a very glamorous occupation and questions would revolve about that and not whatever else I might be doing. In time, Lo Ban also began to buy and sell antiquarian books and thus began our informal bookdealing partnership.

But time had changed the world and the changing world situation had less and less need of our former expertise. We gradually backed out of this field and our Old Group dispersed. Some were dead and some had chosen to isolate themselves, to remove themselves as far as possible from their past activities. I suppose this was a wise decision for we had made serious enemies and sooner or later some would be looking for revenge. Others from our Old Group, such as Maria and Veronica, were perfectly content to keep in touch and could be counted on to help out if Lo Ban and I needed an assist. We still took on the odd job and dabbled a bit, but only a bit. Old habits die hard and we had the skills. It was a shame to waste them, especially when we could convert them into large amounts of money.

For a decade or so after the Old Group separated, we continued our rare book business, only occasionally getting caught up in more dangerous activities. Lo Ban was based in Hong Kong, where he lived with Amanda; I was in Vermont, where I relished the isolation and privacy. I think we both were pleased to let parts of the past recede a bit to be replaced by our book-trade identities. The rest was permitted to drift away, letting the opacity of time obscure more and more of it. Or perhaps, like Osman Bey's door, acquire a coat of grey paint only to have the layers underneath blister through. But only occasionally.

Lo Ban and I found the rare book business both pleasant and interesting, and we became rather good at it, he specializing in oriental manuscripts and I in antiquarian maps and early printing. We were successful and we joined the appropriate trade groups, notably the Association of Antiquarian Book sellers. The AAB organized book fairs that were very successful and, as members, we were able to exhibit at them. The fairs also provided a venue that let us also keep in touch with some of our colleagues from the earlier days.

Antiquarian book fairs are curious events. A half-century ago they were truly antiquarian book fairs. Then, most of the books for sale were old and important. In the intervening years, inexorably, antiquarian stock gave way, probably responding to a version of Gresham's Law, to general secondhand books.

The sale of general secondhand books, of the five-year-old cookbook variety, or 1950s book club editions, used to be confined to lesser, local book fairs held in minor venues. It was here where dealers in such material met to exchange their wares and to sell to the general used-book collecting public. Here, too, specialist dealers such as I would go to pore over the stock on display, looking for valuable or highly specialized material unfamiliar to the local dealers and for which they had no other market. In those pre–internet days, it was the job of the specialist dealer to scout these minor fairs and try to buy items either directly for their clients or for inventory. In this way books moved up the food chain. In these post–internet days, anybody can list books for sale and that list will be seen easily by any interested collector. As a result, the provincial fairs have declined in importance since the average secondhand book is far more plentiful than imagined, and a collector has generally a much larger selection to choose from on the internet than at a provincial fair.

If the recent, out-of-print book of the $25 variety turned out to be plentiful, what about the recently out-of-print book of the $2500 variety? There is a subset of book collecting that concentrates on "modern firsts," or first editions of books by living authors or those of the recent past. One of the elder statesmen of the antiquarian trade in the United States refers to this part of the trade as the "dust jacket trade" and the dealers who participate in it as "dust jacket dealers." These comments relate to a curious system of valuing modern first editions, a system that is based almost entirely upon condition. Thus, if you were to buy a first edition of author X and merely wanted the book in average condition and did not want a dust jacket, you might have to pay $100 for it. If it had a dust jacket with a tear in it you might have to pay $1200. If the dust jacket was pristine and the book virtually unread the tab might be $2500. This gives the dust jacket an undue degree of importance in determining price, especially since there are known examples of dust jackets that have been reproduced. It is quite impossible to fake an entire book, but the dust jacket is another thing. The printing technology used to produce the original dust jacket is still in use and the same paper is readily available, and a single printed sheet is relatively easy to reproduce. Another neat trick is get a dust jacket from a later edition and put it on a first edition that you bought without jacket.

The internet punched a hole in the modern firsts trade. As soon as minor dealers, or collectors, or house-clearing agents could list books on the internet and reach a vast audience it became apparent that many modern first editions, even in great condition, were not rare at all. They were not even uncommon but were, in reality, plentiful. A lot of collectors who had bought $2500 books and who were now seeing them on the internet for fifty bucks had a lot of questions!

Nonetheless, even at the better book fairs in the United States, vast numbers of dealers exhibit shelvesful of these books and seem to find buyers. Some of these dealers have large businesses, with tens of thousands of books listed for sale on internet sites. True antiquarian dealers might exhibit a hundred or so books, perhaps a few hundred, but these dealers are now in the minority. The flavor of the trade, and consequently that of the book fairs at which we exhibit, has changed.

Lo Ban and I used to exhibit at the AAB fairs until some got so large and so filled with ordinary books that we felt swamped. Can there be, using any reasonable measure of the term "antiquarian," 400 antiquarian dealers in the country? Probably there are not half that number in the world! Besides, it was becoming a bit of a chore to drag inventory to these fairs and set up the booth, deal with diverse customers ("Do you have any film star autographs?") for several days and then pack up and go back home. We both preferred the paper catalogue or personal contact with our old clients.

The river of time keeps moving and I am still not certain if it flows around us, if we move through it, or if it just drags us along. Just as we changed from adventurers to book dealers, we gradually backed out of that on a public level. Both Lo Ban and I kept our private clients but did not advertise for more. Only occasionally did we yield to the temptations from the past, for we both liked the peace and quiet private bookselling had brought us.

Now, sitting in a park in Istanbul, Lo Ban was about to pitch me a curve ball.

"Manasek," he said, "I think there will be serious trouble for us very soon."

"Who is us?" I asked, as though I didn't know. "And what kind of trouble?"

"Back in Hong Kong, some people at the Club were trying to chat up Amanda, asking her about me, about our friends, where we traveled, that kind of thing. Not really polite conversation, rather more of an interrogation. Amanda twigged to it quickly and fed them shit. A few weeks ago she was shot."

"Badly?" I was miffed that I wasn't told about it earlier.

"No, a graze. It didn't require any medical attention, thankfully. I didn't report it. Amanda is in hiding right now. For the time being she is absolutely safe."

"And who shot at her?" I did not ask where Amanda was hiding. I suspected she was in one of our old safe houses. But since I had no need to know, I just let that one slide.

"Right now, I don't know. The people who chatted her up in the Club are unknowns. Very curious, but nobody remembers them and they are not members and no member admits to having invited them."

"And why are you meeting me here in Istanbul? Why not back in the States?"

"Old friend, I know why you are here. I do not wish to intrude on you and your pilgrimage, but this may involve the lives of our friends, and there is a connection here—at least I think there might be."

"We have a bit of time?"

"Absolutely. Let us eat well, enjoy life here a bit. Perhaps we can wander along the Bosphorus up to Bebek and eat at that wonderful fish restaurant and watch the ships go by. Shall we meet and think lunch tomorrow?"

I wanted to put off dealing with trouble. "Not now, not here," I fervently wished. I decided to buy myself a day.

"Can we do it the day after?"

"Agreed." Lo Ban's face showed just a bit of curiosity, but he didn't pry.

"And I'll meet you at...?"

"I'm staying at the Hilton."

"Good. Shall we say noon? Lobby?"

Lo Ban and I walked slowly across Taksim.

"Lo Ban, I hate to bring this up at this time, but there's something else brewing and I've been asked for help. I put it on the back burner, but it's serious.

"Red came to see me before I left for the island. He asked for help. He wants to ask our group for some serious help with a problem he's having keeping his people alive. Then, while I drove him to the airport, someone shot my dog. We had been followed but I was overly cavalier about it."

Lo Ban remained silent for a while.

"We'll talk about it."

Lo Ban didn't say more, but we looked each other in the eyes. When we parted, he headed north, and I walked slowly back down the Isticlal. It had been a long day and I looked forward to an early bedtime.

The city indeed was sporting a new coat of paint, I thought. But perhaps it had a devious purpose. Without new paint there could be no blisters from underneath.

Chapter 4

Mehmet

Breakfast in the Pera Palas offered me yet another chance to revisit the past. Goat cheese, black olives, bread, tea. It was a glorious way to start what appeared to be, as viewed through the large windows now for the first time in my memory reasonably clean, a bright day.

My introspection was broken when I saw a Turk enter the breakfast room, look around, spot me, and smile. I recognized him—it was Mehmet, and he headed over to me and extended his hand. I got up to greet him.

"Mehmet! What a surprise!" To myself, I wondered what he wanted and why he should suddenly "find" me here. I had been to this city dozens of times over the past couple of decades and he hadn't looked me up. Nor I him. How the hell did he know I was here?

"Hello!" He seemed genuinely pleased at his reception. "I heard you were in town and thought I'd stop by and see you on my way to work. Might I join you?" Mehmet seemed more distinguished, a bit heavier and a bit grayer than I remembered him. But then again, I hadn't seen him in about 20 years.

"Of course." I gestured to the vacant chair. "I just got in yesterday. Glad you looked me up." I purposely did not ask him how he knew I was in town. That could wait for later.

We exchanged pleasantries for a while. Mehmet was now an editor at a travel magazine that targeted the emerging, and ever more robust, Turkish middle class. He asked about Lo Ban and Amanda, wondering how and where they were.

"Amanda is at home," I replied "and Lo Ban is here, in Istanbul. I saw him yesterday. But no doubt you knew he's here."

A fleeting look of worry flashed across Mehmet's face, it blended quickly into a somewhat forced smile. "Good! It would be great if we could renew old ties—perhaps we all can have dinner together before you all leave. My place? Ahh, but you don't know where I live now, do you?" He produced his card. It had a near–fashionable address in Üsküdar. "Please call me and I can arrange a nice evening. Tell me, any of the others here this time?"

I smiled at my visitor. "I shall ask Lo Ban, but I'm certain he shall be pleased to join me and visit you. It will be pleasant to catch up on things. It is good you dropped by, Mehmet, and I am sure Lo Ban will enjoy seeing you again."

He seemed relieved at my cordial demeanor and walked out smiling. He either ignored my non–answer about the others or did not get it.

Mehmet was a curious character. Some 20 years ago he had helped us out when we were trying to effect an exchange. One of Theirs for one of Ours. But completely unofficial. No governments or governmental agencies were to be involved.

The Italian Red Army terrorist, Alonzo Septichema, had been in prison so long he had become useless and there was no reason for Us to keep him. The one of Ours, Geoff Klinefelter, had likewise had his cover blown completely and since he appeared so inept he was thought not to have done any apparent harm before being spotted, They didn't want him. They thought him a harmless bungler. An easy swap of no consequence and it got rid of some baggage that neither side wanted. And we had reason to believe that Klinefelter was not as big an inept as he seemed and that he might have acquired some serious information. Perhaps there were really many layers of motives on each side, but that didn't really concern us. We were in business and our concern was for the bottom line.

Lo Ban arranged the deal. At the time he and I were in Vienna, exhibiting at the International Antiquarian Book Fair. Our shared booth had a number of long-staying visitors as the details of the swap were being worked out. The fair was a perfect meeting place. Many people from many different countries wandered in and out; business was conducted in huddles and lots of serious book business was being conducted throughout the fair. Our huddles seemed perfectly normal and they appeared no different than numerous other huddles in other booths. We could discuss the prisoner trade without fear of discovery. The only problem was minor. One of our American colleagues, Derek Lope de Nada, a dealer in modern firsts, was visiting the fair and seemed to have latched on to us. He spoke no German, couldn't get the exchange rate into his head—he kept getting it reversed—and, in general, was making a pest of himself. He also had trouble with foreign food and became, as the fair went on, quite flatulent. (Another American dealer, Bryce Donaldson, an internationally known dealer in incunabula, observed that Lope de Nada was now flatulent from both ends, but made more sense from the lower.) We suggested to Derek that he try McDonald's. His face lit up. Lo Ban drew him a little map so he could find the place. Lope de Nada, smiling broadly, propelled himself out of the fair in search of the Big Mac and fries, leaving behind only the slowly dissipating evidence of his presence.

"One of these days he'll graduate from Little Golden Books," muttered Lo Ban.

"Not, as you say, the brightest porch light on the block?" Karl von Unterhosen, one of Europe's major collectors of erotica, was looking at a small volume from Lo Ban's case and had overheard Lo Ban's muttering. "This is quite remarkable," added von Unterhosen as he paged through the little, late 16th-century 12mo book filled with copperplate engravings "I had no idea that Antonio Tempesta did things like this. I will take it." He added it to the small pile of books he had selected from Lo Ban's stock. The pile included such works as Hirschfeld's *Die Transvestiten*, von Altmann's *Au! Erlauschtes über, unter und neben schoenen Frauen* and Paul Geraldy's well-illustrated *Toi et moi*.

Von Unterhosen examined carefully Fingesten's 20th-century work *Improvisationen*. The color plates were in fine condition and all were present, unusual for this work. Putting it aside he quickly looked through Pellar's *Der verliebte Flamingo*, also a 20th-century work. "I'll take these two as well. Now, what about the *shunga* you usually have, my friend?"

Lo Ban pointed to a small pile of Japanese bound books on the shelf. "Help yourself. You'll be the first to look at them. Take them to a comfortable chair and look through them at your leisure. They are all identified and priced." While von Unterhosen, quite delighted, settled in for a long look, Lo Ban and I discussed the deal he had just negotiated.

One of the terms of the agreed prisoner exchange with our Syrian counterparts was that it take place at the Turkish/Syrian border. Since no governments were to be involved officially, we had to take pains to make the whole event seem, on the surface, a private deal. If something blew up, we were on our own. That's where Mehmet came in.

Mehmet was a native of Diyarbekir, an old, walled, caravan-stop city in the eastern part of Anatolia, where his father was a teacher. As a young man, Mehmet had moved to Istanbul and eked out a living as a translator and it was in this capacity that Lo Ban had hired him. Satisfied with his work and rather liking the earnest young Turk, Lo Ban recruited him to do occasional jobs for us. Nothing vital or dangerous, mostly gathering information on individuals we were tracking. We wanted to know with whom they met while in Istanbul and Mehmet became quite good at finding out those sorts of things. We began to trust him with more important jobs and he acquitted himself well in his new assignments. The money we paid him, modest as it was, materially improved his life-quality and he seemed a lot more cheerful. He was also perfectly content to do his job, mind his own business and not be concerned about what others were doing. He seemed to understand that he was small potatoes and he apparently didn't want to push his way up.

"Please, take these with you so I won't have to ship them. I'll post you a bill when I return home." Lo Ban wrapped several choice *shunga* and the rare little 12mo volume and the German and French works that von Unterhosen had selected. He was very pleased with his purchases and, needless to say, so was Lo Ban. They shook hands warmly and Karl von Unterhosen departed.

"Nice sale," I commented. Lo Ban agreed.

The fair was going well for us and we both had substantial sales. In addition, I had bought a splendid Ortelius atlas. The atlas, a 1602 edition, was in magnificent condition with the maps in fine original color. That purchase alone had made the fair worthwhile from a financial standpoint. And, of course, there was our other business...

About three weeks after the fair and our handshake agreement on the exchange of the prisoners, Mehmet and I were driving a Land Rover across Anatolia from Ankara to Diyarbekir. We had flown to Ankara, picked up the Land Rover, stocked it with supplies for the trip and headed east. I had never driven here before and was looking forward to getting the flavor of rural Anatolia. The countryside was rugged and our progress was slow, and given the Land Rover's suspension, less than comfortable. Whenever we could we fell in with short caravans of lorries and managed to attract no undue attention. I was pleased that Mehmet was with me—I felt too visible and naked in this barren, alien world and the presence of a Turk smoothed over many of the minor problems of travel. He was my passport.

Diyarbekir, the ancient city surrounded by looming black stone walls, rose in the distance, silhouetted against a dark, brooding sky. Approaching it, I imagined how, for hundreds of years, caravans saw the same sight and looked forward to a bit of comfort and rest within its outwardly forbidding walls. Mehmet drove through an ancient gate and followed a twisting path to his father's house. In case we were being observed, and I always assumed we were, we played it straight and acted the part of visitors without ulterior motive.

The modest stone house had a small courtyard walled with mud brick where Mehmet's father entertained us. A polite man, he seemed pleased that his son was doing well for himself in Istanbul, but was puzzled and a bit worried about the reasons for our trip east. A major US air base was near Diyarbekir and no doubt there was the unspoken worry that we were somehow involved with either its military business or with its other activity—electronic spying on the Soviets. His sympathies seemed to be a bit to the left and we all stayed away from political conversation. Nonetheless he made us feel welcome and we stayed with him for a few days, resting and sightseeing. Mehmet was a splendid guide, showing me around the old city of his childhood.

44

We took leave one morning and drove southeastward. Near Mazidagi, we saw another Land Rover by the side of the road. I pulled over, opened the back door and we got our passenger. Alonzo Septichema. No words exchanged, no handshakes or waves, just stop and go.

Septichema spoke fluent English. He was foul tempered, arrogant, as well as a fanatic and voluble Communist. The near-decade he spent in Italian prisons probably contributed to his ill temper. He did not have the common sense to stay quiet and I finally threatened to cut his balls off if he didn't shut up. His time in Italian prisons had taught him such things could happen, so he shut up.

Mehmet was remarkably subdued as we drove on. We skirted Mardin and picked up the road to Nusavbin. The last few kilometers to the Syrian frontier made Mehmet nervous. I could not tell if something other than the mild danger of the trip was worrying him. I was driving slowly as the road deteriorated but no matter how slow I went the ride was uncomfortably rough. Septichema began to complain but I turned around and looked meaningfully at him. He shut up. Finally, Mehmet pointed to a small trail leading off to the right. I turned the Land Rover and as we went around an outcrop of rock we saw them. A small gathering of people in uniform, A small truck and a car. "There they are." Mehmet almost whispered. His throat sounded dry. I thought he sounded afraid.

Slowing the Land Rover to a crawl, we approached closer and stopped. "Please stay here with him, Mehmet, I need to first go alone."

I walked up to the gathered group and saw Klinefelter, looking haggard. His head was hanging down and he was unshaven. Next to him were two men in private's uniforms, but I doubted they were privates. And to my surprise, walking toward me was someone I recognized immediately. Colonel XX.

Colonel XX was one of those people who was well-known in my business. He had been assigned to his country's embassy in several different European countries, and I had met him several times. We got along well and I enjoyed his company as well as his stories. Colonel XX was a great raconteur and wove wonderful tales around innocent and otherwise trivial events. He also had a fondness for good Scotch whisky, and once, about a half dozen years ago, I had left a bottle of Glenfiddich at the Embassy for him, knowing that his birthday was approaching. I don't know if he was expecting me here in this remote transfer place, but I certainly did not expect him. It puzzled me why someone of his rank would be effecting such a seemingly trivial exchange.

I signaled Mehmet to bring Septichema to us, and the two of them got out of the Land Rover and walked over. The colonel and I had not acknowledged each other and no words had been spoken.

"Go on over." I nodded to Septichema and he walked to the other side. At the same time the colonel motioned Klinefelter to come over to us.

"Cut my balls off? Ha! You capitalist bastard! Try it now!" Septichema screamed at me once he was safely behind privates and in the presence of the colonel.

Colonel XX raised an eyebrow and looked at me. There was more than a twinkle in his eye.

"What the hell," I thought, and, stepping forward, I extended my hand to the colonel. "Hello, again." I smiled at him.

The colonel stepped forward as well. He now had a broad smile and shook my hand. I saw a slight wink of an eye, a friendly gesture, but then a sudden, slight change in facial expression. He looked at Mehmet.

Out of the corner of my eye I thought I saw Mehmet reach into his coat, then seemingly thinking better of it he dropped his hand. It looked like an aborted move to draw a weapon. Or maybe not. But it could have been interpreted as such if one wanted to. And despite the outward calm, this was not a family picnic and all our antennae were on maximum gain. Clearly the colonel had seen it and was sufficiently alarmed to change his expression. But he decided to disregard it and the smile returned. "Hello yourself, Manasek." We said nothing more, but parted.

Klinefelter was sick. He had chills and diarrhea. He looked miserable and dehydrated. Mehmet drove the Land Rover and I gave Klinefelter a handful of diphenoxylate tablets. "This'll stop your trots long enough for us to get you back." Then I gave him several cans of tepid Coke, which he drank quickly.

On the road back to Diyarbekir we passed another Land Rover stopped on the shoulder. We pulled up in front of it and I told Klinefelter, "This is it. You get in there with them and we go. Goodbye."

Mehmet and I drove on silently. I needed to know if he had a weapon, which we had expressly forbidden. "No weapons of any sort on this trip, Mehmet. No gun, no knife, no nuttin'." Lo Ban and I were both explicit.

"Mehmet," I asked, "do you have a gun?"

He looked sheepish. "Yes, I brought my automatic. I'm sorry, I know you didn't want me to, but I was worried. I was afraid that something might happen at the last minute."

I was silent. This was a major breach of trust and would be the end of working with Mehmet. I didn't know the reason for the suspicious move he had made, but I sure as hell didn't want to drive back across Anatolia to Ankara with a guy packing heat. I really didn't want to drive back to Ankara, anyway. My butt was sore from the slab seat in the bouncing Land Rover. "Mehmet, I shall leave at Diyarbekir and fly back. You can drive the Land Rover back to Ankara and return it. I really want to leave and go home." Mehmet nodded. I think he was relieved that I didn't say more.

When the flight from Diyarbekir landed in Ankara, I sent Lo Ban a two-word coded fax just to let him know that all had gone well and that Klinefelter was back alive. I would let the rest hold until we could talk.

The whole transaction had gone very smoothly, with the exception of Mehmet's curious behavior. I also wondered, from time to time, why the Colonel was there. If this was simply a trade of small-potato people, why the colonel? Did he know, somehow, that I would be there? Even if so, his presence was not explained. Unless, of course, Septichema was more important than we thought.

Lo Ban was paid for the caper and he, in turn, paid off Mehmet. A handsome amount was wired to my London account and, for all practical purposes, that should have been the end of it. But neither Lo Ban nor I could ever quite figure out if Mehmet was telling the truth and really was just worried about being unarmed or if he had some other plans that, for some reason, he abandoned. There was also the problem of Mehmet owning a gun. Why? We filed this away and never used his services again. Mehmet, in turn, never contacted us or asked why his services had been discontinued.

Years later, Maria emphatically stated that we should have "disappeared" Mehmet. Now, decades older, hopefully a bit wiser, I still haven't decided if Maria was right. But I do remember how startled we all were that she was so emphatic about getting rid of Mehmet.

Chapter 5

Charlotte

After Mehmet left, I put him out of my mind for the moment and lingered deliciously, savoring both the strong black coffee and the *International Herald Tribune*. The trouble to which Lo Ban alluded was also easy to push away. I knew we would have to confront it, but today... Today I wanted to be alone and to relax. I toyed briefly with the idea of looking up Charlotte but set that thought aside, hoping it would not intrude again. Or maybe hoping it would.

I finished breakfast and went back to my room, where I coded a message. I used our old code. It took a while for me to do it, I had forgotten much but eventually I got the message translated. Our code would not have been difficult to break if a professional cryptanalyst had ever tried. But its genius was in that it was not obviously a code and therefore the coded message would not attract attention. We did not use a cipher so the message appeared quite innocuous. It had been years since we used the code, giving further support to my belief that this message would not be compromised. Later that morning I emailed it, from a cybercafe, to Veronica. I hoped it would make sense to her. In it I simply urged caution, warned her of snoopers and asked her to spread the word to our Old Group. At least, I hoped that's what I said. My visit to Istanbul, undertaken for very private reasons, was beginning to assume the trappings of an escapade from the Old Days. I sighed, paid the cybercafe, and walked into the bright day.

The Pera Palas is located in the southern edge of the old embassy district. The large embassy buildings, from the time Istanbul was the capital, are still dotting the district and many are now consulates. From the upper stories of the hotel one can look out to the Old City and it is but a short walk to the Golden Horn, that narrow inlet that separates new Istanbul from the old.

Heading south, I slowly walked down the steep hill leading to the Golden Horn. It always impressed me how the Galata Tower, a structure that dominates the skyline, is virtually unseeable from near. The maze of narrow streets and tightly packed buildings effectively blocks out a good view. I skirted the tower today, not being interested in the view from its observation deck nor the pricey restaurant on its upper stories.

When the new Galata Bridge was put up across the Golden Horn the roads leading to it were altered and I haven't gotten used to the new layout. The pattern of streets leading to the old bridge has been imprinted on me and, unless I pay attention, I will follow that pattern without thinking. Once again, I didn't pay attention and, lost in thought, wandered down familiar streets that used to lead to the bridge, but do so no longer. Vexed, I finally made my way to the bridge, cutting through the machine tool district, where grimed shop windows displayed lathe parts, drill bits, and mounds of stuff mechanical.

The old Galata Bridge was a wonderful, creaky structure. Under the roadway was a lower level that had some decent fish restaurants. Boats going by, traffic thundering overhead, a creaking bridge, and good fish served well created a memorable combination. The new bridge creaks less but still boasts a row of fishermen dangling their lines over the walkway's side railing. Some even have plastic buckets containing newly caught fish. In common with the old, the new bridge also has a lower restaurant level and one can still eat well, watch the boats go by and occasionally see flapping fish pulled up by the fishermen on the level above.

I stopped to buy a simit from one of the ubiquitous vendors and ate it while looking over the railing at the busy boat traffic below. From the corner of my eye, the outer limit of my peripheral vision, I thought I saw someone familiar. I couldn't place him, and dismissed the whole thing, concentrating instead on the wonderful view of the old city, with its minareted mosques looming, their domes dominating the surrounding rooftops.

The sun was warming the city nicely and the crowds at the open stands that seemingly lined each street of the old city moved slowly, picking away at merchandise piled high. It was wonderful to be able to just wander about and to savor and enjoy again the flavor of the city.

Behind the Yeni Cami is a small park, ringed by small shops and containing an outdoor restaurant. I headed there for lunch and was rewarded with a nicely located empty table, situated under a vine canopy. Sunlight filtered through and I was happy reading more of the *IHT* and nursing a cold *Efes* beer. The waiter assured me the sandwich I had ordered was on its way.

"Frank! Can it really be you?"

There was Charlotte. Smiling broadly.

I stood up to greet her; we embraced each other. A very long hug. There was none of the awkwardness of our last meeting. She seemed genuinely pleased and, admittedly, so was I. I pulled out a chair for her and she sat down, still smiling.

"Osman Bey told me you were in town. I saw him yesterday."

And I bet you weren't going to look me up, stinker!

"Nice to see you. Really nice. You look great!" As indeed, she did.

Charlotte had matured into a very handsome woman. Not pretty, girl-next-door, but handsome. Her eyelid still had the barely noticeable ptosis, but it was her smile that dominated her face. Charlotte put her hand over mine, tilted her head a bit and said, "I really hoped we would connect this time. Heard you come to Istanbul a bit and I've been researching at the Topkapi off and on for years. But we never were here at the same time."

Curious. This meant she was keeping tabs on me. "Well the least we can do is have lunch together. That is, if you can spare the time. Plenty of room at my table."

She smiled. "You're on!"

I signaled the waiter. Then Charlotte and I began, tentatively at first, to fill in the past few decades. Soon we were as before, sharing thoughts and even teasing each other.

After finishing at Radcliffe, Charlotte had been married briefly to a B-school student, but that ended quickly. It almost didn't "count." She then got her doctorate at Oxford, in Oriental History.

I wondered if we had overlapped at all when I was there working in the bug lab. But I didn't ask.

Another marriage and another divorce. Then a very attractive offer from NYU and her career was launched.

"I've all the time I need or want for my research. I have one graduate course each year. I love it. I also hear bits and pieces about you, sometimes from the damnedest people, but mostly from Osman Bey. Never a whole lot. He's tight lipped and I can't even seduce the information out of the dear old queen. Are you really a rare book dealer?"

Somehow I doubted that she didn't know that I was a book dealer. How could she and Osman Bey be such good friends and not be aware of this? Also, it might be just my vanity but I thought most scholars who work in her area know of me as a rare book dealer.

Charlotte put one hand behind her head, seemingly to straighten her hair. Or was it to show off? Her chest pushed forward. I am certain this was for my benefit, but, quite obviously, she had something to boast about. She wasn't wearing a brassiere and I imagined her breasts to be as firm as they were years ago. I looked at them and she looked at me looking at them.

"You haven't changed."

She shook her head. "I hope I have. For the better. They say I used to be a real shit and I've tried hard to change. And that's as introspective as I want to get with you," she smiled, "for now."

It was a nice smile. It made me feel very glad that we were here, in this city, in this light filtered, flickering, feeling comfortable with each other, decades after being lovers.

Charlotte suddenly started. "Look at the time. Three o'clock." She stood up. "Gotta run. Have to go to Ankara tomorrow. I'll be there at the University for a week. And I have to get to the Topkapi before it closes and ask them to hold the manuscripts for me until I return and not put them away. Look, can I take you to dinner tonight? Can you," and she sounded very tentative, "possibly do that with me?"

"Love to. I have a terrible feeling that tomorrow is the start of something for me and I'd like seeing you tonight very much."

"Pera Palas did you say?" I hadn't, but I nodded. "I'll come by for you in time for drinkies. Then we'll go to a nice place I know. I'll make the reserves."

We hugged briefly, exchanged light kisses and I felt her breasts pushed lightly to me. Then Charlotte strode off, in the direction of the Topkapi.

"Osman Bey was right. She looks good," I thought.

I had another *Efes* beer and sipped it slowly while thinking of Charlotte. "How the hell did she know where I was staying?" But Charlotte had always been one up on me. Even long ago she seemed to have a huge network of friends and acquaintances that constituted a private world—a world that only opened a few cracks to me from time to time. Such as now. In all the years I have known Osman Bey, he had never once mentioned Charlotte. And now he must have told her about me and where I was staying. I wondered why now, and then I wondered if it was indeed Osman Bey who had told her where I was staying.

I had a few hours to kill and took advantage of them by wandering the area's back streets. Narrow, sidewalks obstructed with cluttered displays of all sorts of secondhand goods. Mostly rubbish, such as odd pairs of plastic rainboots, old leather shoes, and bits and pieces of housewares. The cacophony of bargaining sounds was everywhere; the typical Istanbul background noise of districts such as this. I never bought anything from such sidewalk vendors but found the existence of this trade fascinating. Despite the seeming prosperity of much of the city, this kind of economy was still necessary. Clearly, I was an outsider to all this and attracted the stares of the merchants, many of whom squatted down on their heels next to their goods. The stares almost always turned to smiles when I made eye contact. Yes, I like Istanbul. Crowded though the area was, I was completely anonymous. I felt invisible and that was a curious, somehow delicious feeling.

I wandered slowly back to the Pera Palas, giving me enough time to shower and think of Charlotte.

There is a narrow mezzanine overlooking the lobby of the Pera Palas and I waited there for Charlotte. She arrived, entering the lobby with long, purposeful strides. Her legs were still beautiful. Her black dress matched her hair and her smile was genuine when she saw me approach.

The bar was nearly full and the murmur of voices, the smell of cigarette smoke, and the clink of glasses seemed to make it easier for us to share our thoughts. It was a throwback to America of the '60s, our America, a time when bars such as this permitted smoking as well as drinking. And both of us, once again back in Our Time, easily exchanged resumes over glasses of Chablis.

"Hell of a profession you've chosen." Charlotte was blunt. Just as I remembered her. "Sorry, Frank, didn't mean to make it sound that way. But over the years I've heard bits and pieces of gossip about you and your shenanigans. And I don't only mean dealing in rare books. There are people in the academy who despise you even though they really don't know exactly what you do. Yet you're a mystery—I still don't know how to figure you out. Ever think of peace and quiet?"

"Yeah, all the time."

"Sorry again." Charlotte put her hand on mine. "I don't mean to sound that way. I guess I put my foot into it again."

"No offense. I really don't know about my career. Never thought of it all that much in any analytical way. It all just seemed to flow naturally. One event led to another. It's almost as though I was a bystander. An observer. Except I wasn't, of course." But I liked her hand on mine.

"And now you hang out in Istanbul?"

"I get here every once in a while. Seems you do, too."

"I love this city. I love working at the Topkapi. I don't even dislike Ankara—nice university. Funny we haven't bumped into each other here, before now. How long will you be here this time?"

"I honestly don't know. Something seems to be in the wind and I haven't the foggiest what it is. I hope it's really nothing. I didn't come here trying to dig up excitement or adventure. You said you'd be in Ankara for a week?"

"And then back here. Osman Bey's letting me stay at his house. Sweet man. He doesn't like Bosphorus House for some obscure reason and doesn't think I should stay there. It's spartan, but I like the company. There are usually a half–dozen or so scholars there at any one time and it's quite fun. But now I'll be at Osman Bey's when I get back to Istanbul. In about a week."

I think Charlotte caught her repetition and blushed slightly. I pretended not to notice. But I had, and was pleased.

"Change the subject?" She still had her hand on mine and I still liked the feeling. "I picked out a small restaurant not too far away. I've eaten there a bit and it's quite nice. Short walk, too."

Traffic was dense. Charlotte and I held hands as we skipped between cars and light trucks, dancing that short ballet that is required every time one crosses a street in Istanbul.

"Up this street," said Charlotte as she guided me into a right turn. We ducked into the side street, dodged another taxi, and walked uphill through a succession of dimly lighted, ever-narrower streets. "Watch out for the chuck–holes." Charlotte put her arm around mine and we walked closely together.

The restaurant was small and quite clearly an "in" place. Charlotte had arranged for a table in the corner and the owner took us there, obviously showing us off to his other patrons, all of whom were Turks. Charlotte's Turkish was pretty good and she showed off that a bit too.

Charlotte had already ordered the meal—apparently necessary in this small restaurant. Course after course of wonderful food, washed down with wine and laughter. Our old habit of making silly puns was rediscovered and we each tried to outdo the other, becoming more outrageous as the meal wound down.

The last of the food gone, the bill paid, we stayed and lingered a bit over coffee. I certainly didn't want the evening to end, and I fervently hoped she didn't either. I imagined that I saw her eyelid droop just a tad more. But candlelight can play tricks of that sort. We finished our coffee and left, exchanging mutual thanks with the owner.

Outside, she took my arm and pressed close to me.

"Walk you home?"

"Sure." We walked downhill, down the narrow streets with the bad pavements and the stacks of curbside boxes and the cats that prowled amongst them. Very slowly toward the Pera Palas.

We stopped midway there. Charlotte turned and held me close to her. I was certain now that her eyelid was telling me something and when we kissed, her breasts, pushed tightly against me, said the same.

"Remarkable what this city can do!"

"Mmmm," said Charlotte as she held me closer.

We spent much of that night pretending that the episode at the Hayes-Bick had never happened.

Charlotte and I were still in half–sleep as the morning intruded. "I have to be in Ankara by late this afternoon." I put my arm around her, she snuggled in and we both went back to sleep in a losing battle to stave off the day. Reality won out and forced itself upon us in a half hour and we sat up, finally forced to acknowledge that the sun had risen.

Even the magic of our night was not powerful enough to stop time, and finally breakfast had finished its dawn and had to come to an end. All the dawdling in the world would not keep Charlotte from leaving.

We stood outside the Pera Palas and I couldn't think what to say.

"Walk you over to Bosphorus House?"

Charlotte smiled weakly. "I'd better taxi. Still have to pack" then, perhaps as an afterthought, "but thanks for the offer." She kissed me lightly on the cheek and slipped into the lead taxi in the rank. A nice bit of her leg showed, for perhaps a second or so too long for it to have been inadvertent.

"What the hell," I thought, "is this the Hayes-Bick all over again, or what?"

But then I thought of her leg and smiled and waved to her as the cab drove off.

More Charlotte-speak.

By now, it was almost noon. I dropped off my key at the desk and wandered back outside. Feeling curiously empty, puzzled at the turns my visit here had taken, I nonetheless resolved to keep to my original plans as much as possible.

"Sahaflar Çarçisi." The taxi driver nodded and we slipped into the passing stream of cars. He picked our way across the Atatürk Bridge, drove under the dignified ruins of the aqueduct of Valens and swung east, toward the old mosque at Beyazit.

A courtyard next to the Beyazit Mosque holds the city's oldest surviving book market, the Sahaflar Çarçisi. The pleasant square, with trees and other greenery in the middle, has small shops and stall around its perimeter, many owned and operated by third generation or more book sellers. In years past I had done a lot of business with some of the antiquarian dealers here, but in more recent times have found little to buy. But it was nice, nonetheless, to visit and renew old acquaintanceships.

I was struck immediately by how touristic the place had become. Years ago it was where serious bookbuyers would deal with serious book sellers and but a few tourists came through. The square was now, in contrast, choked with foreigners and many of the old shops had become glorified souvenir shops.

Ordinary manuscript leaves from ordinary Ottoman-period Korans were on display by the hundreds. However, these ordinary leaves had become embellished with marginal hand–painted decorations to make them more saleable. In addition to making them more attractive to tourists, these added decorations destroyed whatever value they had as original manuscripts in their own right.

There were stacks of palimpsets, old paper manuscript leaves of no consequence that had copies of Turkish miniatures painted on them. In many cases the leaves were from old Turkish student exercise books and the overpainted illustrations had no relevance whatsoever to the text. But few tourists would know that and most assumed them to be genuine Turkish miniatures. In reality, there are very few real Turkish miniatures, and I would guess that the number of fakes in the stacks for sale in Beyazit at any one time far outnumbered them!

Many of these recent miniatures were quite attractive examples of a type of modern folk art and their manufacture provided a livelihood for some rather skilled artists. But they were being marketed as the real thing. Some had even been painted for specific audiences. In one stack I found some "16th-century" views of Jerusalem with the Star of David on flags flying from the walls! One attractively done example was priced at roughly $500. When I put it down, it was snatched up by an American couple. With a determined walk, they took their trophy into the shop and emerged shortly after, clutching their wrapped leaf and looking very smug. Clearly they had bested the dealer inside!

In one corner of the courtyard was Mustafa Ozak's shop. Mustafa Ozak, now dead, had been a charismatic Dervish, an Imam. He was also a rare book dealer and in the old days I did quite a bit of business with him, usually through his manager, Ibrihim Akoklar. I would also go to his mosque and worship with him on occasional evenings. But now, his shop was locked. When I peered in I saw a portrait of Ozak on the wall and a few cartons, but no sign of active enterprise.

Seeing the changes that had taken place in the book sellers' square saddened me a bit, but at least it was still there and, who knows? Perhaps some day it would lose its touristic veneer and re-emerge as the strong core of Istanbul's antiquarian book seller community.

The entrance to the Sahaflar Çarçisi is right next to the Grand Bazaar and although I would have liked to go in and wander about the day was getting on and I didn't want to be late to dinner with Lo Ban. So instead, I headed back to my hotel across the Golden Horn and up the steep hill to Pera.

Stretched out on my bed I allowed Charlotte to re-enter my thoughts, putting me in a happy state as I dozed off, to awaken an hour or so later in time to head north to dinner with Lo Ban.

Chapter 6

LoBan and I revisit bookselling

As I walked up past Taksim and on to the Hilton Hotel, anxiety began to surface and I feared that my dinner with Lo Ban might presage the beginning of some unpleasantness, that some lukewarm leftover intruding from the past would end my holiday. The incident with Amanda seemed to point in that direction. And there was Blaser. Whoever killed Blaser would regret it enormously and I hoped whoever did it already realized he had made a serious error.

"I like this hotel." Lo Ban looked comfortable as he stretched out in the lounge chair, sipping a glass of white wine. "In the old days I used to stay at the Park Oteli, but when they ripped it down, seemingly for no good reason, I moved up here to the Hilton. Have a drink?"

"No thank you, Lo Ban, I'm mostly off the stuff. Occasional beer, wine with dins, but not much more."

Lo Ban nodded. "Ah, yes. And so should I. But I limit myself to a glass or so of wine and I don't feel it too much. But the martinis of old are out for me."

"Same with me. Pity. You know, I really miss them. I miss the Scotch as well. But one of either and I lose my edge for the next day. Not good. Of course, I still whine about it a lot. Sign of age. Sign of impending death." I meant that last one lightly, but Lo Ban frowned. I don't think he believed in mortality.

"A sign of age is when we look back a lot. In my case, another sign of age is my creaking joints and desire for more creature comfort. I would rather lie in bed another hour than start another adventure."

"But they were splendid times, Lo Ban. What sport! I can't believe that you lie about in bed, anyway. Listen to us, we sound like the old guys playing chess in the park outside. Now confess, what brought you to Istanbul, and what happened with Amanda?"

"Amanda, as I said, is in hiding. Not too uncomfortable for her, mind you, but she is staying off the streets and nobody knows where she is. Not even her friends. I never reported the shooting to the police, but had friends in the Department keep their ears to the ground and let me know if anything of possible relevance turned up. Something did. A short time later a foreign corpse was found. No papers on him, but he had some Turkish banknotes in his pocket. They were in a little buttoned inside pocket—some sort of mad money, perhaps. Whoever killed him and removed his ID must have overlooked it. None of his papers were ever discovered. Was this evidence? Was he related to the shooting? I don't know, but it was the only thing I had to go on. It certainly wasn't enough to keep the police involved so I thought I would come here to Turkey and snoop a bit. I'm really glad you're here, too. I was going to ring you last night but thought better of it.

"Good thing, too," I thought.

"What brings you to Istanbul this time? Elizabeth again? Or," with a sly smile, "someone else?"

"Yeah, Elizabeth. All is OK, but every once in a while I need to go there myself and check on her grave." Did Lo Ban know about Charlotte? How fast could gossip spread, if it was indeed gossip? I decided to ignore his implication. "Did you find out anything here in Istanbul since you arrived?"

"Yes and no. None of the usual contacts know much but they are all very vague. It seems that something is in the air, but nobody knows what it is for sure. It isn't even certain whether it does or doesn't involve me, or Our Group. Consensus is that somebody ordered a job and it was given to a petty crook from Izmir, but nobody here seems to know much about him, what the job was, or if he's the guy who got whacked in Hong Kong. But he appears to have gone missing.

"This is still Istanbul and I put out a call for information to the hotel clerks. Supplements their income. I've been here a week or so and no doubt word of that had gotten out. Information travels in both directions."

Lo Ban did not volunteer what he had been doing the past week, but it clearly did not involve Mehmet. Nonetheless, it might be useful to know what Mehmet had been up to and what he was doing now.

"Maybe this is why Mehmet took the trouble to look me up. Did you find out anything about him?"

"Mehmet really is a travel editor now. However, and this is a big 'however,' he still does jobs on the side. He has a small cottage business, I gather quite profitable, and has two people working for him, data-gathering. It seems that nobody of interest can pass through Istanbul without him poking about their business. He does for others what he did for us. He's a contractor, not ideologically involved, and he doesn't do violence. He doesn't contract hits. He only sells info. That much is definite."

"So we should see him? In Üsküdar?"

"Would you make the arrangements to see Mehmet for dinner? I don't care what day. You say he's in Üsküdar? Haven't been there in years. Understand it's quite fashionable in places. Now, old friend, let's get some supper."

Our conversation changed to bookselling. We quietly shared memories of the fantastic "scores" we made, lied about the quality of our material and gossiped about the friends we had made among the dealers. I felt nostalgia grasping at me.

"We haven't done a book fair together in years, Lo Ban. Matter of fact, I haven't done one alone in years. The AAB still sponsors them and they're well attended. In California the fairs still have hundreds of exhibitors."

Lo Ban roared with laughter. "I still think that's very funny! Hundreds of antiquarian book dealers! Hundreds of rare book dealers! And most of them with thousands of their rare books for sale on the internet. Ah, me. Or, as they say here, *inshallah!*"

"Maybe *oi vay?*"

Lo Ban ignored this and continued. "Have you been to the Sahaflar Çarçisi yet? Wonder who's running old Mustafa Ozak's shop. He's been dead for some years and I haven't been there since he died. I guess old Ibrahim is dead, also.

"The shop hadn't had much really good stuff for sale in years. Or at least any that was offered to me. On the other hand, it doesn't take much if it's the right stuff," mused Lo Ban. "I'd always had the feeling that Ozak's book business was a front for something else."

"Yes, in a way it was. Ibrihim would try to keep visitors as long as possible—perhaps to closing time and then invite them to the mosque. Years ago I used to pray with Mustafa Ozak—his mosque was in some derelict area out along the Golden Horn. I needed guides to get there and I could never find it again if I had to."

"Speaking of fronting for something else, I stopped by at Osman Bey's, off the Isticlal. Had a very pleasant non-book chat. Rodney Oufle was there. I think he's living there now, or at least staying there. Anyway, Osman Bey would like to see you—didn't know you were in town." I had no more said this than it occurred to me that Osman Bey most likely knew Lo Ban was in town but for some reason didn't want me to know that he knew. And logic then dictated that he had somehow guided Charlotte my way? Charlotte. I was thinking of her again. "Let's go together to call on Osman Bey tomorrow. Always nice to see him and maybe he has something we might buy."

"See? We're practically back in business together again!" Lo Ban smiled. "Perhaps we'll do another fair together!"

"If you're serious about it. It might be fun. I think the last one we did together was the New York AAB fair about five or six years ago. I seem to recall that was the time they tried to throw you out for 'incivility unbecoming the profession.'"

This memory caused Lo Ban to smile. Then he threw his head back and laughed. "Yes, I made some dust jackets out of newspaper, took a felt marking pen and labeled them 'Original DJ in fine condition' and put them on my incunables."

"Then you put up the big sign that read 'Incunables. Without DJ as priced, with DJ add $2000.'" We both laughed again. "And they failed to see humor. Imagine that."

"And that Lope de Nada guy sent me a seven-page letter full of invective, threats, and ill–breeding. After all I did for him in Vienna when he was farting like a motorboat."

"Yeah, you sent him to McDonald's."

"So, I should have sent him to the Korso already?"

The thought of Lope de Nada in the Korso made us both smile.

"Have you much inventory left, Lo Ban?" I asked. "I still have a hundred or so nice-ish items tucked away."

"Same here. I think I have somewhere between a hundred and a couple hundred items. Good stuff. They haven't been flogged around. The stock is old enough to have become fresh again."

This diversion was beginning to sound interesting—something we could do together. My semiretirement had been pleasant. Sitting on the back porch in early morning watching the sun come up over the distant hills, the occasional visit from an old client, the occasional very satisfying business transaction, time to pursue other interests, friends, to travel without the specter of violence shadowing me. Lo Ban had voiced the same feelings and when occasionally, the Old Group met, usually somewhere in Europe, Veronica and Maria looked more relaxed each year. We rarely talked about the Old Days but once in a while it was fun to indulge in reminiscence. Over the years we had lost some wonderful friends and comrades and we remembered them well. And there were those who were still active but of necessity had severed ties with us. We still treasured those past friendships. Over the past decade or so we four survivors, Lo Ban, Maria, Veronica, and I, along with Amanda, had taken on ever fewer jobs, but Lo Ban and I had continued our respective antiquarian book businesses. But these too were allowed to wither a bit over the years and now we were proposing to have another hurrah. I looked forward to it with some mixed feelings. Yes, we knew our stuff and could probably still muster a good presentation at a book fair, but the trade had changed. The moving window of collecting keeps going forward in time and book fairs were now overwhelmingly filled with twentieth-century items. It is hard for many of us to consider them "antiquarian." This is not necessarily Gresham's Law in operation, but it reflects a change in the tastes of American collectors. It seems, although there are no studies I know of to back me up, that younger collectors are more comfortable with maps and books in English and that are not too alien in appearance. Many times I have witnessed the inability of a collector to even determine the language on a map. They cannot tell if it is German or French or Latin! These collectors are far more comfortable buying 19th- or 20th-century American maps or books written in English. They like maps of America from this period. The geography is more familiar than that of very early maps, say from the 1500s, and many collectors derive great joy in locating the region where they live currently or where their families lived fifty or a hundred years ago. It seems that much of the change in character of book fairs in the past few decades reflects simply the realities of doing business—dealers sell what collectors will buy.

"But none of this, Lo Ban, gets us closer to who shot at Amanda. Let me suggest we chat up Mehmet. If that doesn't get us anywhere we can try calling in some old debts, but I would rather not."

We both agreed to eat in, and had a rather nice dinner in the hotel dining room. Afterwards, over cups of fresh, decaffeinated coffee, we killed several hours catching up on gossip.

I ended our evening by telling him about Red, Blaser, and the pheasant shoot.

"I don't like two things going on at once and I think Amanda takes precedence." I continued with the thought, "even over Blaser."

Lo Ban nodded. "But let's not rule out helping Red with his problem."

I nodded, got into a taxi and went back to the Pera Palas.

A faint trace of Charlotte's perfume lingered in my room and blissfully, I went to sleep. And wondered.

Chapter 7

A tourist in Istanbul runs into trouble

Patience was something that had been hard for me to learn, but I had gotten pretty good at it as the decades rolled by. I hadn't been entirely convinced that there really was a plot to kill Amanda, and I wasn't sure that Lo Ban himself was convinced. We didn't speak about these doubts, but I think that was why we were letting the scenario unfold at its own pace rather than try to force it. Patience. And an unspoken mutual agreement had been forged and we would go into this together.

After breakfast I rang up Mehmet and left word that Lo Ban and I accepted his invitation and when did he want us to come by?

The day was another splendid one and I walked slowly down to the tünel, walked across the new Galata bridge that spanned the Golden Horn and wandered into the Old City. Time to be a tourist again and revisit some of my favorite places. I savored the sounds and smells of the Old City.

Near the Blue Mosque is a small building that has a staircase leading down to a damp, curious, giant underground cistern. The ancient water reservoir has a forest of stone columns supporting the ceiling and footed in water. This was a favorite place for Victorian travelers and a vast amount of Victorian fantasy revolved about this place. Legends sprung up of bold young men rowing off into the night carrying only a few torches, never to be seen again, never to find their way back from the endless jungle of ancient columns. There must have been epidemics of the vapors when these stories were printed back in England. The legends of the underground cistern represents an artificial mystery—essentially a ghost story invented for the sole purpose of mystifying even more, to Europeans, this unusual and possibly strange city, a city unlike anything elsewhere in Europe. But in truth it was a mysterious place. When I was here last a feeble light bulb shed enough light to see but a few rows of columns and then darkness enveloped the cavern. Now, a major restoration project has been completed and there is a well–done presentation of the entirety of the cistern. One can walk through its vast interior on a catwalk over the water, the columns are properly illuminated, and there is opera music in the background. Although this all sounds bizarre, it actually works and, much as I miss the feeble light and mysterious darkness, my non–Victorian soul appreciates being able to explore the entire structure. Despite the fact that the bold young rowers have never been found, I've visited this place every time I've been in Istanbul.

The sunlight made me squint after I came up from the dim light of the cistern. Although I do not believe the stories of lost boatmen, the place is still sufficiently unearthly to make the daylight above a welcome contrast. I ambled along, past Trajan's column and toward the covered bazaar. Another one of my ritual stops. There is little in the bazaar these days that I would want to buy, but it is a bit of good fun to wander through and look at the latest in tourist trinkets, leather jackets, gold armlets, carpets, and of course, copper. Of all the items for sale in the covered bazaar, copper is my favorite. In my younger days I used to ship much of the stuff back to the States and I still have some nicer pieces scattered throughout my house and office. The copper merchants are located in, oddly enough, the region called the Copper Bazaar. But this time I was astounded to see how few copper dealers there were compared to my last visit. What had been a large and thriving part of the bazaar was now reduced to a handful of copper dealers who were barely surviving. Much of the rest of the old Copper Bazaar is now occupied by leather jacket merchants. But one can still find very old copper pieces, heavy and often tinned, dating to the times of the Caliphate. I stopped in one of the remaining little copper shops and looked at a very nice group of old tinned pots. Made of very heavy sheet copper, these pots were unlike new ones and had a wonderful massive feel. The proprietor began his sales pitch but I really was not interested in carrying home a suitcase full of metal. This time, I promised myself, I was not going to burden myself with heavy items and I left the copper bazaar, headed toward a wonderful restaurant that I hoped still existed.

As I left the shop I caught sight of someone who had been, I thought, also waiting near the underground cistern. He was idly looking into another shop window, but occasionally looked my way. He was tailing me. He wasn't very good at it. But lunch was next. I ducked around the corner and slipped through a wooden doorway set into the market wall. It opened onto a small courtyard with tables and chairs. A small number of people were already taking their noon meal. This little restaurant had the best lamb dishes in Istanbul and I ate very well. I had been introduced to it years ago by a book dealer colleague—I would never have learned of it on my own since the restaurant has no sign and there was no outside indication that it exists.

My tail had gone by the time I left the restaurant, but he had spoiled my day. Now I knew I had to be careful. But careful of what still wasn't clear. Patience.

I slipped into a cybercafe and checked my email messages. Veronica had gotten the one I sent her and, indeed, had notified the Others to be careful. Or at least to be aware that something might be brewing. Some minor bits of e-business were taken care of quickly. Then came a real shocker—I received an email detailing my entire activities for the past two days. Times, places, routes, all were itemized. There was no signature and it had evidently been sent through a laundering site, so I could not readily trace its route. Was this a threat or a warning? Clearly, Lo Ban and I had been followed and, overall, it must have been a pro job because, except for today's tail, we both had been completely unaware of being observed. I forwarded the disturbing message to Lo Ban with a request that he meet me at my hotel. Carefully.

"Time for us to get proactive rather than responsive," I muttered to myself as I walked out of the cybercafe, "but not to show it." My vibrissae were picking up all the early warning signs. I wondered if that email really was a threat or was it a warning from someone watching out for me.

I stopped for a cup of coffee and let myself catch a tail again. This guy was much better than the last and I had trouble convincing myself that I was being followed, but a few tricks confirmed it. My tails were being changed as I meandered back across the Golden Horn, dodged the roaring traffic, rode up the tünel and headed back to the Pera Palas. I counted four tail-switches. This must be very important to someone, whatever the "this" might be. And the "someone" had money enough for good people. And Charlotte. Did this concern her in any way? I tried pushing that thought away but couldn't stop the uneasy feel of worry from creeping in.

The thought of Charlotte made me ache. A dull ache, just like the one I felt decades ago when she and I parted on a street in Cambridge. I thought of her and ached and smiled and worried. Charlotte. With me again.

Lo Ban was waiting at the Pera Palas when I arrived and there was also a message from Mehmet, suggesting we dine with him the next evening. Lo Ban and I went up to my room. I felt safer there than in the public spaces downstairs.

Nothing had been disturbed in my room. The maid had done her thing but there had been no obvious search or snooping. I took a small portable RF detector from my suitcase and began to sweep the room. My machine was not very sensitive, but it was good enough to pick up an ordinary bug if there was one anywhere in the room. Lo Ban kept speaking so that if there was a bug, it would be transmitting and my detector would pick it up.

We located the bug on the back of my headboard. I didn't disturb it and Lo Ban did not alter his monologue and I kept walking about as though pacing, and continued the sweep of the room. We fell into a routine that we had used several times before upon discovering a bug. It was especially useful now, when we had no idea who was doing this and all we knew was that they were good and very competent.

"OK, let's cut to the chase, Lo Ban." I announced. "I don't like what's going on here. I think I was tailed today and I recognize one of the goons. We can get our man "T" to hit him. That'll send a message. They've made their moves, now we do ours. Second act in a two-act play."

"Yeah, but I have a better hit to make," Lo Ban paused. "Let's go after Himself. We know enough to make serious trouble and once they're all busy putting out fires, we make our real move."

Of course, both "T" and "Himself" were our inventions, but we hoped it sounded as though we had some real knowledge and the ability to use it. The only trouble was that it might also be so incorrect that it would reveal to the opposition that we really didn't know anything. And even if we could we certainly would not disappear a tail. Nothing would be gained and it might have the same effect that throwing a rock into a bees' nest has.

"Now, let's eat!" I motioned to the door and we left.

We took the mahogany elevator down and walked out into evening Istanbul. I had my little RF detector in my pocket and we decided to check out Lo Ban's place.

Two changes of taxis later, we were in the Hilton, in Lo Ban's suite. Here too, we found a bug, and in the same place as the one in my room. ("Not very creative," muttered Lo Ban later) We left this one in place also and left the room.

"This is getting worse and I'm beginning to worry—there are just two of us and we're seemingly up against somebody real, and whoever they are, they're moving. Let's eat in the hotel tonight. I don't feel like wandering the streets after dark. And tomorrow I'm going to move in here. Let's try to get a suite together. Close ranks." Lo Ban agreed.

The hotel dining room was sparsely populated because the hour was so early. The maître d' suggested a table for us, but Lo Ban pointed to one in the opposite corner. "That one."

"I am sorry, sir, that table is reserved." He again steered us toward the table he had suggested originally.

Lo Ban repeated himself. His voice carried a mixture of icy hostility and command. "That one." He pointed to the table. Few ignored him when he spoke in this manner. The headwaiter did not either. With a shrug he led the way.

We were silent for much of the meal. "Do we stay or do we leave?" Lo Ban didn't answer. "What about Mehmet tomorrow night? Is it worth the risk?"

"I don't know. We should find out who's so interested in us. Mehmet might be a key. It's likely, or at least possible, that he's being paid to spy on us.

"Going to his place for dinner might be worth the risk." Lo Ban paused. "Here is something we can try."

Lo Ban then outlined a scam. He had with him a small tape recorder and some tapes of various sounds. Among the sounds were several weapon noises, such as cocking a revolver and chambering a round in an automatic. Lo Ban proposed that we play some of the sounds to the bug so that whoever was listening would think we were armed. We would be thought less vulnerable. Then we would feed the bug some verbiage about the rest of our group coming in tomorrow. Whoever was bugging us would not have time to verify and this might delay whatever, if indeed anything, was being planned for us. The visit to Mehmet might be just safe enough under these conditions.

After dinner we contented ourselves with decaffeinated coffee. I sorely wanted a brandy, but couldn't afford what it would do to my reflexes. We didn't say much over the coffee, but we both were lost in thought. I don't know what Lo Ban was thinking, but I was having serious doubts.

"Why in hell are we here? Unarmed, out of practice and creaky and we don't even know what's developing around us. Is this still a sport?" I think this was the first time I ever felt this way when an adventure was unfolding.

Back in Lo Ban's room, we fed the misinformation to the bug. Lo Ban's little tape recorder played the sounds of an automatic being loaded while Lo Ban said to me "Here, catch. This one's for you. We'll each have one for tomorrow. Too bad the rest of our group won't get here in time for backup."

"But it'll be close, at any rate. They're due in early evening, aren't they?" I added that one for good measure.

Lo Ban scribbled a note—"Let's leave together."

We walked about the lobby where Lo Ban suggested our next move. "They aren't going to try anything major tonight or tomorrow before we go to Mehmet's—they will want to find out what we know and, if Mehmet's their lapdog it'll be his job to find out. The most they'll do is follow us to keep tabs on where we are and whom we see. So I think we'll be safe at least until after Mehmet's dinner. But tonight, we'll go to the Pera Palas in a taxi together. You jump out when we get there and I'll go back to the Hilton. Tomorrow you can check out of the Pera Palas and move into the Hilton. They're not nearly full and I'll get us a large suite that we can share. I think we need to stay close. There are only two of us."

"How many of them?"

"How the hell should I know?" At least Lo Ban admitted he was as uninformed as I. In the Old Days he would never have admitted it. I smiled. "And who the hell's 'them'?" he added.

Lo Ban showed the driver a US century and the driver was quite willing to weave through the tangled, twisted streets of Istanbul in response to Lo Ban's directions which consisted mostly of "Left" and "Right." I jumped out two blocks from the Pera Palas Oteli and the taxi roared on.

I searched the room thoroughly when I returned, but again, there was no sign that anyone had been in my room during my absence. No bombs. Still one bug. I left it alone and sleep came quickly.

Getting up earlier than usual, I carefully packed my suitcase, locked it and put a hair across the join near the back hinges. This location I prefer to the more obvious hair across the latch, since if anyone snooping is in a bit of a hurry, they are more likely to overlook it than if it were right near the latches.

I had my last nice Pera Pelas breakfast, checked out, and paid my bill.

"Would you like a taxi, sir?" asked the receptionist.

"Yes, thank you. I am going to the airport."

The receptionist raised her eyes a bit. "Are you leaving Istanbul?"

"Yes. I'm on an early flight to Athens. I'll be down right on, I just need to get my bag."

The hair on the suitcase was still there. I checked the room to be certain I wasn't leaving anything, took a last look at the bug but it had disappeared. It had not fallen off and I could not find it anyplace else. Sufficiently intrigued, I opened my suitcase and took out my little RF detector and swept the room. It was clean. It was irksome to have this much traffic going through my room, but the loss of the bug may have been a good thing. I am always tempted to yield to the child inside and say naughty things to bugs. At the time I always think it funny but invariably, I later wish I hadn't. At least my anonymous visitor had prevented me from doing that again.

For a brief moment I wondered if the bug was there when Charlotte spent the night with me.

The wonderful old elevator took me down once again, I left my key and stepped outside where a taxi was waiting.

"Airport, effendi?" The taxi driver was waiting.

"Evet!"

A few blocks later I took a US twenty-dollar bill from my pocket and showed it to the driver. "Quickly, turn right here!"

He stomped on the brakes and made a quick turn into a narrow street. I saw him smile—he evidently knew the routine. A few more sharp sudden turns and he owned the twenty. Another twenty got me to Taksim, where I changed taxis and went to the Hilton. There was really no need for these precautions since the Hilton was doubtlessly staked out but I hoped it would send a signal.

If I was going to be Mouse, then Cat had better be on its toes.

Chapter 8

How Osman Bey helps us

Lo Ban had selected a wonderful suite for us. Not only did it have a splendid view but it also was large enough for us to not get into each other's way. I put my bag into my bedroom and leaned back in a very comfortable chair in the common room, waiting for Lo Ban. The day was still young and I wondered if he had any plans. We really should, I thought, go visit Osman Bey and see if he had any books for us or at least catch up on book trade gossip. We certainly would have enough time for that before we were due at Mehmet's.

"A ferry ride. That's what we should do. Take a ride on a ferry." Lo Ban's suggestion stunned me. But he was really serious about this and I knew that it would be pointless to argue. Osman Bey would have to wait, and whatever we might be able to do as far as our other problems in Istanbul would have to wait. Lo Ban, of course, was being wily as usual and I had to agree that if we spent the day playing it might give our followers some pause.

And play it is indeed to ride on a Turkish ferry. Istanbul straddles the Bosphorus and one part of the city is in Asia and the rest in Europe. The Old City lies below the Golden Horn, a blind inlet of water leading to the west. The Old City has long been connected to the northern part by bridges, but until sometime in the 1970s there was no bridge across the Bosphorus. That, along with the congestion on the narrow roads that run along the Bosphorus's shore, made water travel preferred and a wonderful ferry system was the core of Instanbul's public transportation system. Decades ago many of the ferries were still old, Dutch-built steam ferries. I loved their near-silent propulsion, their engine boilers stoked manually by sweating stokers shoveling lumps of soft coal into glaring fireboxes. Belching huge amounts of dense black smoke that eventually settled over the entire city, these low-gunwaled boats would move silently from their slips, occasionally uttering a mournful deep-throated call from their steam whistles. Gone forever, these wonderful old steam-powered polluters have been replaced by diesel-driven ferries that, although more efficient, pollute in other ways. The wail of the steam ferry whistle is gone, that wonderful throaty sound no longer reverberates off the ageless domes and minarets of this city, mingling with the imam's calls to prayer, to produce sounds that are forever etched into my memory and will be, to me, forever Istanbul. Instead we now hear a diesel horn signaling progress.

"Where to?" asked Lo Ban as we walked toward the water.

"Bebek for lunch?"

We agreed and wandered down to the ferry slip to await the northbound boat. The ferries are still convenient, but not nearly as in the old days when they ran frequently—one needed only to wait for a few minutes for a ferry on the major commuting or travel routes. This time we waited a bit longer, but soon were on board and sitting on the starboard side watched the shore of Asia slip by, the banks dotted by large old houses built over the shore of the Bosphorus.

"Everything all right on the island?" Lo Ban was referring to the reason why I was here at all.

"Yes, Elizabeth's grave is well tended, I spent some time chatting with some of her old friends and had lunch with the priest who was going to marry us. He's a lot older now—at that both Lo Ban and I smiled—but still the same nice guy. The island itself is virtually unchanged, still unspoiled, still virtually no tourists, still wonderfully insular. The old, and only, bed-and-breakfast is still there and takes in the occasional visitor. Nonetheless, I may not go back again. I just needed to touch bases, so to speak, once again. Elizabeth's been dead a long time. Her spirit, well, it's still there. You know, Lo Ban, when I'm there I see her again but she hasn't aged. She's still like she was in those days when we were together. And she's still happy."

Lo Ban grunted. "Jackie Kennedy never grew old either. Whenever I saw her, even later in her life, she looked to me like she did during Camelot."

I let that one go by. Lo Ban could quite conceivably have been a friend of hers, although I hadn't known about it. But yes, there is a Camelot. That's why I go back to the island. The sun always shines, still bounces off her golden hair blowing in the wind and her smile and inner joy still outshine the sun. If fleetingly, Camelot appears. It is real. And I know it in my very heart.

"Elizabeth's parents are both dead now. I used to visit them every once in a while. We always got on well. Her brother now has the title. I saw him just a few months ago when I was in England."

"I only met him very briefly at the memorial service for Elizabeth. Not long enough even to get a read on him," responded Lo Ban. "What's he like?"

"Huntin', shootin', fartin'. No, I shouldn't say that. He's actually quite bright and is doing a lot with the lands. The tenants like him. I like him a lot. But he does like shooting and he finds farting terribly funny."

"Manasek, so do you, I might point out." There was just a hint of annoyance in Lo Ban's voice.

A few toots on the diesel's dreadful horn announced our arrival at Bebek. Despite the sunny day the deck had been cold and we were glad to be on land where the wind was less and we could get warm again. We wandered over to a restaurant that jutted out into the Bosphorus. Specializing in fish, it was well known and we were fortunate that there was space for us.

"You know, of course, that we were tailed on the ferry?"

Lo Ban had indeed noted it and we both surmised that our tail was very disappointed because our trip was clearly for lunch only and not for any other business that might be of greater interest to him. He sat at an outdoor cafe across the street and drank innumerable glasses of hot tea while waiting for us to finish lunch.

"I don't think it would help a bit to try to plan for Mehmet's dinner tonight. I have no idea what he wants, if anything."

"I don't like it." Lo Ban spoke softly. He always spoke softly when he felt danger. "We need a driver. I don't want to be stuck in Üsküdar late at night with no car or driver. I'm not going to trust a taxi and I don't want to drive."

"Nor I. Let's finish up and see if Osman Bey is around. Maybe we can get his man to drive us. At least we can trust him."

Lo Ban nodded. He got the bill and settled quickly. This time we took a taxi back along the Bosphorus to Istanbul, down almost to the Isticlal where the alley opened to Osman Bey's. Fortunately he was in.

We sat down on the overstuffed, carpet-covered divan and sipped his very strong coffee while we caught up on trade gossip. Unfortunately he had nothing to sell us this trip, but promised to let us know if something came his way. Osman Bey would always kept these promises. He was also very discreet. He did not mention that I had visited him not too long ago, even though Lo Ban was well aware that I had.

Was he still interested in early 19th-century plate books? "Yes, of course," responded Osman Bey, "Pardoes and Alloms. Always." I knew we could do some business. I had a dozen or so of these back in my office.

"Is Rodney still in town?" I needed to know out of sheer nosiness.

"Yes he is," replied Osman Bey." But he said no more. Perhaps to counter my nosiness, or perhaps to suggest I was a tad intrusive, he asked me, "Have you seen your friend Charlotte?" He again had that curious twinkle.

"What the hell," I thought, "was he up to?"

"Osman Bey," said Lo Ban, thankfully interrupting, "we have a favor to ask. We are going to dinner in Üsküdar tonight with someone we don't completely trust and really should have transportation to and from. This might be one of 'those' kinds of trips."

Osman Bey smiled. "So this isn't only a book-buying trip, is it? I should have suspected. Yes, of course I can help. I will arrange for my nephew to drive you. As a favor only. No pay. But tell me, Lo Ban, should he have backup? What is the story?"

"We don't know, Osman Bey," I answered for Lo Ban, "but it might be a bit dicey for us. We don't know what is going on or why someone is taking so much interest in us." I then filled him in on the history of Lo Ban's concern, Amanda's incident, and the two of us being followed. And our rooms bugged.

Osman Bey paused and sat back, pensive. "It sounds like private work, not the secret police. It sounds like someone just wants to fact-find about you. I know your man Mehmet a bit and my take on him is that although I don't like him and wouldn't trust him, I don't think he's dangerous. He's a bit of a suck. Still, I think my nephew will take a friend along with him."

Lo Ban wrote down Mehmet's address and the name of our hotel and the time we were due at Mehmet's. We shook hands and took our leave. This time, the "click" of the door sounded comforting.

"It always surprises me, Manasek, how intertwined this community is. Osman Bey clearly has a finger in more than one pie."

We had some time to kill so we decided to walk up to the Hilton. The crowds were thick on the Isticlal. The little restored trolley, with urchins hanging onto the back for a free ride, clanged its bell as it entered the space made for it by the dividing crowd, space that closed behind it. The trolley was like a slide moving through a zipper of people. Lo Ban and I speeded up a bit, dodging in front of some strolling Turks. Then, adroitly slipping into a shop entry, we waited for the tail to come by. He did, clearly disturbed that he couldn't see us. We slipped out into the pedestrian traffic again and worked our way behind him. Lo Ban darted in front of him and stopped short. The tail crashed into Lo Ban and I crashed into the tail and stumbled. With great apologies, I backed away from the tail, who looked at us with a mixture of fear and surprise. Lo Ban walked away as I continued my profuse apologies, but all the while smiling broadly at the hapless tail.

Lo Ban and joined up again a few blocks up the street and we did a "high five." "Well done, Lo Ban. The last time we did that was in Spain. Good move!"

"Anything on him?"

"Nothing. No heat, no wallet. Completely clean. But I did put a few US greenbacks into his pocket. Maybe they'll get him into trouble. Or at least make someone wonder about him. If his keepers find the money they will wonder. A small thing, only, but enough small things...."

Chapter 9

We dine with Mehmet

Osman Bey's nephew, a great hulking man of about 35, and his friend picked us up at the Hilton and began driving to Üsküdar, the Asian side of Istanbul. They had taken Osman Bey's large black Mercedes and the car purred gently as we crossed the bridge to Asia. Nephew knew Üsküdar well and had no trouble finding the address. It was a seemingly small house, appearing quite modest from the outside. Nephew and friend let us out and agreed to come back in two hours and wait outside for us, however long it might be for us to finish our dinner.

"Have a pleasant evening." Nephew smiled and drove off. I had a suspicion he wasn't going to go far. Osman Bey was indeed a good friend.

Mehmet opened the door as we approached. He smiled broadly. "Haven't seen you together in a long time. Glad you could come.

"For some reason, I thought you might have left town." Mehmet looked at me when he said this. I wondered how much he had paid the clerk at the Pera Palas for this bit of misinformation.

We shook hands and I noticed that Mehmet's was cold. A bit like a fish. Mehmet never did have a strong handshake but this was much worse than usual.

"Drinks?"

Lo Ban and I both opted for something soft. We settled for two ginger ales while Mehmet poured himself a healthy Scotch.

"So, what brings you to town this time? Skullduggery?"

Lo Ban frowned a bit. "Not really. Manasek just happened to be here and I'm here on some private business. We ran into each other. This is a very nice place you have here, Mehmet. Had it long?"

"No, just a little over a year. Let me show you around." He took us through the house and out the back that opened into a small, but nicely done, walled garden. He showed us also a small, but well-appointed octagonal room, with a fine inlaid wood ceiling. The room was a small library and Mehmet had some nice manuscript Korans that he unwrapped proudly and displayed for our enjoyment. Pulling down a 19th-century volume of Donovan's *British Insects* he said, "Since I do a bit of gardening I am building a small collection of garden books." He opened the Donovan and pointed to an insect on each page. He said nothing, just pointed to insects. Putting the book away, he took down a butterfly/moths book and did the same, pointing wordlessly to the creatures.

I did not speak to the images but I managed to compliment him on his garden. "It must be a lot of work. I can see why you're collecting garden books. Great fun. I could never identify either plants or the bugs that grow on them."

The three of us, Lo Ban, Mehmet, and I, exchanged a fleeting look. I am sure I was right. Mehmet was telling us something and I hoped Lo Ban understood as well.

Mehmet's hand shook a bit as he poured himself another Scotch. "Were you back on the island before you came here?" He did not look at me when he asked this. A good thing, too, because I am quite certain that he was not privy to that information. Mehmet was never either a friend or part of our Old Group. He did odd jobs for us, but that was all. I didn't answer. Elizabeth was none of his business and his query was impertinent.

"I'm here looking for the person who shot Amanda." Lo Ban's voice was low. "Heard there might be someone in Istanbul who knows about it." Mehmet looked more than a bit uncomfortable. I don't think he wanted to be here with us.

"And your work must be going well, Mehmet. This is a lovely house." I tried to interview him as we walked in to dinner. "Are you still doing outside jobs?"

"I'm working for a magazine now. That takes up a lot of my time." Mehmet was evasive. "And you? Still books and hush-hush?"

"Yes. I'm doing books, but not as much as before. And now I'm helping Lo Ban find who shot Amanda." I was blunt. "And not surprisingly I think we will."

"Well, if I was useful to you in the old days, perhaps I could help a bit now. It might be interesting to try to do some information-type things for you again."

Mehmet was offering to work for us! After we had not used him for a very long time, some 20 years, he wanted back in. There was no point in bringing up the gun issue again.

"I think we're on to something on our own," said Lo Ban, "and we'd like to let it play out first. However, if I were to ask you who you thought might be tailing us, who would you name first off?"

Mehmet paled and was more uncomfortable than before. "I know nothing at all about that. As I said, I haven't been doing outside work."

The rest of the evening was spent playing cat-and-mouse games with information. We let Mehmet know we were working, but we couldn't get any hard information out of him. There was clearly something in the wind, but it never materialized. All we knew was that he warned us about bugs. Or so we thought.

Dinner was characterized by small talk. Whenever Mehmet tried to turn the conversation to our activities we parried and finally he gave up. Once that happened, dinner became a lot more pleasant and social. Nonetheless, Lo Ban and I were both glad when it was over, and we were heading toward the door.

"Thank you for a delightful evening, Mehmet. I'm glad we've touched bases again. Let's have a drink together some evening before we leave Istanbul." Lo Ban tried to leave the door open to another contact with Mehmet, as we were about to leave his house.

"Splendid. Let's do that. And when do you leave Istanbul?"

"Manasek leaves in a week and I in two. So we'll ring you up in a day or so and set something up." Lo Ban was spreading some misinformation again.

"Wonderful! And thank you for coming." Mehmet seemed relieved and we shook hands and left. I was pleased to find Nephew and the Mercedes waiting. Mehmet walked us to the car and managed to whisper "Later" to us as he closed the door of the Mercedes.

"Phew!" was the first thing Lo Ban said as the car drove away from Üsküdar. "Was that a warning about bugs, or wasn't it?"

"I think it was. I also think Mehmet's been compromised and had to try to get something out of us. I suspect, though, that he really wants to be on our side, if for no other reason than I didn't kill him after the prisoner exchange."

Nephew suddenly stomped on the brakes and with squealing tires the Mercedes turned violently into a narrow side street, turned again, and roared up an alley not more that a few centimeters wider than the car itself. We hurtled out of the alley into a large thoroughfare, thankfully missing the other traffic, which with horns blaring managed to swerve around us. Nephew turned into the flow of traffic heading north and said, "We're being followed. I really don't like the looks of the guys who were behind us. I think I shook them, but that's not the point. Do you want to go back to your hotel or to my Uncle's place?"

We opted for the hotel and hunched down as far as we could for the remainder of the trip. Lo Ban and I leaped out of the Mercedes in front of the Hilton and sprinted down the walkway into the lobby. "I think we really need some weapons, Lo Ban." I was out of breath from the short sprint. "Now is when we need them. I'm feeling boxed in—somebody very aggressive is interested in us and they hold the high ground right now."

"I don't want to mess with the Turks on a weapons charge. Remember, I told Mehmet you were leaving in a week and I was going in two? Well, let's both leave tomorrow. Our time here isn't productive and we might get killed. I'm too old to get killed. We're alone and we don't even know who's after us, or, really, why. Not good. I say let's run and regroup somewhere else."

"Such as?"

"Doesn't matter. As long as we finally get to Madrid. To Maria's. I think we should stick together. It would be best if we can get on the same flight. We can watch each other's backs. If they want to take us, it's easier for them if we're alone, and we don't owe them that favor."

"Madrid it is and together if possible." I agreed with Lo Ban's logic, and assumed he had some valid reason for picking Maria's place in Madrid. The prospect of seeing her again appealed to me. Maria was one of our Old Group and she and I went back a long way. We liked each other's company and things felt very easy when we were together. To my surprise, once again the thought of Charlotte intruded. Things had been very easy between Charlotte and me, and that night...

Once in our suite, we pushed the TV cabinet, the heaviest movable piece of furniture there was, in front of the door. "I'll take the first shift if it's OK with you. Three-hour shifts, as we used to do?" Lo Ban agreed.

The night passed without incident. During my time on watch I sat thinking about Maria and it was all pleasant. I also thought about Charlotte and that was pleasant also. At six the next morning we checked out, awakened a sleeping taxi driver and went to the airport to wait for the ticket counters to open. The first flights out of Istanbul were domestic and we were able to get two seats on the shuttle flight to Ankara. Not our first choice, but at least we'd be moving. And that made us harder to hit.

In Ankara we checked outbound flights on the monitor. The next flight would be a Lufthansa to Frankfurt. We were lucky and we got two adjacent seats on the nonstop flight.

"Manasek," said Lo Ban after our flight had taken off, "since we're talking about doing a book fair, perhaps we should stop and see Eberhard. I don't like Frankfurt enough to hang around in the city but I'm tired after all that stuff in Istanbul and could use a few days of peace and quiet and perhaps pick up some good books. A visit to Eberhard might accomplish a lot."

Lo Ban was certainly playing the whole thing cool, and it still wasn't clear to me if we were hunting or only being hunted. Our activities were certainly not predictable.

"What you really want to do is eat some good German food." It was my turn to be the cynic. "But it sounds OK and I could use a few good nights' sleep, anyway."

Chapter 10

We go to buy some books

We arrived in the Frankfurt airport on time and after getting through passport control stopped to buy a newspaper. Lo Ban got a *Frankfurter Allgemeine* and I was looking for the *IHT*. I happened to glance over the shoulder of someone reading the day's *Cumhuriyet*. I no longer knew enough Turkish to even get the gist of a newspaper story, but I recognized Mehmet's picture on page three. I bought a copy along with my *IHT*.

"Nierenstein, bitte." The taxi driver grunted and we headed for a town on the outskirts of Frankfurt, in the foothills of the Träume Mountains.

Sitting next to Lo Ban I opened the Turkish newspaper and pointed to Mehmet's picture. Between the two of us we managed to surmise that Mehmet had been killed and his corpse found in the waters of the Golden Horn.

"And where you guys wanna go?" The cab driver leaned back and waited for our reply as we neared Nierenstein.

"Hotel Sonnenschein, bitte."

"Yeah, sure. I know it."

It seemed that every German from bank presidents to dustmen knew idiomatic English and found it easier to speak English than listen to my labored efforts at speaking German, no matter how hard I tried. Again, I gave up, but then had another thought.

"You know any Turkish?"

"Naah."

Nierenstein im Träume is an insular bit of Germany. A wealthy residential town, it is close enough to Frankfurt to be able to function as a bedroom community but far enough away and sufficiently expensive a place in which to live, to preserve its own way of life, especially its insularity. The town is guarded by the great hulk of a ruined castle squatting on the highest hill. Destroyed by Napoleon's troops on their way to Moscow, the castle's ruins are worth the climb. And the view across the valley to the ruined castle at Blasenstein is quite splendid. A plaque on the wall of a building on the Hautstraße commemorates the stay of Marshall von Blücher, on his way to reinforce Wellington. The Hautstraße has a delightful mix of shops, quite good restaurants, a splendid bakery where the clerks still wear starched white aprons and white bonnets to cover their hair. The taste of their pastries brings back memories of a German childhood. Real cream and real butter. Just a few doors down is a quite good bookshop where I used to buy my newspapers and the occasional German paperback thriller until I got tired of the rudeness and arrogance of the owners. They would have been more comfortable in a Germany of 65 years ago, so I take my business elsewhere. Yes, Nierenstein is a most comfortable place, at least for some.

Of the several hotels in town, the Sonnenschein, located on a large estate on the edge of town and abutting a large wood, is the most comfortable. And dramatic. The Sonnenschein was built originally in the 19th century as a summer house for one of the Rothschilds. Seized by the Nazis, it was returned after the war, but apparently in dreadful condition. The story also has it that the German government presented the Rothschilds with a bill for back taxes. The place is now a hotel, the building owned by the town but operated privately.

"Hello, Mr. Manasek! Nice to see you and welcome to the Sonnenschein!" Then she paused and a look of panic appeared. "Oh my goodness, is there a reservation for you?" The desk clerk, who has been there for years, had a moment of concern.

"No, this is an unexpected visit. Have you two rooms? Adjacent, if possible."

She looked relieved and moved a few reserved rooms around to come up with a pair of adjacent rooms in the old part of the house. It was perfect.

The rooms each had a small terrace that overlooked the garden and in the distance was the haze of Frankfurt and to the right the double hills of Leistenberg. We both looked forward to a relaxing couple of days.

Our trip to Nierenstein was, of course, not purely for recreation. A distinguished dealer in rare books had his premises there and we usually were able to buy some good items from him.

I went down to the front desk with my Turkish newspaper, leaving Lo Ban to telephone Eberhard, our bookseller friend in town, to arrange for us to see him the next day. As expected, the Sonnenschein had a Turk working at the hotel and he was quite able to translate my article.

Indeed, Mehmet's body had been found floating in the dirty waters of the Golden Horn. It had been savaged and he had been tortured severely before he died. The report hinted at a most unusual mutilation, but didn't go into further detail. There were no suspects and again there was just a hint that it might have been a sexually provoked attack.

The Turkish lad, a local *gastarbeiter*, who translated the article for me looked at me quizzically. But my fifty-euro bill erased his doubts and he went back to his job.

"I suppose," said Lo Ban, when I had passed this information to him, "we might telephone Osman Bey to see if there is any more that he might know."

I picked up the telephone and began to dial. At this point I really didn't care if his line was tapped. I just wanted to know what was going on.

Luckily, Osman Bey was in and indeed, he had information. Mehmet had been tortured and had died a horrible death. He had been impaled. Osman Bey sounded somber. I heard someone in the background make a comment.

It was Rodney. "But not the hook, it was the pole. Tell him it wasn't the hook."

"My god!" I blurted out. "How horrible. What was he involved in? Also, Osman Bey, we ourselves might be in some trouble. Lo Ban and I were there the night before he died. We had dinner with him. Then we quickly left the country. That could easily look suspicious. And your nephew drove us. We cannot have him implicated in anything—it's not fair."

"Do not worry," Osman Bey assured me, "remember Nephew's friend? He is special police. I asked him to go along as a favor to me. He has already testified that Mehmet was alive when both of you left his house and that you both went back directly to your hotel and didn't leave it all night. He swore to it. You see, Manasek, this time it was we who had you two watched! And," he added somberly, "thank you for your concern about implicating my nephew."

"One other thing, Osman Bey, could you please convey my apologies to Charlotte. Once again I skipped out on her."

I heard a slight chuckle. "I shall give her your forwarding address."

I was glad we had been followed and I was even more thankful that Osman Bey had additional skills and interests that I had been unaware of despite our long friendship. Nonetheless, I wondered who the "we" were.

"This time," I said to Lo Ban when I had rung off, "I'm glad we ran."

Lo Ban concurred.

Chapter 11

Nierenstein holiday

We relaxed as best we could, given the events, in the lounge area of the Hotel Sonnenschein. Lo Ban had a glass of white wine and I abandoned abstemiousness to join him. We looked out the large windows and quietly enjoyed the view.

"Do you think we need help?" Lo Ban didn't answer and I didn't repeat the query. I think I knew that we did and that the question was really unnecessary. "I'm going into Frankfurt tomorrow and buy a cell phone. With some luck we've dropped out of sight and I'd like to keep it that way."

"Good idea. What about Eberhard?" Lo Ban was concerned about our appointment with our book seller colleague.

"Screw all of this stuff, Lo Ban. I'm going with you to visit Eberhard and we can get the phone the next day. I think I want to avoid just sliding into this pit entirely." Then I remembered that Lo Ban and Amanda had a greater stake in all this than I. "Sorry Lo Ban, That was selfish. I'll go get the phone early tomorrow morning. I'll come right back and we can both see Eberhard in the afternoon."

Lo Ban and I met for breakfast in the splendid dining room of the Sonnenschein. As usual, the coffee was superb, the German cold cuts and the fresh Frühstück Brötchen perfect. And there was a selection of stinky cheese. Despite the tempting selection of food, I ate hurriedly and left for Frankfurt right after breakfast. I decided to walk to town rather than have a taxi come to the hotel. The day warranted a nice walk and I did want to stay as anonymous as possible. I was beginning to have doubts about the wisdom of having telephoned Osman Bey using the hotel telephone. But as far as I knew that was our only security breach and except for that we, if we kept our fingers crossed, should be relatively untraceable here.

I walked down to the center of town and got a taxi from the taxi rank near the public parking lot. My taxi driver spent the entire trip to Frankfurt telling me, in idiomatic English, about his condo in Florida and how wonderful and beautiful he finds Florida. I, of course, could do nothing but agree. In Frankfurt I got out of the taxi from Nierenstein and quickly hopped into a local cab and asked the driver to take me to a shop that sold cell phones. He complied and 30 minutes later I had two of them.

It was a good feeling to be able to move about unfollowed and I spent an hour window shopping and had a nice late morning coffee before taking another taxi back to Nierenstein where I got off at the Hotel Vergelegen, my two telephones in a plastic bag.

Mobile telephones are, in my opinion, a mixed curse. I remember some years ago when they were new on the market and it seemed to me that every Londoner who had delusions of importance stood proudly on prominent street corners talking loudly on his cell phone. We passersby were, no doubt, supposed to be impressed. This phenomenon still occurs, but there are many more important people now than then, and they infest busses, restaurants, theaters, and seemingly every ecological niche occupied by humans. But a distinctly bright side to the cell phone phenomenon is that we can make telephone calls that cannot be readily traced—although possible, it is hard for someone to track a signal from a cell phone. But instant gratification is of little importance—certainly there have been very few times that I needed to make an immediate call that couldn't wait until I got into a telephone booth. And now, I had two of the beasts with me—one for me and one for Lo Ban. And I was still in time for a late lunch. A quick telephone call to the Sonnenschein, using one of my new cell phones, got me Lo Ban and he agreed to meet me down in the Staatsmitte by the bus stops. Here is a wonderful Bavarian style restaurant, the Kur-Schänke, that serves real German home cooking—just like Mutti made.

Over a splendid lunch we planned the rest of the day. Eberhard and his hoard of rare books and then perhaps some time off with a stroll around town. But first, right after lunch, a telephone call to Maria was in order.

Lunch was wonderful and very filling. After our coffee we walked across the street, past the taxicab queue and went into the little grassy park to sit and digest. Lo Ban used the cell phone to ring up Maria and, fortunately, reached her on the first try. I was about to leave to let them discuss their business in private when Lo Ban motioned me to sit down. He invited me to eavesdrop. I was startled to learn that Amanda was there, in Madrid, with Maria. Both Maria and Amanda were pleased to learn we were all right and liked the idea that we were going to do some book business before continuing on to Madrid. They were both safe and did not think they had been spotted, but were sufficiently concerned, following Mehmet's death, to be very careful. Neither sounded worried and they were both having a quiet, comfortable time.

Then, it was Maria who made a connection. "So Mehmet was impaled? We should talk with Luther if he's still alive and findable. Let's bounce it around when you get out here."

Lo Ban rang off, looked at his watch and got up. I joined him and we both walked slowly up the little slope, past the bronze tablet commemorating the reunification of Germany, on to Eberhard's office on Handelstraße. Neither of us commented on Maria's observation. I think we both didn't want to deal with it at the time. No point in ruining a nice few days in peaceful Nierenstein.

Eberhard had, as usual, a fine selection of antiquarian books. Lo Ban was able to buy (handsomely, he later told me) three items and I found a splendid Münster *Cosmography* and a pristine Gilbert *De Magnetica*. Not cheap by any means. Indeed, not even reasonable, but nonetheless I would be hard-pressed to find nicer copies elsewhere at any price.

It was also good just to see Eberhard again. We used to be regular customers but recent years proved us recidivists and we spent several pleasant hours catching up on trade gossip. Eberhard took great delight in showing us a newspaper clipping with the obituary of one of the trade's most nefarious modern firsts dealer. In German, it read: *R. Schlough Book dealer Dies* and related a bit of the history of Robert Sikes Schlough, a dealer in modern first editions who fled the United States after being convicted of fraud. He had quite a business printing up dust jackets for various jacketless books he owned and increased their value substantially by putting the new jackets on the old books. He was finally caught red-handed when he accidentally put two identical new jackets on the same book. Evidently the newly printed jackets had stuck together and when he "aged" them, they were identically aged: tears and chips matched. Needless to say, his irate customer, who finally realized what was going on, tried to get his money back, but the arrogant R. Schlough refused. The collector then went to the trade ethics group, but they were too busy at the time to help. But Schlough had underestimated his ex-client, who went to the Attorney General. Schlough was awarded three years for fraud. However, before he was jailed he fled the country and continued his business by mail from Europe. Book-related theft and fraud are not taken seriously enough by the authorities to force an extradition, and Schlough was never extradited. However he was thoroughly disliked by European dealers who put him in the same league with Lope de Nada. The European trade, proud of its stiff requirements and the depth of knowledge individual dealers have, largely dismiss American dealers unless they know them personally and have reason to respect their knowledge.

"And," added Eberhard, "these guys wonder why we don't want them around or why we don't pay any attention to them!"

Eberhard had always surmised that Lo Ban and I were involved in other activities in addition to bookselling, but never pried. It was also obvious that he was wondering why we were here in Nierenstein together, unannounced. Splendid chap that he is, he simply said, "Let me know if you need help while you are here." As one of Germany's leading antiquarian dealers and a major citizen of Nierenstein, this was no small offer.

Lo Ban and I walked around town a bit after leaving Eberhard's office. We played the standard tricks to see if we were being followed but it appeared that we still had no tails. The relief we felt was wonderful. At one point I tried to jump up and click my heels but only succeeded in almost falling to the sidewalk. But I did garner disapproving glares from several substantial middle-aged German burghers. Another misbehaving *auslander*. Right here in Nierenstein! There goes the neighborhood.

"Lo Ban," I said, "let us dine in tonight. I feel a good night's sleep is due me and the restaurant at the Sonnenschein is not too bad. I could use an early dinner and a long soak in that incredibly large tub in my bathroom and a night's sleep without worry. If whoever is after us knows we're here, they haven't arrived yet and that means a night without war clouds. What say?"

Lo Ban agreed. "Manasek, we need to clear our heads so that we can see, and think, and maybe figure this all out. And, hopefully, your suggestion will do just that. Join me in an espresso?"

We ambled down the street to the Hautstraße and hooked a left into the park. *The Kurhaus im Park*, the former town library-turned-café had just been renovated and we went inside, eschewing the outdoor tables since it had gotten a bit brisk. Inside, we got a window seat overlooking the valley below. Off to the left was a large sequoia tree. Although growing on a hillside in Germany, far from its native shores and family, it seemed happy enough. I liked that tree and found its soft, thick, deformable bark pleasant to the touch. I could push my finger deep into the yielding bark but it was normal: not pitting edema.

Lo Ban and I said very little to each other as we sipped our coffee. I looked across the table at my old friend, my old comrade, and took comfort in our being here. Alive, well, and working together again.

Lo Ban looked up at me. I think he divined my thoughts. "It does get good sometimes, doesn't it?"

I smiled and nodded in response. I put Blaser out of my mind.

"Well, hello! May I join you?" It was Rodney Oufle. "I just got in. I telephoned Eberhard about some books and he told me you were in town. Glad I found you."

"Sit down and join us, Rodney." Lo Ban was overtly hospitable. He then leaned over the table and in a low, icy voice murmured, "And I hope you are not following us. That would be very unwise."

Rodney shuddered slightly. "That's not necessary, Lo Ban, I know your reputation and I have no intention of messing with you. I don't care why you're here. The both of you. Either of you." Rodney was getting a bit histrionic. "See that tree over there?" He pointed to a large tree with a curious tangle of branches. "That's why I'm here. That tree."

Lo Ban looked pained. "Trees. Are you nuts? The both of you are. Manasek, here, thinks he's best friends with the sequoia, and you travel a thousand miles to look at branches."

"Ah," Rodney replied, "not just branches, Lo Ban. That tree's branches held the remains of the garroted victims of the Nierenstein Terror. The first victim was found hanging there when the leaves fell. He'd been hanging for a month or so and nobody had noticed. They cut him, or rather what was left of him, down. In a week he had been replaced by another victim. This went on a few more times. Then it all stopped."

"I heard about that. Eberhard once told us the story over dinner. Nobody was ever caught. Yet, if you walk out along the Kugelhernstraße to the Karlstraße, you'll come to a row of delightful 16th-century houses. The third one down has a peg in the old door jamb. That's where a garrote was found shortly after the murders stopped. And there was a severed foot leaning against the jamb, underneath the garrote. Just the foot. The rest of the body was never found and the authorities could never connect the garrote and the foot to either the Terror murders or to anyone living in Nierenstein."

"Correct," added Rodney. "And each Terror victim had been garroted in exactly the same way. I've seen the pathology reports and the killer was very good—clean and proper. A signature, if you will, of an expert with the classic garrote technique. No doubt about it. Nobody gets that good with only a few tries. He had to have done many more. No amateur. Anyway, I need to look at the approaches to the tree—how did the Terror get his bodies up there without being noticed? How does one learn the classical garrote these days? Are there mentors? So many questions!"

"And so few answers?" I paid for the three of us and we walked out together, into the deepening dusk. "Where are you staying, Rodney?"

"At the Hotel Hinterteile. Stayed there for years running each time I come here to buy books. You big money types like to stay at the Sonnenschein, no doubt?" Rodney meant it as a joke. He could probably buy all of us with ease.

"Do you believe him?" I asked Lo Ban as we trudged up the hill, back to the Sonnenschein.

"Yes, I do. After all the years I've known Rodney, I'm convinced that what you see is what there is. A big old queen obsessed with strange ways of inflicting death. On others. But he's quite harmless. I think he browned when I sent him that warning, and I, of course, did that just to make certain he stays out of this affair and doesn't talk about us to anyone."

"What about the 'Nierenstein Terror'? Has that anything to do with us?"

"I don't think so," answered Lo Ban. "That's a small-time aberration. Someone got into killing and needed to display his handiwork. I wouldn't be surprised if the killer finally had to try it out on himself, and hanged himself. Perhaps on a tree."

"The ultimate in self-gratification?"

"Sort of."

The Sonnenschein dining room did well by us. I broke down and had a nice Napoleon brandy after dinner. Feeling well, and, for the moment, at peace with the world, we retired.

There was no real reason for me to pull the bureau in front of the door, but I did so anyway and I slept particularly well that night.

There was still no evidence that we had been followed to Nierenstein. None of the tricks we played, the doubling back, the splitting up and rejoining, gave any indication we were being tailed. For the moment, at least, we could move about normally.

Lo Ban and I would fritter away another day. The Sonnenschein provided us with a nice picnic lunch, packed, along with a bottle of white wine, into a smart wicker basket. Late in the morning Lo Ban and I began walking slowly up the wooded hills behind the Sonnenschein, picking our way along the barely-marked trails. We spent a very pleasant hour and a half, wandering beneath the canopy of hardwoods, whose branches caused the sky to wink at us as it tried to dodge around their leaves and to reach the forest floor. It was all uphill, so we walked slowly and finally reached the ruined castle of Blasenstein.

We were the only visitors that midday and it was quite pleasant to sit on the ruined walls and enjoy the spectacular view. Across the valley was the ruined castle of Nierenstein, still on duty, still standing guard above its town below.

"This might be a good time to review." Lo Ban was right. We were each in a good frame of mind, we had slept well and in no discernible danger from whoever had been stalking us in Istanbul.

Unfortunately we could only repeat the sequence of events and that exercise did not lead to any theory that might prove useful to us. The attempt on Amanda's life still confounded us. Lo Ban and I had been followed and Mehmet had been killed. Tortured, probably to try to elicit information. But what information? Fortunately for us Mehmet had none to sell or give away. He had seemingly been trying to get information from us. Particularly about our former group. He knew the group existed, but he did not know the individuals. Was it their names that his killers wanted?

If this was true and whoever was after us wanted to find out who had been in our group, then we might all be in danger.

But we still needed the "Why?"

Chapter 12

The story of Luther

There was something else that puzzled us about the death of Mehmet. It wasn't that he was killed, since small players often get killed when their usefulness on one job is over, but it was the way in which he was killed. Osman Bey had described wounds that could only have been inflicted by impalement. It was Maria's comment that we should think of Luther that kept us thinking along this thread. Now, sitting on the walls of a ruined castle in Germany, beginning to enjoy a great German picnic lunch, our discussion of Mehmet's death brought back memories of one of our jobs, one that we pulled off about 30 years ago. The whole affair was so sordid we all tried to put it behind us as quickly as possible.

There existed at that time, as it does even now, a market in captured persons. Some were sold into sexual slavery, some sold for other uses. Lo Ban and I had agreed to do a rescue of one such captured person.

An American officer, in the field, had been betrayed by one of his agents and had been captured. His captors were not ideologues, but rather businessmen trading in living people, and they sold him to the highest bidder. But the highest bidders were not to be his final owners. Intelligence suggested that he had actually been sold several times, first to hostile governments and finally to a private buyer, who had some sort of operation in the jungle of Southeast Asia. Just what kind of operation was not known at that time. Even the name of the group, or individual, running it was not known. However hard we tried, we couldn't find out much about it. Our Side flew some aerial reconnaissance flights and sent in some agents to interview locals. Collectively, this intelligence suggested that our man was being held by his ultimate owner, a private buyer of living people who kept him in a pen on the Cambodia/Thailand border. The owner was someone whose reputation had only been whispered before. Most were unbelieving when any discussion of him arose; others were simply afraid. Those bits of rumor; those bits of anecdote that did circulate about this operation seemed so staggeringly unbelievable that local governments didn't want to touch it. Better to ignore than to deal with this monstrosity even if it was as great as was rumored to be.

But it was different now that one of our own officers was in the clutches of this person, possibly some sort of maniac. His plight and the whole situation really couldn't be ignored anymore. I recall meeting with Lo Ban after it was decided that Luther must be rescued and Lo Ban had been approached to do the job. I was home in Vermont when he telephoned me and chatted idly about some book-related things. Two code phrases were used and I acknowledged understanding them with another simple code phrase. Two days later I was flying out of Boston on my way to Southeast Asia.

I met Lo Ban in the lobby of the Oriental Hotel in Bangkok. He looked harried and this job, whatever it would turn out to be, was of utmost urgency. At check-in, I had my two Globe-Trotter suitcases taken to my room, but I stayed downstairs with Lo Ban. Tired as I was, this could not wait and we had best begin right now. We went to the Bamboo Bar and picked a table in the corner, from which we could survey the scene. The entrance was in our direct sight, and our backs to a secure wall.

"Good flight?" asked Lo Ban.

"The hell with the flight. What's up? Some big infusion of cash?" I tried to sound flippant, but it didn't work.

Lo Ban smiled wryly. "Yes, a very big infusion of cash. One of our biggest jobs. And one of the worst. Here's the matter in a nutshell. One of Ours, a man by the name of Luther, has been caught. Quite literally, caught. He was captured in an animal net, wrapped up and sold like a slab of beef. Put on the auction block."

"Auction block?"

"Yes. Auction block. No longer in Bangkok, but just a ways up-country there are regular markets that provide a useful service, at least for some people. Catch someone who might be of use for any reason, to any government, or any individual, and there's a market for them. There's a surprising number of third, second, and, most interesting, first-world people brokers at these sales, bidding for bodies. But the bodies have to be alive. Usually they are available for examination, but some of the more established dealers have enough of a reputation that they don't need to exhibit their wares. Their word is good. In the case of our man Luther, he was exhibited wrapped in a net suspended from a hook in the ceiling or maybe from a tree limb. There were about a dozen others displayed in the same manner. Our Side was caught short here—we hadn't the intelligence and didn't even know that he was on the block until it was all over. It would have been easy to buy him and that would have been the end of it all. In any event, he was sold first to a small potentate in Southeast Asia. Really a warlord.

"Why would he buy Luther?" I asked, just a bit dumbfounded.

"Speculation. Luther had all the appearances of someone of substance. He was therefore valuable for a number of reasons. Ransom, blackmail, or selling upstream to a foreign government who wanted an edge in some deliberation. But they probably never figured on Z. He's called "Z" because his real name is completely unknown. Not a clue. This guy bought people so he could kill them. Like he was buying clay pigeons for target practice, or some sort of sporting animal. And Luther had appealed to him.

"Sexually?"

"Probably. But most likely Luther was just cheap enough and was also someone of some import. Just the kind of trophy Z wanted for his death games.

Lo Ban and I spent the next hour or so going over the terrain maps and aerial photos of the region where Luther was being held.

The best we could make out was that there was a large "U"-shaped compound about a kilometer from the nearest road. There were some defenses along the road and around the compound. And the compound was where Luther was presumed to be held.

I studied the maps and photos for a while. Lo Ban finally asked, "How many?"

"Five, and an armored vehicle and a driver for the AV. Smoke and concussion grenades and the right stuff to take off doors and building sides. I get it tomorrow and we do it in two days. No later.

We can't be here too long without word getting out. We also need Luther's picture. Also, let's get Veronica to come to Bangkok, take a hotel suite and just be there for us in case we get into trouble on our way out. We may need some help at that time, or a place to hide for a day or so."

"And maybe get patched up, too." Lo Ban was being a realist. I didn't need that right then. "I'll get started on it right now." Lo Ban, I knew, would deliver. The "five" were understood to be commandos. Ours. Under my command.

Two days later, at five o'clock in the morning, Lo Ban drove us to a clearing north of Bangkok where a helicopter was waiting. We flew a few hours north and settled lightly into a jungle field. Parked near the perimeter was our armored vehicle, camouflaged nicely. Five American Special Forces were sitting in it, smiling and feeling very full of themselves. Colonel "A" was there, waiting for us. Colonel "A" was a no–nonsense (he would have described it as "no-shit") career officer who loved strange and dangerous assignments. He had an image of himself that had probably been forged when he was 12 and had not changed since. He was a warrior and loved fighting. Although we had worked together several times, he didn't quite approve of us and the way we did things. Actually, it was the fact that we did these things that bothered him—he always thought that regular military men ought to do them. He had not much use for political realities. I had a personal respect for him that was enormous.

Colonel "A" had always coveted a knife I owned. It had been made by an old knifemaker in southern Indiana. The guy used centuries-old Japanese blade-making techniques to make knives that were simply wonderful. The blades were virtually unbreakable and kept their keen edge extremely well. In his younger years he produced three or four a year, now in his 70s, he worked only enough to make one a year. He was not very well known in ordinary knife circles, his work was perhaps too esoteric, too expensive, but guys like Colonel "A" knew of him and lusted after his knives. But the waiting list was so long that if one wasn't pretty high on it, the chance of getting one before the knifemaker died was close to zero. A few years ago I spoke to this old Hoosier and explained Colonel "A" to him as best I could. The old man looked at me.

He understood. The next day he went to work and six months later Colonel "A" had his knife. It cemented an unspoken bond between us.

Now, standing in the jungle, Colonel "A" introduced me to the commandos and read them the rules of engagement. I detected a few disapproving glances my way when he told them I was their commander but I ignored them. Now was not the time to deal with that kind of stuff. Nonetheless it was clear that the guys thought Lo Ban and me a couple of pussies.

All necessary precautions had been taken to cover any governmental asses should the mission fail. All five Special Forces guys had been reported AWOL two days ago; our AV reported stolen at the same time. None of us carried any IDs. If we were captured we would be alone and, no doubt, in deep weeds. If we succeeded, each SF guy would get 50,000 US dollars. Cash in a big manila envelope. No record of the payment. And the AWOL rap would disappear. My take would be an obscene multiple of that. Lo Ban's? Who knew?

Jumping into a forward seat of the AV, I gave a signal and we rolled out. Pulling out my maps, I guided us along narrow trails and roads, my holstered .45 digging into my hips as the AV struggled with the terrain. Two hours out, I called for a stop. We relieved ourselves and some of the guys smoked. I mostly stretched and tried to put new life into my extra-large long limbs.

I spread out a large-scale map and we huddled around it. It was a tracing from an aerial photograph.

"I don't know how good this map or the information is, but it's the best we have. We think guards are here, prisoners in this compound. The 'owner' seems to live in this cluster of houses." I pointed to a small group of buildings. "Our job is to forget everything except the prisoner compound, and we are to rescue this one guy. His name's Luther." I passed around photos of Luther. "Kill anyone who gets in your way. No discussion or questions. No interrogation, no prisoners. Just kill them. There will be dogs. Kill them as soon as you see them. We think them to be particularly nasty so be certain to kill any dog you see when going in. We have to be in and out quickly. We're talking about minutes, so don't stop to think. Kill everyone you see except the prisoners. It doesn't matter if they appear hostile or not. If they aren't prisoners, kill them. However, if you have to kill a prisoner in order to save Luther, do so. Any prisoner that gets out will be given space in the AV as available. We'll take them away but will have to drop them off quickly. I have cash money—US dollars—for them when we kick them out. Enough to get them to some safety. But, remember—they are not why we are here. Luther is. And only Luther. We kill anyone we need to in order to save Luther. We are now 15 minutes away. Let's take 10 minutes to do the job, so in less than half an hour we'll be rolling out. When I let off a red flare, that means to get back on board, 'cause we're rolling out. No stragglers. If you miss the boat there's no second chance."

There was no cheering or high-fives when the AV rolled away. This was no picnic and there would be no parades, drums, or banners. Just a crappy operation in a fetid part of the world. And a lot of money at the end.

In about ten minutes we picked up a better-maintained trail and a few minutes later, with the AV growling in low gear, we roared into the compound. There were defenders, probably uncertain about us but we soon felt and heard the "ping-ping" of rounds hitting the AV. We returned the compliments. But ours were in the form of a withering fire of 50-caliber stuff; some no–joke big-boy rounds.

We sent some heavy explosives at the buildings of the owner's compound and a lot of damage was done. The SF were throwing lots of concussion grenades and noisemakers to add to the confusion. Dogs aplenty were released by the defenders and began to tear into us. From the top of the AV I began picking them off. I took out a few guards as well, and some stray figures that were running around the owner's compound, which was now burning nicely. Dull thuds, screams, and shouts emerged from the smoke and confusion. Two of our lads appeared from the smoky mayhem carrying a figure I assumed was Luther. Several other men, in rags, were running or limping, some almost crawling toward us, and several others were being helped along by the SF. I had the AV backed closer to them. We kept the .50-caliber fire going and the buildings, now burning, were raked time and again. I was shooting slowly, deliberately, and was picking off dogs and whatever else was moving. A lot went down.

"Luther on board! We got him!"

I let off the red signal flare and we began moving out. A few of the other prisoners made it on their own, some only with help from our lads who now turned all their efforts to getting themselves aboard. After a quick head count we roared out of there. We heard occasional pings off our armor as the stunned guards and other survivors of the camp began to get our range. But the jungle intervened and we were out of sight.

Two hours later we stopped at a crossroads and sent the rest of the prisoners away, with 200 US dollars each. All in 20s. That should have been enough money to get them to a city where they could then fend for themselves. They didn't want to leave but there was no choice and we just drove away from them. Our job was to get Luther out and safely home. We had accomplished the first part.

Luther was weak, dehydrated, and feverish. He also stank to high heaven. He had suffered from severe diarrhea and there had been complete absence of any washing facilities. He had crusted feces on his legs and feet; his clothing rags were saturated and his bare feet had large sores. We stopped the AV and took Luther outside. One of the lads stripped off his rags and splashed some tepid water on him from a jerry can. From somewhere a bar of soap appeared and Luther was busy scrubbing away, occasionally getting rinsed by more tepid water. I'm not sure it made any difference to his stink—he didn't seem to smell any better when he climbed back on board but his spirits were certainly higher. Especially when he put on some clean clothes. Chinos, a shirt, and sneakers. He wolfed down several candy bars and a couple of cans of Coke. Then he fell asleep, leaning against a rescuer who, given Luther's odor, was not all that pleased with the honor.

There was little conversation and we were all left to our personal thoughts as we drove on. I wasn't thinking about much—I felt too tired. The operation had taken a lot out of me and it wasn't yet finished. But it had another effect on one of our men. He suddenly retched and vomited all over the floor. Shivering and trembling, he began to weep silently. Lo Ban and I got to his side. We both knew he had been hand-picked by Colonel "A," and could we not understand this behavior.

"I saw what they were doing there. I saw it." He sobbed lightly.

"And what was that?" I asked.

"When we ran into the compound I saw the prisoner's cages. They were set up around a dirt courtyard. There was a gallows, something that might have been a chopping block and a couple of posts. There were two guys on the posts. Still alive."

"What do you mean on the posts?" Lo Ban was now asking.

"Hard to describe. They were on the posts, but the posts were in them. They had their hands and feet tied and the posts were stuck up their asses. They were writhing and moaning. But just barely. I think they were still conscious. It was horrible."

"Sounds like impalement. Dear God. What did you do?"

"I shot both. It was the only way I could stop their pain. Even if we got them down, and there was no time for that, there wouldn't be anything we could do. They would have been all torn up inside. So I killed them. I shot each one in his head."

"Thank you. That was well done." Lo Ban rarely gave out such compliments, and it had a good effect. We rode on in silence. I shuddered occasionally.

Two more hours on, we stopped. There in the road was a dusty Land Rover. Jim, the lad who was serving as Luther's pillow, gently woke him. We got Luther out of the AV and helped him into the Rover. Jim, Lo Ban, and I stripped off our camouflage and we each put on similar worn chinos and oft-laundered blue shirts and climbed into the Rover. The SF lads would take the AV back, get passports and good IDs, a wad of cash, and they would be out of the country within 20 hours. The rest of their money would be waiting for them. Cash, of course. Jim volunteered to go with us— we needed another set of hands. Lo Ban drove off.

We spoke very little as Lo Ban headed south. Dusk was deepening as he neared a medium-sized village. He took a sharp turn, entering a short driveway. Lo Ban had rented a house and we now had a bit of time and a place to pull ourselves together. I later learned that Lo Ban had rented three additional houses in villages farther north. It would take any pursuer a while to figure out that we were not going to be at any of them. Here, we again stripped Luther and stuck him in a large tub. Lo Ban and I lathered and scrubbed him and rinsed him many times. I had given him something to stop his diarrhea and his overall pain and we fed him several multivitamin capsules, more candy bars and more Coke. Luther was beginning to feel better. We stood him up to dry him off and Lo Ban dumped some Bay Rhum on him. Luther yelped as the astringent stung his sores, but he didn't protest too much. I bandaged the worst of his sores so they wouldn't ooze through his trousers and arouse suspicion if we were stopped for any reason, but I didn't bother to treat them. Luther would very soon be in hands far more competent than mine.

"Will we stay here tonight?" asked Luther. "Get some sleep? I haven't even thanked you guys yet." Luther's head began to sag.

"No." Lo Ban was adamant. "We have to move on and get you out of the country. Two more hours' drive and we get picked up. Now, we have to fill up the petrol tanks before we leave." Lo Ban and Jim dumped several jerry cans of petrol into the Land Rover's tank, checked the oil, and we were off.

Lo Ban navigated the Land Rover across meadows, along trails, and narrow roads. Finally he stopped. "Here is where we wait. No lights. No noise." Luther was asleep, shivering and making low whimpering noises. We let him alone.

We soon heard the "whap-whap-whap" of helicopter blades in the distance. They got louder as they approached and I waited with some apprehension as we heard them begin to fade. Lo Ban and I nodded to each other and I let off a red flare. It arced high in the sky and headed down before dying. The "whap-whap-whap" grew louder and we soon saw the helicopter itself. The pilot didn't see us, so I lit a magnesium flare and tossed it into the meadow. Lo Ban meanwhile had gone back to the Land Rover and placed an incendiary canister under the dashboard. He pulled the canister's lanyard and closed the Land Rover's door.

Helicopter on ground, Jim and I half-carrying Luther, Lo Ban, on board already, helping us get on. We lay prostrate on the floor as the machine lifted off and veered steeply to the south. An hour's flight brought us to an unnamed military base, we landed, traded Luther for a receipt, were given a car and we drove off, into the night, headed for Bangkok. Jim stayed behind. He would rejoin his unit and we never saw him again. Didn't even learn his last name.

The operation had gone extremely well and, seemingly, we had gotten away cleanly. When Lo Ban and I walked into the lobby of the Oriental Hotel, we noticed Veronica sitting nearby. Even though we didn't need back-up, it was a very good feeling to know that it was here. We didn't acknowledge Veronica—not even eye contact.

The next day, Lo Ban and I were on a flight to Hong Kong and we kept our low profile. We didn't talk about our job, nor did we show any of the exhilaration that we both felt. But we were very pleased. Job done and nobody hurt. At least none of Ours. Whoever "They" were, they certainly took some big hits. Lots of bodies.

I began to wonder a bit about Luther and the impalements. But one of the things about this kind of job is that one learns not to wonder about such things. They are for someone else to ponder and for us to get paid. Right now Lo Ban and I looked forward to some downtime. And I was looking forward to soaking in a tub and getting some sleep and some good food before flying back to Vermont.

Not much wiser, but certainly a bit richer.

Chapter 13

Taking stock

During all the years after Luther's extraction Lo Ban and I had never discussed the issue of impalement, nor did we speak of the captives who had been held in those cages deep in the Asian jungle. But now we did since it appeared to be the only link we had to the murder of Mehmet and possibly, by an even longer stretch, connected to the attempt on Amanda's life. After some 30 years it was hard to remember details about that jungle rescue but we could both agree that we really didn't know much about Luther or his captors or his ultimate jailer, even if he was still alive. Or about any of the tortures that might have gone on in the strange compound. But we did remember, and would forever, the observation related to us by the weeping SF lad who had, out of mercy, shot the two near–dead victims he had found writhing, impaled on posts.

"Maria mentioned we need to find Luther. She's right. Suppose whoever impaled Mehmet had something to do with that crowd in the jungle thirty years ago—the ones who had bought Luther. If so, Luther is the key to finding out whom those guys are, or were. We need to see if Luther is still alive. If Colonel "A" is still alive, he might know something. Remember, we never did learn Luther's last name. None of the commandos would be of any help, either."

There hadn't been impalers or impalements in our other experiences. We might as well start with the only one we know of.

"And, we can't just run some ads!"

We sipped the last of the wine, repacked the wicker basket and began the walk back through the forest to the Sonnenschein, where we returned the basket.

Lo Ban and I then wandered downhill through the extensive park in front of the hotel to Eberhard's office on Handelstraße. Eberhard was in, and although not too pleased with our unannounced visit, was polite nonetheless. I noticed Rodney's briefcase on the table. Stacked near it were several old vellum–bound volumes. Eberhard was evidently showing them to Rodney and it was a bit of a surprise that Rodney felt he had to absent himself when we came in. We only stayed a brief time. Lo Ban and I thanked Eberhard for the books we were able to buy and told him we were leaving the next day.

"Back home?" asked Eberhard.

"Yes," Lo Ban lied. "I'm off to Hong Kong and Manasek is back to Vermont."

"I never understood why you live there." Eberhard turned to me and sounded annoyed, as though some part of a puzzle was missing—and that the missing part was the only piece needed to endow him with perfect understanding.

"Come and visit and you'll understand. It's a lot like living in Nierenstein."

"Oh, by the way," added Eberhard, "I got a request for a book catalogue from a friend of yours." He looked directly at me. "Someone named Charlotte Lippe. She telephoned and was interested in some Levant books I have in stock. Particularly the Thelot *Views of Constantinople*. I don't know her and she gave me your name as reference."

"Yes, that's her field. I think she's in Istanbul now. Or possibly Ankara. Did she ask after me?"

"No. Just used you as reference."

Lo Ban and I walked slowly up the hill to the Sonnenschein. So, Charlotte again! It was nice to be reminded of her, even though I was only her reference.

I was deep in thought as we walked along, but not so deep that I didn't see Lo Ban look at me curiously. "Just coincidence?" he asked.

"Probably. It would have been more worrisome had she shown up here."

"Oh sure. I bet you'd have been worried if she were here."

I let that one go by.

The next morning Lo Ban and I took a taxi to the Frankfurt airport and caught an early flight to Madrid. Maria was waiting for us and drove us back to her house in the old part of the city.

So many pleasant memories embraced me as we entered her house. I think I must have been grinning like an idiot because Maria burst out laughing when she looked at me.

"Am I still so transparent?" I asked her.

"Paco, to me you are." And she gave me a nice little hug. I think I blushed. Decades ago, Maria and I had lived together, in this very house, two lotus-eaters never thinking of tomorrow. Then we were separated when I went to work on the anti-germ warfare project at Oxford. And, as the fates would have it, we were reunited when she, Veronica, Lo Ban, and some others who do not now wish their names to be used, joined together to form our most unusual Group. I think Maria and I still shared an unspoken fantasy that we would someday be together again. And pick up our lives as though 30-plus years had not intervened. It certainly seemed possible as we sat opposite each other at dinner that evening. I saw her as she looked then, and I hoped she saw me in the same light of the same magic candle.

The next morning the four of us, Lo Ban, Amanda, Maria, and I discussed our strategy. Although Maria had not participated in the jungle raid that liberated Luther she was familiar with it and we didn't have to retell the story. She also had an uncanny memory and was often able to link seemingly disparate, unconnected events.

Maria recalled one night, several years ago, when she and Veronica had dinner with an old mutual friend, a former officer, now retired and living in France. He was an amateur military historian whose specialty was the Turkish invasions of Europe. At the time he was working on Vlad of Transylvania. Vlad the Impaler, who allegedly, when the Turks were invading, lined the road with stakes and each stake had an impaled peasant on it. The Turks were unnerved by this and fell back. Impalement did not seem to be, observed Veronica, a modern activity.

The officer had disagreed. "Still around, not in wide use as torture, to be sure. Probably because once an impalement is started it cannot be stopped. That doesn't make it a good torture. You can't stop an impalement and reprieve or revive the victim. Or keep him alive for any length of time to get more information out of him. As such it's not very useful except in inflicting a very painful, drawn-out death. Or as sport."

Both Maria and Veronica were intrigued by the concept of impalement as sport and pressed for more detail. Their officer friend knew Luther had changed his last name and moreover had an idea where Luther might be living. The officer had been associated with Colonel "A," who had been our military connection to Luther's rescue. Colonel "A" had just recently died so there was no chance of getting more information from him. Maria remembered that Luther was thought to be living in Des Moines, Iowa. She also recalled his new last name.

Lo Ban and I choked back a laugh. There was something preposterous about the idea of Luther living in Des Moines, but we couldn't pin it down. A bit more reflection, however, and it made sense. Des Moines was probably the antipode of his experience in the jungle.

Amanda shared with us the story of the attack on her in Hong Kong. "The more I think about it, the more interesting it seems that I wasn't killed. No—not a matter of luck. It seems more like by design. The shooter could easily have killed me. He was close, presumably knew what he was doing, and yet just gave me a minor wound. I wonder why?"

Maria wrinkled her nose. "Remember that job in Rome? We shot a Red Army guy in the leg so he would lead us to his cell. Could have killed him, but a winged bird looking for refuge was more useful."

"So whoever had Amanda shot, might have wanted her to lead them to the rest of the Group? Makes sense. If they got that close to Amanda, they must have known about me, so getting me can't be it. But if the theory is correct then we can assume they don't know about the rest of us. Except possibly about Manasek, and we don't know when they figured that one out." Lo Ban's summary seemed to have some validity.

"Mehmet was a bust as a source for their intelligence. Even though he had worked for us he didn't know much about our Group. He was pretty clumsy when we had dinner together—it was clear that he wanted names. The poor bastard was going to rat us out."

"Maybe not. Remember he tried to warn us. Or so we think. Anyway look what happened," added Lo Ban.

"Our world is a very small world," Maria was pensive, "and I find it surprising that whoever wanted to find out about our Group had that much trouble."

"Maybe it means that whoever wants to find out about us isn't part of our world. Don't forget too, that we haven't been overly active in the recent past. It has to be hard, for whoever this guy is, to reconstruct our Group of 20 or 30 years ago starting now. We never advertised our connections, most of the time we acted like ordinary book sellers and if they've been trying to work through all those connections it would be years of dead-ends. No, if they were trying to reconstruct our Group, they would have to start with obvious connections—connections that were open relationships, not our covert ones. Like me and Amanda. Years ago it would have been you and Elizabeth. And they never tried to just kill me or you. Curious." Lo Ban was trying to reconstruct a plausible scenario.

"Elizabeth's death was an accident. She fell off a ledge while she was painting. I saw her body." I couldn't believe that there was a connection. And I didn't want Lo Ban to go down that road again.

"All right. I was just using that as an example. If, for instance, someone wanted to connect us, then perhaps by attacking one of us, the others would become identifiable. But that still doesn't help understand why not just shoot one of us? Manasek or me? Surely the others would do something?" That should be enough to flush us out."

"Maybe," I mused, "but what if our deaths were not their only objectives? Suppose whoever did this wanted, or wants, something more. Our destruction, yes, but in another sense, or with another dimension. Perhaps he, or whoever, wants to torture us, too. Also, don't forget that someone did shoot one of us. Amanda. And it has indeed flushed us out. Or almost."

Maria pursed her lips. "But why? Because of the raid 30 years ago? Possibly. Let's look at the chronology." She took out a pad of paper and drew a long vertical line, ticking off equal segments. "Five-year intervals."

She began adding events in their proper chronological location along the line. "First was the raid to rescue Luther. Then a long gap until the attack on Amanda, and the death of Mehmet. It's a far fetch to connect what's happening today with what happened some 30 years ago. And the only connection we can come up with is impalement. Whew!"

"Put in Elizabeth's death also." Lo Ban leaned over the time-line. "Notice that even if we do put it in, just for the sake of argument, there is this huge gap of about 20 years."

"Why make the assumption of murder? Thinking Elizabeth's death was murder bothers me."

"Elizabeth's death always bothered me." Lo Ban spoke very gently.

Maria looked out the window, sadly.

Chapter 14

Reunion with Luther

Lo Ban and I checked into the Des Moines Embassy Suites Hotel. The clerk looked at us with curiosity.

"Where you folks from?"

"Mongolia," answered Lo Ban.

"I don't know where it's at and I never been there, but I hear it's real nice." The clerk finished checking us in. "Your suite (pronounced "suit") is ready. Take the elevator to the third floor and it's just at the end of the corridor. Enjoy your stay."

Des Moines is a generic city plopped onto a generic landscape, and populated largely by generic people. Lo Ban and I both felt the oppression engulf us and clutch at us, like an animated miasma rising from some vast subterranean void. And we'd been there less than an hour.

"This place gives me the creeps." Lo Ban nodded agreement, as though reading my thoughts.

"And now we wait for Luther." It was my turn to nod.

Lo Ban and I had located Luther. It was not hard to do—he had a listed telephone—apparently he had it since moving here some 15 years ago. We wrote him a letter reintroducing ourselves to him and asking if we might spend a bit of time trying to tie up a loose end that had emerged recently. We did not, we assured him, wish to intrude on his privacy, and would appreciate any time he could spare us. We received, rather promptly, a short courteous reply, agreeing to a meeting in our hotel. Not his home.

We had a few hours to kill before Luther was due to show so we wandered outside and walked about a bit. It was nice to stretch my legs after the flight but we soon headed back to the hotel to wait for Luther. We didn't want to miss him in case he came early.

The lobby was a comfortable place to wait. Lo Ban picked up the hotel copy of *The New York Times* and I busied myself with the *Wall Street Journal*. At precisely the time of our appointment, we noticed a tall, slim man enter the lobby, look around and walk to the desk. He was dressed in oft-laundered work clothes, but his carriage betrayed something else. The clerk behind the desk pointed to Lo Ban and me sitting in a corner of the lobby, and he walked over to us. Indeed, it was Luther. Even after 30 years, I could remember enough of him to morph the old eidetic image I carried with me into the new image that stood before us.

We were all awkward at first. Luther tried to thank us, but it didn't work and we tried to convince him that was not why we were here. Finally, I took the bull by the horns.

"Luther, someone is trying to kill or harm us, our associates, and those dear to us. We've been followed, someone's been shot and someone else tortured to death. The only link to anybody we can come up with seems to be the torture death. A chap in Istanbul who had done some work for us years ago and who seemed to still be in the business was killed after we had dinner together. He was clearly trying to get information from us, but for whom we don't know. That's what we're now trying to trace."

"How was he killed?" Luther spoke very softly.

"He was impaled."

"Look, this is going to be very hard for me. I retired from the Agency right after that episode and have for decades tried not to think too much about it." Luther was gathering himself. "I do owe you, though and that's why I'm here—I also appreciate the fact that you let me alone all these years."

He continued. "I've been out of intelligence for a very long time. I still remember the drill. It's sort of like psychoanalysis—I talk and talk and talk and you put together a story. Reality? Who the hell knows. But anyway, you go away with a story. You feel better and maybe I feel better. Maybe not. Me feeling better doesn't matter right now, but your story does."

"How about in our suite? We can get room service if we need to." Luther assented and we took the elevator up. I pulled three comfortable chairs forward so they faced each other, Lo Ban and I broke out yellow legal pads, and the 30-year-old debriefing began.

Luther began his story.

"I was on assignment trying to trace the flow of hard drugs. We were supposed to be trying to stop them, but I was never too sure just why I was there. After a few months it became clear that we could've put a big crimp into their operations, but it never happened. The trade was so open that it meant it had to have been protected and I was too young and naive to figure it out. So I did my job. I collected data. Mostly names, connections, times, amounts, money, the whole thing. I had lots of information but nobody back in the Company really wanted it. In fact, I was beginning to embarrass them. That's when this little punk, Queng Tree, whom I had hired to translate, do minor surveillance, and things like that took a bribe. He sent me off down a trail that seemed to be perfectly safe. It was midday, and I was to meet a contact. A big one. I think that I had gotten careless and was tired of the whole operation, or whatever. Maybe a death wish. Anyway, I let my guard down. I walked down the trail and bingo! Suddenly I was up in the trees in an animal net. Just as quickly I was lowered down and the net was quickly wrapped around me, I was blindfolded and gagged and felt myself being carried off. Next, I was thrown into a truck, I remember landing on some other soft bundles, they began to thrash and grunt. Obviously also tied up and gagged. I remember thinking that I was now in a truckload of tied-up humans, going where? To slaughter?

"We were driven along some pretty rough roads and it was very painful. The truck had no working suspension and the other captives were doing a lot of thrashing. I had given up thrashing about since it did no good and only made me tired and even more sore.

"Anyway, after a time, I don't know how long, we stopped. They ripped off the gags, for some reason cut off our clothing and dragged us—they dragged us because we were all still bound hand and foot—into an open area. I saw about 20 or so others, all tied and stripped as were we. Groups of men were walking about us, looking us over, occasionally kicking us or turning us over. I then realized we were in a market. These guys were people-buyers!

"I tried to say something, but one of them kicked dirt in my face. I was blinded and choked. It caked my mouth, I was coughing and hacking and my eyes hurt and stung. That was the last time I tried to speak. I was grabbed, wrapped in another net and hoisted up. Hung from a hook in a tree limb. It was utterly frightening. And the buyers kept looking and prodding.

"The next I remember is being cut down by two men and, still wrapped in the net like an Easter ham, thrown into the back of yet another truck. Another ride, this one so bumpy that I got huge bruises and began to bleed from cuts inflicted by the truck bed. The rest is less clear. I remember being transferred to at least two other trucks, each time there were guys looking me over, sometimes kicking me, and I heard them asking questions about me. I think I was bought and sold several times. To whom, by whom, or for what reason, I didn't know.

"For the next few days I was kept in a hut. Just a bit of damp rotted straw over a bare earthen floor. I was still tied up and had not been untied since I was captured. Once each day someone dumped a bucked of water on me. That cleaned me and gave me a quick drink all at once. A wooden bowl of watery rice gruel was put on the floor, and like a dog, I inched over to it and lapped it up. Sometimes it spilled and I got nothing. My cuts and bruises were getting infected and the pain in my joints was unbearable. I hurt too much to scream. I think I passed out and was unconscious much of the time, so I don't have a clear idea of how long I was in the hut.

"Then another move. Another truck ride, this one quite long, but again I don't know just how long since I was unconscious much of the trip. I do recall being thrown into a cage and someone reaching through the bars and cutting my binds. Now, for the first time since I was captured, I was untied, but I hurt so much I couldn't move arms or legs. The pain was so severe that when I tried to move, I blacked out.

"When I came to, I found that I had some clothing on. Really just some rags, quite filthy and half rotted, but at least something. Someone was giving me some water—I couldn't hold the bowl nor could I move my legs. But although the pain had subsided a bit I still could not stand up. I had to look up to see him on the other side of the cage."

114

"Who is 'him'?"

"Some guy, a Westerner, standing outside my cage. He was speaking to me, I think."

"Welcome you piece of scum. I'll show you why you're here." I looked up and saw neatly pressed khaki shorts, a khaki shirt, and a neatly shaved, average size person, at least average European in size and appearance. He had a swagger stick under one arm. He kicked a cloud of dust in my face and moved on. He seemed to be making an inspection. I then became aware of my surroundings a bit more. There were several separate cages, made of bamboo, iron rods, lengths of old pipes, boards and whatever seemed needed to fortify and strengthen them. Each cage contained pathetic-looking individuals, dressed in rags much like mine. They were dirty, unshaven, emaciated. And then the man with the swagger stick pointed it at a creature huddled in the corner of the cage adjacent mine.

"Him!" barked Swagger Stick.

"The wretch yelped and tried to burrow under some straw. Then I saw the dogs. Two guards, one dog, went into the cage and like an experienced cowboy hog-tying a calf, they bound the poor fellow. He was quickly immobilized. One of the guards, the one without the dog, half carried, half dragged the fellow outside. His hands had been tied behind his back and then to his ankles. His spine arched backwards. His eyes bulged out in pain and fear.

"I remember seeing just a bit more. The rest of the outside area. I saw blocks, poles, all made of stout wood. Swagger Stick pointed to a large block of wood and without saying a word, the two guards carried the tied fellow over to the block and put his neck on it.

"Swagger Stick laughed." He came over to me. "Look at him, you shit," he screamed at me, "think about this and enjoy it!"

"I tried not to, but could not help watching. Another guard came out, and with an ax, casually chopped off the fellow's head.

"The head rolled over to one side and great gushes of blood shot out of the stump of neck. The body leapt about, reflexively thrashing, all the while making a gurgling sound as the lungs sucked in blood and spewed it out, the effluent joining the diminishing flow still pumped by a beating heart.

"I wretched—vomited—or tried to, and passed out.

"The next day, or I think it was the next day, I woke up. Bowls of weak soup were being pushed under the cell doors. I could still barely move and whenever I did, the pain wracked my joints. But I was hungry and managed to get a bowl. Some of the other captives came over to me and we managed to converse a bit. One of them was reasonably fluent in English and he began to explain to me what was happening. We were, it turned out, in the clutches of someone named Morgagni, a genuine madman who set up this group of cells for his own pleasure in torturing people to death. The decapitation we had witnessed the previous day was mild as far as what else he did. Morgagni used it to introduce the concept to the newcomers. It really was the quickest and least painful of his stunts, but perhaps the most dramatic. Vomiting and passing out, I was told, is what every newcomer does. And every newcomer gets to see a decapitation. Morgagni occasionally hanged people, but impalement was his favorite activity. I was told that we each had about a month's life expectancy here. There was a steady stream of replacements and Morgagni's appetite seemed to be growing.

"We had no sanitary facilities whatever. No water for washing. Our clothes were rotting rags. The stench was unbelievable. I tried to look out between the bars—I put my hand on a bar and was pulled back, just in time, by another captive. As soon as my hand touched a bar, one of the many massive mongrel dogs leapt at me and tried to bite. Everyone was afraid of the dogs and rightly so. I was told they had ripped off arms. I believed it. I did the experiment a few times of putting my hand on a bar and immediately a dog leapt at me with the full force of his body. Apparently one prisoner, some time ago, had gotten a long stout splinter of bamboo and when a dog leaped at him, he stuck it into the dog. The prisoner took three days to die, impaled on a stake, in full view of all of us.

Morgagni came by periodically to watch us, as well as the captive who might be on the stake. He sat on a canvas camp chair, often sipping a drink.

116

"Every captive was sick. Dysentery, lice, all sorts of parasites, some malaria cases, I had large sores that oozed. Prisoners who had been there a week or so became listless. And always the dogs. We were like fish in a Japanese restaurant's holding tank. Every once in a while one of the fish would be selected and taken out for the enjoyment of the patron. There was nothing at all we could do. I played every possible scenario and none worked. Even if we could kill a guard, or a dog, there would be more. And most of us were too weak to resist. Morgagni always picked a victim who was just on the edge of total despair. Someone who had been in captivity a while and had been weakened physically and mentally. Semi-starvation dulled us into lethargy. I hit on a way to get a little extra food. There were some flat rocks in my cage and once I turned one over. I saw some worms and slugs on the damp underside of the rock. I ate them. No, I didn't even gag. I just swallowed them whole and they were slimy and slid right down. Tasted a bit sweet. Once or twice a day I harvested my worms and slugs. That extra nutrition made a difference and I slowed my wasting.

"The impalements were most horrible. They were Morgagni's favorites. Guards and a dog would come into a cell and grab the se-lected victim. They would tie his wrists tightly behind his back and only loosely bind his ankles. Two guards would then pick up the victim and carry him out to a stake, lift him up, rip off his rags and seat him firmly on the sharpened top of the stake. A few yanks on his legs would drive the stake into his rectum. The victim's writh-ing and kicking would then simply work his body further down the stake. If he were lucky, the point would head toward his spine and possibly sever his aorta. This would take an hour or so, then merciful death. Unlucky were those in whom the stake worked its way toward the abdomen. Sometimes it protruded through the belly wall, sometimes it worked its way into a lung. These were the long-term sufferers. The screams were unbelievable and some of the prisoners went mad listening. They couldn't shut out the sound that told them what their turn would be like.

"Morgagni sometimes hanged his victims. He had that down to an art also. No drop, just a very thin rope around the neck and the victim would be hoisted up. Hoisted very gently so his neck wouldn't snap, and just high enough so he could find a little relief by stretching down his toes. They just touched the ground and by exerting a huge effort the victim could prolong his life. But slowly, inevitably, he fatigued and more weight was transferred to the thin noose around his neck and he slowly strangled. No screams from the hanging victims—just an hour or so of gurgling and eyes bulging out of their heads. He had a variant. The victim wasn't bound at all. Feet and hands were left free. These victims would try to hold onto the rope. But the rope was too thin and too slick to get purchase for very long, and then began the dance. Like some marionette, the hanging man would leap about, legs kicking and arms flailing, trying to grab the rope and climb up it. And Morgagni would laugh."

Lo Ban interrupted. "Was Morgagni present at all the executions?"

"Absolutely yes. He selected the victim personally each time."

"Anything sexual?"

"Yes. He often masturbated."

"So it was for his pure enjoyment?"

"Yes."

"Do you know how he got his prisoners?"

"I am not certain, but I surmise he bought them."

"All of them?"

"As I said, I don't know, but the ones I was able to speak with had all been bought."

"As were you."

"As was I."

Lo Ban had brought Luther back from his memory of the impalements. We all relaxed a bit and Luther looked a bit less drained. Lo Ban took out a menu and we each picked something to order and Lo Ban called room service.

"You realize, of course, that we could not get access to your original debriefing. All this is new to us. Forgive me for going over material you've already covered with others. Tell me, Luther, what are you doing now?"

"I quit the Agency. Got a good disability. Then, I joined the Salvation Army. I work there still. I have a small apartment nearby and walk to work every day. I rarely leave Des Moines, I don't aspire to anything else. Once you leave, I will go back to my routine."

"Are you happy?"

"I am neither happy nor unhappy. I just am. Something got lost in those cages and it never came back. I've given up looking for it. I'm not sure that I even know any longer what it is."

Room service came. Lo Ban signed for it and tipped. We ate and talked a bit about things in general, not specifically relating to Morgagni, the impalements, or the raid. When we had finished eating, Lo Ban took us back to the debriefing.

"There isn't very much more, except recalling various individual deaths, the behavior of some prisoners, Morgagni sitting there, watching them all. Then, of course, was your raid."

"Did Morgagni survive?"

"At the time I didn't know. Later I discovered he had."

"When and how?"

"About two years ago, I saw Morgagni. Alive."

"Where?"

"In this country."

"Where?"

"Chicago. He was riding the escalator in Marshall Field's."

"Positive?"

"Absolutely."

"Did you follow him?"

"Yes."

"Why?"

"I'm not sure. I didn't know what I wanted to do with him."

"Where did he go?"

"He got into a taxi and I got into the one behind his. We played 'follow that cab!' He went to an address on the Near North Side.

I saw him get out and I took down the building number. I paid off my taxi around the corner and walked back to the address. It was a small building with three flats. One was a speech therapist, another a couple with an Indian surname, and the third was just a name. Not Morgagni."

"What was it?"

"E. Golgi."

"What did you do then?"

"Went back to my hotel. The Allerton, on North Michigan. Looked up the name in a phone directory. It was there. I telephoned him and recognized the voice when he answered. It was Morgagni. I recognized it even after all these years."

"Anyone else know about it?"

"Yes. I told some old contacts in the Company. I needed to get help to find out about him."

"Find out what?"

"I wasn't sure what I was looking for. Just some info about him. What was he doing in the US? Just who really was he? That kind of stuff. I had no real idea what, if anything, I was going to do."

"What kind of response did you get?"

"Oh, some old friends helped me get the info on him. Unofficially. But officially? Officially nobody wanted to hear about it."

"What did you find out?"

"Morgagni was a native–born American. From a rather wealthy family. Really very intelligent, budding scholar. Yale class of '55. Did drugs. Then disappeared for a while. You know the part about his compound in Southeast Asia. He survived your raid, and again disappeared for a while—just for a few years. Then he surfaced back here in the states and was arrested and served a long prison sentence."

"For what?"

"Torture and murder. He was living in western Arkansas and a neighborhood woman disappeared. She was found dead, having been tortured to death. The trail led to Morgagni and he was arrested and tried on circumstantial evidence. The evidence was pretty strong, but not enough to convince a jury to give him the death penalty. He spent 25 years in jail and got out just a few years ago. About the time I ran into him in Chicago.

"You know, Lo Ban, I had been trying to forget this whole thing. It consumed so much of my life and changed me incredibly. Now, it all starts up again. I don't think I can escape it again and I feel that I have to do something, just for my sake. I could kill him, you know. I'd have no trouble with that now that I've seen him again. Five years ago, in the abstract, I think I would have said that I couldn't kill him."

"Everyone struggles with that." Lo Ban said this so matter-of-factly that I was startled. Indeed, I knew he struggled with it, and I struggled with it, but did everyone? Just how many people did our kind of thing? And, most important, if the people who did this sort of thing all have the struggle, how many gave in? And to what? Do they all become self-appointed killers?

Luther leaned back and stretched out his legs. I had been observing him carefully as he did his dog-and-pony act with Lo Ban. He was obviously trying to cooperate and he answered Lo Ban easily, not putting up any barriers. I felt we could trust his answers. Luther had let his eyes half close and he seemed to be in a mild trance.

As the session wore on, there was a perceptible change in Luther. He was being transformed from a burnout who had found himself doing good works for the Salvation Army in a podunk town in the midwest to someone who had a new self. Or was it the old self, but resurrected?

"My turn," said Luther. He handed me an envelope." Firstly, this is the most recent picture I could get of Morgagni. It's his prison release portrait. It's pretty good—it catches the essence of Morgagni and is very close to what he looked like when I spotted him in Chicago. Secondly, why, after all this time, are you guys interested in Morgagni? I know that when you busted up the compound and sprung me you weren't after him particularly—your job was to get me out. I know you got paid well for that. Not to diminish my gratitude you know, but it was only a job. Hey, I don't really mean 'only' what I mean is that.... oh, hell! You know what I mean. But here's a question. Why now?"

"Yes. Please don't worry about words. We know what you mean. Yes, it was 'just' a job. We did not have personal involvement with you because of your job or your political philosophy, but I personally am glad we did it, pay or no pay. I've often wondered how the other guys we turned loose fared. That was a gift. We had no responsibility to them other than our own personal honor. I wish we could have done more for them, I truly hope they got away.

"Anyway, somebody seems to be after us now. It looks serious, right now, for us. Whoever it is, has an organization and money. And does torture. Impalements. At least we think so. We really have very little to go on and we might be clutching at straws. But at least it's something. Your guy is the only one we know who was an impaler, and certainly the only impaler we crossed in any of our activities. We really had no idea who he was or if he was even alive. You were the only link we had. Nobody at the Agency was interested in helping—we couldn't even pull in some old debts.

"Your picture will help us. It is probably the most important thing we've unearthed."

"Any idea where Morgagni is now?"

"No. I tried to keep tabs on him but he left Chicago and disappeared. Maybe not disappeared, but I lost him. Really didn't try too hard to follow him around at first, I confess."

"At first?"

"Yes," responded Luther. "But then the whole thing began to gnaw at me. I called in some favors again and tried to have him located. The Agency couldn't find him. They shouldn't have even tried to do it, especially for a private guy like me, but they did and came up with nothing. Everywhere they looked. Morgagni had disappeared. He had done all his time in jail, and been released, so there was no parole involved. I couldn't come up with a passport, or evidence of his death. I couldn't penetrate the IRS so I have no idea if he's still paying taxes. Some friends run a private service. They tried also and lost his trail after Chicago. The whole thing got to be an obsession with some of the guys. How can you lose someone like Morgagni? They went after him whole hog and I suspect that he had to be aware that someone was looking for him. With all those guys checking around he had to be aware of it. And I suspect that he really couldn't figure out who it was who was looking for him. Must have bothered the hell out of him."

"Think he was scared?"

"I really don't know. Apprehensive because he couldn't control something that affected him, perhaps. But scared? I simply don't know."

"Think he knows it was you?"

"I have no idea. Did he know I was still alive and did he know where I was? I just assumed he couldn't connect me with the guys I had looking for him. I hadn't even considered that possibility."

"I would." Lo Ban's words chilled me. He could sometimes say simple things in icicles that engendered numbing fear in those who heard. Luther heard.

I took up a yellow tablet and pencil and drew Maria's time-line, again segmented in five-year units. I filled in dates—the raid, Morgagni's prison sentence, Luther's discovery of Morgagni, Amanda's episode, our tail in Istanbul, Mehmet's death. Then, against everything I wanted to believe, I penciled in a small asterisk. Elizabeth's death. It was just before Morgagni's conviction and beginning of his prison time. Surely it was a coincidence. But Morgagni was on the loose when all these things happened. I tossed the pad over to Lo Ban.

Lo Ban looked at it and sighed. "A good correlation. But just that." He passed the tablet to Luther.

"None of us really know Morgagni." Luther was being practical. "Except that we know what he did in his compound before you raided it, and what he most likely did in Arkansas. But we know nothing about him otherwise that would help understand this, or help us decide if he's behind your troubles. Anyway, I don't know what I'm going to do about all this, but right now, I'm very tired." We looked at the clock. It was 2:30 a.m. "And I'm going home and to bed. Get in touch with me if you want to go over anything else. If I think of something, or if I need to bounce something off you, I'll be in touch with you. Good night."

"Good night, Luther. Thank you." We shook hands all around and traded addresses and telephone numbers.

Luther left and I walked him to the elevator. "Really appreciate your help."

He smiled at me. "Really appreciated your help." He stepped into the elevator and the door began to close. Luther stopped it with his hand and looked as though he wanted to tell me something. "Oh, nothing. It'll keep." and the door closed fully this time.

Lo Ban and I were equally tired. Listening to Luther had drained us both and we packed it in for the night.

Chapter 15

We go proactive

Over breakfast, Lo Ban and I discussed Luther's information.

"I hope Luther doesn't decide to try to do anything to Morgagni." Lo Ban seemed worried. "If Morgagni is behind all this, he's got too big an organization and is probably too well protected. Luther would get wiped, working alone."

"Any need for us to see Luther again?" I hoped Lo Ban would say "no," I wanted to get out of Des Moines. Today.

"No," said Lo Ban, and then, as if reading my mind, "and let's leave as soon as possible. I have to do something about Amanda—make sure she's OK. She's a tough broad and I don't think that anybody's on to us in Madrid, but, just in case..."

"Well, Maria's there too and she can handle herself pretty well. I don't think she ever goes out without her little .25. Amanda and Maria would be a double whammy if anyone tried something.

"And, I'm not sure what to do next. I hate to just wait for his next move and then respond. If we could be proactive it might be better. We should try to find Morgagni. Maybe it's time for us to call in some big favors and spread some money around. I wish Morgagni had been an agent instead of a rich pervert. It would make things so much easier."

"Lo Ban!" I had just gotten a thought that might help us find Morgagni. "Somebody with Morgagni's depth of perversion can't be entirely unknown. The guy has money, he lives internationally, he can hire guards, armed compounds, killers. Presumably he can bribe local officials. But more to the point, the guy is educated, if that's something Yale can do, and that means he might have an academic interest in his hobby. And, he's wealthy enough to support it big-time. That means he absolutely has to be known."

"And what is an 'academic interest' in sadistic hangings and impalements? Does he collect famous gallows from the past? Posts that have impaled the rich and famous?"

"No. He would collect books. Prints. Travelers accounts."

"And?" Lo Ban was dense at times.

"And, that means we have the best contacts in the world to find him. Assuming he doesn't collect children's books or modern firsts."

"In which case, he'd be right at home. There're some Godzillas in that field that he would impale on sight." Lo Ban was riding one of his favorite hobby horses, yet again.

"Calm yourself, Lo Ban. We were planning to do another book fair, even if we have to rub shoulders with 'that type of person' and we really can just ignore them. At least for a few days. I do admit, that it's great fun to bait them. The temptation is enormous. But, let's not forget that we have other fish to fry."

"Agreed. We can do a book fair and we can also make some good money. We've been talking about doing that anyway and this is yet another reason. And we can try to find out who buys stuff on old torture and executions. Yes, Manasek, you think logically."

I ignored his attempt at insult. We were still in Des Moines and needed to get out.

Lo Ban became pensive. "I'm still bothered, Manasek. It's fine that we do a fair, expose ourselves to hit men and all that, but I'm still bothered about whoever is trying to get to us now. Here we are in Des Moines, Amanda and Maria are in Madrid and Veronica is in Paris. That leaves us a bit vulnerable. Hard to back each other up. Suppose Amanda and I come visit you in Vermont?"

"Of course. Come and stay as long as you like. But what of Veronica and Maria? If anyone's digging through airline tickets and that kind of stuff sooner or later the trail will lead to Madrid. Shouldn't Maria come here also? Veronica is far more anonymous right now and not likely to be tracked down."

Lo Ban smiled. "I'm not going to tease you, even though the temptation is enormous. I'm glad it's finally working out."

I dropped the subject. Besides, both Veronica and Maria could take care of themselves. They didn't need us as shepherds. On the other hand, if we were all together we could coordinate our efforts and get some serious intelligence, which, at some point we would need.

"Will you go back to Madrid to fetch Amanda?" I asked Lo Ban.

"No, probably not necessary. I'll telephone her and suggest she fly over to Boston. I can meet her and pick her up at Logan."

We checked out of the hotel, symbolically bidding Des Moines good-bye, and drove the rent-a-car to the airport. We got rid of the car and still had plenty of time before we would be physically rid of Des Moines.

Check-in was almost deserted, the flight was mostly empty and we got two good seats. After checking in, Lo Ban made a telephone call from one of the pay phones. The conversation was short. Lo Ban put the receiver down and walked over to sit down next to me. He was smiling. "Amanda's coming." I could see he was pleased. "She'll drop us a coded signal when she gets her tickets."

A couple of hours later I was looking down on the feature-less Midwest unrolling slowly below us, like an e-make scroll, and felt as empty as the landscape. I should have asked Maria to come also.

Chapter 16

Home

It is always a pleasant experience for me to head back home to Vermont. Lo Ban and I landed in Hartford, Connecticut, and rented a car for the drive north. Interstate 91 was virtually devoid of traffic and we sped along, more than a tad over the speed limit. The smooth road wound its way through some very pleasant Vermont scenery, and provided glimpses of the Connecticut River to the right. My home in Norwich is a bit over an hour's drive north of the Massachusetts border and we soon heard the pleasant crunch of gravel under our tires as I drove down the winding driveway to my house, the grey-and-blue cape nestled amongst the pine trees.

"It's still a mystery to me why you don't at least have a pied-a-terre in New York. This is so isolated."

"It's a nice contrast to the rest of my life."

I turned off the primary alarm and once inside deactivated the secondary alarm. The house was cool and had the distinctive aroma of desertion; that strange and characteristic smell that develops in furnished houses long unoccupied. Not unpleasant: each time I smell it I remember my childhood and the annual opening of our summer house after a winter of abandonment. Pleasant memories. Somewhat reluctantly, I opened the windows and let in both the outside air and the sounds of Vermont woods. Lo Ban, for his part, had taken the rental car to return it, and I fortunately remembered to pick him up.

"Any messages?" Lo Ban was anxious as we returned from the car agency.

"Haven't gone into the office yet. Let's check right now."

We went into the little outbuilding that had once been a carriage house and now served as my office. The fax machine had been busy during my absence and there was a spiral of paper curling across the floor. I scanned the strip quickly and, except for some long-delayed book orders, there seemed nothing urgent. Until, near the end, the brief coded message clearly from Amanda giving us the date and flight when she would arrive from Madrid. There were a couple of things in the message that weren't too clear to me, but Lo Ban smiled when he scanned it. I had the feeling it was no business of mine.

The next day Lo Ban and I began setting up a command post in my office. We swept the building for bugs, a precaution we took despite the double alarm system. Bugs could work from outside the frame building. We ran tests on our telephone lines and the fax line and they all checked out bug–free. We each made a few telephone calls to our various contacts and set some wheels in motion. We had been out of action long enough to have many sources dry up but we were able to prime the pump enough times so that we began to feel that we actually had the beginnings of a new network. With any luck we would begin to get a trickle of information and somewhere, in that trickle, if it ran long enough, would be what we needed. Information about Morgagni, about his Istanbuli contacts, impalements, who was tailing us, and what they wanted.

We made yet another of Maria's timelines but this time drew it long enough to enable us to potentially insert a large number of events, put in precise dates and even times if we knew them. I tacked it the wall of our command post. At some point correlations would emerge if we got the right data on the timeline. And we could infer from these correlations and test our inferences.

One of the first bits of information to come back to us was the precise dates and times of Morgagni's incarceration. All the dates and times of his detention in the local jail, then the county jail during his trial and finally the state penitentiary. These we dutifully plugged into the timeline. It was satisfying to fill in blanks—it signified progress.

"Another good day's work done." I thought as I stepped back to look at the long time line on the wall. The little scribbles we put in were comforting. They were icons that told me we had begun to put things together.

As dusk developed the Vermont air cooled quickly. We both felt the chill as we walked the short distance from the carriage house office to my home. Swallows darted about overhead, silhouetted against the glooming sky. Venus twinkled brightly as pine branches, wafting in the wind, swept modestly before her as though their brief occultations were trying to shield her from voyeurs' eyes. I took a last look at her as we went into my house and shut the door on the outside world.

Lo Ban brewed a pot of tea that was sufficient for each of us to have refills. We sat, mostly not speaking, in the comfort of my living room and watched the world outside grow dimmer. I missed Blaser.

"When does Amanda get here?"

"Tomorrow. She gets in early afternoon." answered Lo Ban. "I'll drive to Boston and meet her flight. If I can get to the airport through the mess that the Big Dig has made of Boston and if I can then navigate that airport. Gotta be among the world's worst. What's on your plate tomorrow?"

"FBI. I'm going to meet with Mike Coprinus over in Rutland. We'll have lunch together. I should be back here just about when you get back from Logan."

The quiet, the tea, the comfort of my living room with the oriental that came from my childhood home had an effect. I felt tired and drawn. Old too, maybe.

"In order for us to pull this off, we need to give it absolute attention. Just like the old days. Eat, sleep, and breathe it 24 hours a day. Compulsive unending attention. Nothing else can intrude. We always practiced that. Which is, I think, why we were so successful."

Lo Ban looked at me curiously, said nothing but nodded.

"And I don't think I'm up to it anymore."

Lo Ban nodded again. "Same here. But we don't really have a choice. We didn't put in a bid for this job." I wondered what he thought about the situation Red had asked us about.

Of course Lo Ban was right. He knew it and I knew it. I decided to say no more, to express no more doubts. It was not wise to introduce a psychological negative into all this. We needed to give succor to our strengths. Again, I put off bringing up Red.

130

"What about dinner tonight?" I changed the subject.

"I'm not all that hungry. Maybe we could have a light supper in Hanover. Nothing fancy."

"Molly's?"

"Agreed."

Hanover is located on the New Hampshire side of the Connecticut River and is home to Dartmouth College. It is a sparkling New England town; a quintessential New England college town. A bit on the self–conscious side, it is also a very wealthy town with an expensive inn, expensive shops and a severe parking problem. So when Lo Ban and I drove in for supper at Molly's, one of the town's many restaurants, I was pleased to stumble on some good luck and find a parking space just a few blocks from the restaurant. Lo Ban and I began walking down Main Street, glad that we had put on jackets. The chill was deepening.

Then, I stumbled on some more luck. Bad luck, this time. Suddenly, as we were passing the Dartmouth Book Store, my path down Main Street was blocked by the hirsute hulk of Esau Gedunsen, standing in the middle of the sidewalk. Esau is an in-your-face kind of guy. He kept pushing close to me. I backed up. He advanced. A slight saliva spray showered my face whenever Esau spoke. Or rather screamed. Esau perceived every interaction as a confrontation, and he responded by street-smart aggression. Sort of like a street thug off a dead-end in Brooklyn. And now, I was backing up and he was advancing. And yelling and spraying.

"I have shome books and maps I want to shell." Esau had never learned to recognize a hard 's.'

"That's good, Esau," I answered, looking for a way to get away from this discussion before my jacket needed to be changed. I knew from experience that nothing subtle would work on this guy so I was blunt.

"Esau, I really don't want to do business on the street."

"So what'sh wrong with doing business on the shtreet? I know a lot about old maps. I used to be a rare book dealer. I used to work for a rare map dealer." Esau was getting desperate. He was also a liar.

Passersby gave us a wide berth. Esau had quickly turned my stroll down the sedate street of Hanover, New Hampshire, into the trip from hell. Esau lived a rich fantasy life and thought himself a book expert but he was nothing but a liar who managed to cheat a few unsuspecting people out of the occasional book that he would then flog off to the trade. A thoroughly disliked man, a near-thug and a complete boor. And now I was trapped in public with him.

Lo Ban took it all in and acted.

"I don't think we've met," he said to Esau, "but I don't think I want to. Now get out of our way."

His voice had that steely chill that, rarely employed, always worked. Esau trembled visibly. He wilted. He slumped. He stepped aside and mumbled "Shorry."

"Thanks, old friend. I owe you one."

The meal at Molly's was, as expected, unremarkable but perfectly palatable.

Lo Ban and I drove back across the Connecticut River and back to my house.

I opened the damper, threw some twigs of kindling into the fireplace and started a small fire.

"We deserve it." I poured each of us a bit of Napoleon and we watched the fire catch and begin to consume the larger logs I piled on. Neither of us said much; we both felt introspective.

Pale moonlight outlined some trees against the sky. I saw them and felt a shudder begin at the base of my spine and migrate upward. Lo Ban noticed it.

"Manasek, something wrong?"

I nodded. "Lo Ban, years ago I had a house on Lake Michigan in the Indiana Dunes. I remember a night much like this one. There was also a foreboding but, as now, the foreboding was kept at bay by a small fire. A couple of friends were over and we were talking quietly.

"I recall sitting, looking out, vaguely cognizant of the dim, moonlit scene outside the large window. Somewhat brighter than the one now but not by much. The open space around the house was reasonably well-lighted by the moon, but brush and branches progressively filtered out the light as the land fell away downhill.

"Suddenly I became aware of something outside. An apparition of sorts. A being. I couldn't quite focus on it, but it was large and clumsy and was lurching slowly downhill. I said nothing but watched its progress through the dim light.

"It stopped a few times as though resting, but each time it continued its way downhill. Just at the edge of light and dark, almost where I could no longer see it the creature turned and looked directly at me. I could see nothing clearly except its eyes and it was only by extreme effort that I could turn mine away. Something terrifying connected us when our eyes met. Two beams of hatred, or perhaps evil, flowed from those eyes toward mine. I had the sense that it was waiting for me to beckon.

"Something in a human-like form was wandering the night outside my house and it was able to connect with me but only by some manner that I still cannot understand.

"That creature was an embodiment of something evil, some kind of tangible, particulate substance congealed into near-human form. I have seen such things since, but never before. But each time they were terrifyingly real. I later had a strange experience right here in Vermont. There is something flitting about just beyond my ability to identify that appears to me from time to time.

"That evening changed something forever in me. I had met an evil and was then, and still am, convinced it was real and not my imagination.

"Lo Ban, do you believe in the Devil?"

Chapter 17

The gathering force

We needed data for our timeline. Some we could get by casual inquiry, for others we needed some serious help. We wanted to list every recorded impalement death, every bizarre hanging, and every beheading we could get information on. Torture deaths aren't exactly listed on every database, nor are they common knowledge and we needed to access the FBI databases to dig out these crimes. I hoped we could find a pattern to any such unsolved crimes that might implicate Morgagni or perhaps point us to someone else. Now was the time to try to call in a big-time debt.

While Lo Ban drove to Boston to meet Amanda's flight, I drove out to Rutland and visited the regional FBI office. It was good to see my old friend Agent Mike Coprinus, and to meet his boss, the new regional head, Agent Don Russela. Russela wasn't quite sure why he was meeting with us, evidently Coprinus hadn't gone into too much detail about some of our current problems. Russela was new to the region and was still getting his sea legs. He listened with fascination tempered by a poorly disguised look of disbelief. I slowly fed Mike enough parts of the long story so that he would comprehend my request. Over lunch, joined by Russela, I added more to the story, deliberately doing it slowly so that it could sink in and they had the chance to ask any questions. Mike was buying it; Russela was not. That was fair enough, I've known Mike for a long time and he knew a fair amount about some of my activities. He didn't seem at all surprised by these latest problems. Then I popped the big one.

"Can we somehow arrange for us to get access to the database where we'll find unsolved torture deaths?"

"You mean, off-the-record access." Mike understood.

Russela blanched at the direction the conversation was going, and made it clear that he didn't want to touch our problem with a barge pole. He wanted us to work "through channels." That is, file a complaint with the FBI and let them do the investigating. "That's the only way the Bureau can do things. We simply cannot, never have and never will go outside channels." We let him explain the proper procedure in all his bureaucratic splendor. The English language quivered with shame as he expounded on the Bureau's procedures. It wasn't just copspeak. It was awesome copspeak. Bureaucraticofederalcopspeak.

Mike and I let him finish, whereupon Mike quietly said, "These are the guys who saved the Bureau's ass in Karachi."

The Karachi caper made me smile. Some years ago Lo Ban, Veronica, and I were near the region on unrelated private business when we heard, through the grapevine that four FBI agents had been captured by some ragtag insurgents. The FBI had, of course, no business being there and the whole thing had been a harebrained venture dreamed up by a less-than-bright desk boy. Now the thing could get nasty. An international incident of major import was in the making and nobody in the government or any of the participants knew how to head it off. Even the insurgents who captured the agents weren't too sure if that action served their cause. It wasn't yet public so the political fallout hadn't started, but it was certain to begin very soon unless someone headed it off.

Lo Ban knew some of the power people behind the insurgents and we decided to act on our own. It hadn't been too hard to get an audience with the insurgent backers. They were, on the surface, successful and conservative businessmen and Lo Ban simply presented his card and we were admitted immediately to the offices of two of the most powerful men of the region, neither of whom had any publicly identifiable association with the insurgents or their cause. There was genuine pleasure expressed as Lo Ban and the two bankers embraced. After Lo Ban delicately explained the problem and requested help, he was asked "How much will they pay you?"

"I'm not asking for money and they don't even know we're here. I just think that neither side needs this incident and I seek your help."

"Of course we will help, Lo Ban. It will be only a small repayment of what we all owe you and we agree that however stupid the FBI was to come here, it will not help us to hold them. Hopefully though, you will get paid."

"In kind, perhaps," Lo Ban answered. Clearly the issue had been resolved and no more discussion was necessary. We were treated to a splendid dinner and left the country the next morning. At about the same time, four bewildered and disorientated FBI agents found themselves thrust, blindfolded, into a narrow fetid street in a dense slum area. Even after they got their blindfolds off, they didn't know where they were, but obviously they were free. A street urchin, seemingly innocent, led them out, unmolested by the crowds that parted for them. Even the beggars knew to stay away. And, fortunately for us now, the FBI had learned who had sprung their agents.

So now, sitting in a restaurant in Rutland, Vermont, two FBI agents were in a position to help us for helping some of them. Rusella, although clearly concerned about his career, behaved with honor and nodded a silent approval. Mike Coprinus smiled and handed me the access passwords I needed to look up unsolved torture deaths stored in the FBI mainframe. The rest of the lunch was pleasant and low-key. Russela actually relaxed and offered some good suggestions. I promised to keep them posted, and we parted on very good terms.

"Another good day's work," I thought as I drove back home along Route 4, the winding east–west two–lane highway that snaked across the mountainous center of Vermont. I drove slowly through Woodstock, that charming, somewhat Disneyfied old village with its splendid inn and pseudo-quaint, expensive shops. I fell in behind an overloaded logging truck and couldn't decide if Vermont was lucky indeed not to have a superhighway instead of creaky old Route 4. Thoughts of Red came to me. Red, my old friend sitting next to me and Blaser, my dog sleeping in the rear, all of us driving this very route.

Lo Ban was back from his Boston run—the car was in the driveway and, assuming he and Amanda were inside the house, I walked in.

"Surprise!"

I was stunned to see Maria standing there, an impish grin accentuating her features. Silhouetted against the large window, her slender body invited my embrace.

We held each other tightly. "Nice to see you, Paco."

Maria's soft hair and her fragrance were magical and her body pressed to mine was more than magical, it was wondrous. I kissed her again. "Thank you for coming. I'm so glad."

"So that's what that gibberish in your coded message meant." I turned to Amanda after Maria and I stopped hugging each other. Amanda nodded, smiling broadly.

"I've never been here, you know." Maria held my arm tightly. "Show me our room so I can freshen up."

Lo Ban and Amanda were grinning like idiots as I carried Maria's bags upstairs.

"Tonight, let's not worry about business. Let's celebrate. I reserved a table for us at the Norwich Inn." Lo Ban had made dinner reservations at the town's splendid old inn, whose kitchen was truly remarkable. "Sally thought we could have a table away from others. They're not too busy tonight." Sally Wilson, the inn's proprietor, and Lo Ban were good friends. They both had hit it off well many years ago and enjoyed teasing each other occasionally. Tonight, Sally arranged for our table to be surrounded by empties—the other diners were clustered in the far end of the dining room. I have no idea what Lo Ban told Sally, but she was especially solicitous of Maria and by the time dinner was finished, Maria had become a convert to the Norwich Inn. The food had certainly helped with that.

I think we had duck that night, but cannot quite remember. The promise implied by the game of footsie I was having with Maria's smoothly stockinged foot far eclipsed mere dinner.

Chapter 18

A line for time

Over a leisurely late breakfast the next day, Vermont sunshine streaming through the windows, the four of us reviewed the situation regarding Morgagni. Our own security was discussed since we clearly had concerns for our safety. Lo Ban suggested we travel in pairs and stay armed at all times. It sounded like a sensible precaution despite no evidence that we were now being tailed, or that we had even been discovered here.

Later that day, using the passwords and procedures given us by Mike Coprinus, Amanda and Maria began searching the FBI files using the computers in my office.

Hangings posed a problem. There were hundreds of them in the files and many could not be classified as murder rather than suicide. We agreed to ignore hangings for the time being and concentrate on impalings and beheadings. As expected, there were not many in these categories but it was sometimes difficult to decide if a given murder was by impalement. Many other descriptive terms were in use, and if the person describing the scene was trying to use more polite terms, it was often difficult to determine precisely what happened.

Two days of sifting through FBI records yielded 14 impalings, or at least murders that perhaps involved some form of impaling, and six beheadings. We went back to the timeline and entered them. All the impalings and one beheading occurred at times when Morgagni had been out of prison. The other five beheadings happened when he was locked away. We decided to concentrate solely on the impalings, and if that led nowhere we would go back and analyze the beheadings. The impalement murders seemed to be scattered about but most were in the Midwest. However the two most recent cases, occurring about two months apart, took place in the pleasant horse country of Virginia's broad Cloacre Valley. If this all was the work of Morgagni, he had hit twice in the same place.

The trickle of information continued to come in. Most was irrelevant. Some was even interesting if not important. But when the occasional significant bits were added together we began to make some sense of all this. Morgagni, it seems, could not stand being thwarted. His biggest problem in prison was his inability to do as he pleased. Nobody before had ever crossed him, or blocked any of his plans or activities.

Maria went back and looked more carefully at the victims entered on our list. The last two impalement victims, those at Cloacre Valley, were both stable hands working for the same stable. The police, looking at homosexual motive, had missed an important connection. Both victims had been prison guards before taking jobs at the stables. And both had been prison guards at prisons where Morgagni was an inmate. A quick check on the other victims showed that three other impalements had been done on former prison guards and all had been at prisons that had held Morgagni. The job history of the other victims was not clear from the records.

The timeline was filling in and each entry seemed to point yet another finger in Morgagni's direction. Every time I looked at it, I mentally inserted Elizabeth's death. It, too, was a plausible Morgagni hit.

"But she had fallen, not been murdered," I kept telling myself.

Despite the continuing trickle of data, we could not determine Morgagni's current whereabouts. We didn't even know if he was in the country and were unable to get any leads about his organization. Although we still assumed our Istanbul troubles were related to him, we could come up with no firm connections. It was all still a giant construct that might exist nowhere except in our imaginations. Hopefully it was not the sign of a collective psychosis.

All those ambiguities were put aside for a while. We checked our incoming data each day, but were content to let it sit for a bit.

"If we leave it alone for a while, we'll see it in a clearer light." I argued.

The four of us played, temporarily shelving our project. We had a splendid run of fine Vermont weather—bright blue skies, warm days, and cool nights. We canoed, swam, picnicked in the lush green hills, and walked a bit on the Appalachian Trail. The weather had been perfect for wild mushrooms to appear and, after one picnic, I filled our basket with firm, fresh chanterelles, the orange-colored trumpet-shaped mushrooms that stewed wonderfully. A few early *Boletus edulus* joined the chantrelles in the wicker basket. Growing in profusion were several species of Amanita. There was the spotted *A. muscaria,* that grew locally with a yellowish cap instead of textbook red. We also were hosts to the evil white *A. verna,* source of the deadly alpha-amanitin.

"Didn't Russian peasants used to get high on the *muscaria?*" asked Maria.

"The story is that Russian nobility would eat the mushrooms to get high, then piss out the windows and the peasants would catch and drink the urine for their high. I don't believe it," I continued, "for a couple of reasons. First the muscarinic effects from the mushroom's content of muscarine, are not highs, but pretty dreadful—muscarine makes you ooze from every orifice, and you can drown in your own fluid. Second, why wouldn't the peasants just go into the forest and eat their own freshly picked mushrooms?

"Killjoy." Maria smiled.

Anyway, the *verna* is the real baddie. The toxin in it, the alpha-amanitin, blocks RNA synthesis. A week or ten days after ingesting it, the ingestor runs out of RNA—no more can be made to replace the old RNA and the ingestor dies. It's a horrible death, too. It took a while to figure this out, since it's tough to link death to such a much earlier event, that of ingesting the mushroom.

Maria and I had wandered off, hand in hand, down the trail to a secluded little area, deep in the pine woods, where the shaded moss carpeted deeply the forest floor.

"But your chanterelles are OK?"

"You betcha!"

Maria smiled and held me close. "You betcha? OK, you betcha!"

The forest floor was soft and yielding.

It was growing dark when we returned home. Almost time to think of dinner.

Blood's Seafood is located just a bit down the road from us and they have a large, well-stocked lobster tank. Maria and I picked out four nice pound-and-a-half lobsters for our evening dinner. She involuntarily wrinkled her nose a bit as she watched the tankful of lobsters crawl over each other, the rapidly circulating seawater rippling the surface. "I feel sorry for them," she said.

I found her irresistibly charming and was filled with happiness as we took our lobsters back to my car.

"I hate to break the enchantment," announced Amanda at dinner, while we were trying not to drip butter from the chunks of freshly cooked lobster, "but the time to think about the book fair is upon us. We need to get the contracts signed and sent in. If we're really going to do it, we have to pull together our inventory."

"And you all think you'll locate Morgagni through his purchase of books on torture? Is there any evidence he buys the stuff?"

"No, but it's a chance. The guy is bright and he's good at what he does. Most people who fit that description take an academic interest in their pursuits. I've seen it before. I sell a lot of *shunga*," continued Lo Ban, "and I suspect that a number of my clients are deviants. Or at least are arrested in development. Fascinated by hugely oversized genitalia. There's also a ready market for books such as the *Tortures of China* and, let me tell you, some of the people buying that title are practitioners, not just intellectually curious."

The lobster finished, the Chablis drained, the dishes cleared away. Time to fight postprandial stupor and begin preparations for the fair.

"Can you get your stuff shipped here from Hong Kong?" I asked Lo Ban, hoping he and Amanda would stay until the fair. I didn't want to risk breaking the magic spell that had come to inhabit my house.

"I suppose so. It's easier than going back and getting it. What do you think, Amanda?"

Amanda looked supremely comfortable. "I'd rather stay here and eat lobster than do a round-trip."

"I've got about a hundred decent maps and about eight good atlases to take. Together we can mount an impressive display." I turned to Maria. "Want to come out to the office and we can start selecting them now?"

Our feet crunched the gravel beneath us as we walked, making a pleasant, comforting sound. A gibbous moon illuminated the short path between my house and office building. We stopped to embrace. Maria pressed herself closely against me.

"You're a big smoocher." Maria smiled.

"Uh-huh."

The office was cool and peaceful-looking and the green-shaded lamps over the map cabinets created a warm, comforting island.

Our command center, and all that implied was in another corner, across a dark sea that we chose, at that time, not to navigate.

"So this is where you do your honest work!" Maria laughed. "I like it." We embraced again and held tightly to each other.

Until the fax machine rang. Our collective curiosity didn't permit us to ignore the paper emerging from the squat black box. It was a single sheet, no cover, no sender's imprint. It was a brief police report, sent to us by one of our contacts, we presumed. And it told us more than we wanted to know.

Dazed, we hurried back to the house with the message.

Amanda and Lo Ban were sitting on the living room couch. Wordlessly, Maria handed them the message.

"So Morgagni is in the country." Lo Ban shook his head. "We should have thought of this and warned Luther."

"And they're listing Luther's hanging a suicide?" Maria wrinkled her brow.

"Rope burns on palms from trying to climb up rope or to support himself. That part is typical of suicides who change their mind too late. Few suicides rig a drop long enough to snap the neck and they wind up strangling. That isn't too pleasant so they try to climb back up but eventually get too tired to hang on and get rope burns as their hands slip down the rope. Then they dangle until they choke to death.

"But eighth-inch rope and feet barely touching floor. That's what Luther described as Morgagni's special technique back at his camp. No way the cops could know about that, but there's probably some other evidence that doesn't quite fit. Maybe we can find out tomorrow."

The gibbous moon had set. A few frogs still croaked their occasional call. "You awake, Paco?" Just a low whisper.

"Yeah. I'm awake and feeling sorry for myself and for all of us. We shouldn't need to do this. We didn't ask for it. I have a terrible feeling about this operation. I'm too old for all this."

"No, you're not." Maria moved over to me and with her slender body very gently let me prove it.

Chapter 19

Boot camp

The next day was a hectic one. We all realized that the salad days were over and we needed to take our gloves off, stop playing, and start moving. We had acquired a lot of information, probably enough to act upon. More would be nice but we couldn't wait for more. Besides, we would never get all we wanted—we would have to act on incomplete data. As always.

Under Lo Ban's tutelage we began to brush up on our weaponry. None of us had shot handguns regularly for years. We needed to shake off any rust that might have accumulated affecting not only our aim, but the psychology of shooting. We had twice-daily half-hour sessions target shooting against an earthen mound. Maria still favored her little vintage .25 semi. The rest of us were using .22 semis. Small caliber handguns are looked down upon these days. Most favor larger guns and some argue that the venerable .38 is inadequate. We have always felt that it is more important to know how to shoot well than to throw massive amounts of lead. The biggest disadvantage to small caliber semiautos is the small amount of energy available to operate the mechanism. Good quality ammunition and keeping the gun clean and properly lubed is the key and I have never had a jam or failure to feed. I can also place a shot into a head-sized target at 20 feet. On the move.

Later in the morning, Mike Coprinus rang me up with some information about Luther's death. Seems the police found a partial letter he was in the process of writing. Mike surmised it was meant for Lo Ban although there were no names either in the letter or on the envelope. But there was enough in the text to indicate that Luther feared for his life. He thought he had been located and was worried and wanted to know if could join our group. Partly for self-defense and partly to avenge. This made the whole death scene a different matter. The police wisely chose to continue to play it a suicide and not tip their hand and they did not reveal the discovery of the letter in any of their press releases. For the moment, at least, we could assume, or at least hope, that Morgagni wouldn't find out about the letter.

"Shouldn't we have told Mike about our progress?" Amanda's suggestion made sense to me.

"Too much heat on Morgagni might drive him underground and he might not surface for years. Then, if he surfaces just when we don't expect him, we could be in real trouble. I think it's better to get this thing over with now. Let's just get him."

The last four words sent a chill around the room. We all had heard that tone before, and it always had the same effect. Lo Ban's words were still his alone but he had planted the seed of death.

Lo Ban's books arrived from Hong Kong and together we selected those we would take with us to the book fair. We needed to look good. The AAB fair in New York is America's flagship antiquarian book fair and many of the world's major dealers and collectors either exhibit there or visit it.

"Rodney Oufle will be there. Hope he has a lot of torture plate books."

Lo Ban's comment gave me an idea. "Why don't we invent a unique treatise on impalement? We can get some publicity, maybe a New York Times article about it. If your theory about Morgagni as a collector is correct, he might bite. Especially if it sounds important and he's never heard of it."

"A fake book?" Lo Ban was pensive. "What about the AAB ethics committee? How will they take it?"

"Lo Ban, you disappoint me. We won't actually have a fake book and we won't sell one and furthermore they would never hear of it."

"I like the idea. Let's think about it."

Despite the intriguing nature of this idea, nothing came of it and we never produced a fake impalement book.

We finished by assembling a collection of about a hundred maps, eight atlases, and about 30 of Lo Ban's books from his inventory. That would make the fair easy to set up and also to take down at the end. I am always impressed by the dealers who drag hundreds of books, packed in dozens of boxes and chests to fair after fair. They labor like donkeys setting up and labor like donkeys taking down. For their sake, I hope they do well.

Although our weapons skills were becoming better they were still not adequate. Lo Ban thought we needed more practice so we added a third half-hour to our day's target shooting. We drilled ourselves in shooting at both stationary and moving targets, but just as important, in reloading and shooting on the move. This was much like the Old Days, when our Group was really active. But we were then not so out of training as we currently found ourselves. Moreover, although I discovered that even as some of my old skills slowly returned, the necessary mental attitude did not. I intellectualized the operation. Knew it had to get done but couldn't quite throw myself into it like I could have, and would have, some 20 years earlier. I found myself thinking of Maria and the pleasantness of her warm, slim body next to mine each night. How nice it was to wake up with us still next to each other! And I pondered how it was that mortality had infiltrated me now, and to spring forth as some fifth-columnist, to make me wonder things I never wondered before and to make me wish this all away.

Chapter 20

Elizabeth's line

I stared at the timeline, so deep in thought that I did not hear Lo Ban come up behind me.

"Well?" was all he said.

"I dunno. I keep trying not to think about Elizabeth's death. But it really belongs on the timeline."

"Well, then put it there. Manasek, I could never get this through to you. But you know very well that when an accident like this happens to someone connected to people in our line of work, it usually isn't an accident. And we never ruled that out in Elizabeth's case. I always thought we needed to do it, for her sake if not for yours. She was very conspicuously part of your life—there was no hiding it and then she died. If it was foul play then it wasn't your fault. You have got to know how she died—we all do, including her family—and it's not your damn fault. If Morgagni or someone else iced her because you two were a unit, then we cannot just let that pass. I've told you this over and over again. Now you have to hear it. Now we have to try to deal with it."

I sat for a long time. Then I picked up a pencil and slowly wrote in, over the date of her death, "Elizabeth." The timeline had again grown in content and meaning.

"Now what."

"Can we get her exhumed?" Lo Ban was dreaming about this one.

I tried to pretend that he hadn't asked that question. It took me a long time to answer.

"Possibly, but the chance of doing that is so remote that it's near impossible. The island is small; they don't want to hear of foul play. They accepted Elizabeth and if now she turns up murdered they all take it on the chin. If we could somehow work through the bureaucracy, and get a request for exhumation taken seriously, they would ask the local priest. Unofficially, of course, but they certainly would swing it past him. I would doubt that the priest, however friendly he might be to us and our cause, would give consent and that would be the end of it.

I thought for a while. The silence was comforting.

"However, there is another way. We can try to have her body brought back to England. Ostensibly for re–burial in her ancestral home. They couldn't object to that. For that, I think all we'd need is her family's request."

"Could you get it?"

"I really don't know. Her next-of-kin is her brother. I can always ask him."

Chapter 21

Elizabeth's brother

Getting from Norwich, Vermont, to anywhere else in the world is a tad difficult. Of course, the reverse is true also, and that, in part, is what has kept this place pristine. We haven't got the crush of people that invariably brings with it a disproportionate amount of social problems. I never lock my car and occasionally will forget to take the keys out of the ignition switch. But then, too, although we lack big-city excitement there's none of that big-city electricity in our air. Because of the presence of Dartmouth we have more cultural events in the area than anyone could possibly attend. But there's still no electricity in our air. I pondered this as the bus to Boston drove me through New Hampshire, down winding, hilly, tree-lined Route 89.

Boston's Logan Airport was the bus's last stop. The trip took almost three hours. The line at the American Airlines desk was mercifully short, but that left me with another two hours to kill before the plane departed. Then, six more hours to Heathrow and another hour or so to London's St. James.

London of late has lost much of the allure it used to hold for me. Many of my friends and colleagues have either died or quit the capital and I now feel rather lonely there. It's an expensive city. I guess overall it costs at least half again as much to be comfortable in London as it does in New York. The underground, once a splendidly efficient transport system, is now in shambles; the vehicular traffic is staggering and the congestion on the streets has become physically uncomfortable. I can often walk to where I'm going faster than if I took a taxi or bus. But then I have to struggle against the tide of pedestrians.

Bloomsbury has changed enough to lose some of its appeal and although I am still fond of it, I no longer stay there. The Hotel Montague, just a block from the British Museum, was my last "regular" hotel in Bloomsbury and these days I stay in Pall Mall, in the Oxford and Cambridge Club. It is close to both Purdey's and Holland & Holland.

And the rare book and map trade has changed. Not too many years ago London was the center of the antiquarian map trade with, perhaps, Amsterdam or Paris a close second. This is no longer the case and the change was a swift one. Firms such as venerable Tooley Adams Ltd. closed their London premises and the myriad of smaller dealers, most of whom I knew well, are no longer. A few new dealers have moved in, but I find that I generally cannot afford to buy inventory from them. Much of the antiquarian map activity has shifted to the United States and is spread out, not concentrated in only one city. London has even lost its monthly antiquarian map fair that used to coincide with the PBFA book fair. London prices for rare books and maps are all "American internet" prices.

So my business trips to London have become less frequent, less social and less financially rewarding. But this would be a special trip for me, and it wasn't about old maps or books.

Damon, Elizabeth's brother and now, following the death of his father, the 13th Earl of Shankstonwold, would be in London for a week on business relating to his landholdings. I had not seen Damon in some years and was looking forward to our meeting. By telephone I had briefed him on the purpose of the meeting and asked him to withhold his decision until we could meet. The O&C Club where I was staying was a convenient venue for Damon so we agreed to have lunch there.

I had asked him, as next-of-kin, to request the exhumation of Elizabeth and the return of her remains to England.

"Nice to see you and thanks for taking the time to see me, Damon. I know you're on a very tight schedule. Appreciate it."

"And you, Frank. Five—no, four years has it been? You must come and do a real visit again sometime." The Earl slouched in his chair and looked tired. Our eyes met and we both smiled. The late morning London sun poked into the Club's library and bounced off the book-lined walls, highlighting the well-worn leather chairs and the gleaming mahogany tables. Soothing.

"Thank you. I shall." I knew he meant the invitation. And I meant the acceptance.

We chatted briefly about friends in common and family we knew. It was nice to catch up on this world again.

"Still shooting?" asked Damon amiably.

"Whenever I can. Mostly clays and rough. Grouse. Haven't been on a driven shoot since the last time we shot together. That shoot, Damon, is still the highlight of my shooting experiences. Remember? I drew the guinea peg and the birds were as thick as they are in my dreams. Could have fried eggs on my barrels. But now, at least for some time, my plus-fours have been in mothballs."

We sat. Reflecting. The quiet of the library, the warmth of the books, granted us both a bit of time for reminiscence.

"Now about my sister..." The Earl let his voice fade away. "You know, Frank, I was there on her island a couple of years ago. We were in the Aegean on holiday and put in the little harbor. I checked her gravesite and it was quite all right. They told me you stop by once in a while and keep an eye on it. Nice of you."

"It gives me some comfort. Elizabeth and I were close."

"How well I know it. She and I were great chums when we were little and we stayed about as close as brother/sister can. I still remember the letter she sent me when she met you. It was so wonderful I showed it to the Old Man. He was fond of you immediately."

We both smiled and lost ourselves in a little shared, silent reverie.

"We are both lucky, Damon. Our parents, both yours and mine, lived to a decent age and had quite a good run. Somehow, death at old age is appropriate, but death at a young age is not.

"This is really the reason for my trip here. Many years ago Lo Ban—I believe you met him briefly at Elizabeth's memorial service—and I thwarted a particularly vicious character who was running a torture farm in Southeast Asia. It is possible to conclude from the available information that he has been tracking down those involved in wrecking his playground. Over the years he might have killed numerous people whom he thought had gotten in his way, and also possibly their friends as well.

"Now, we have no proof at all, and, frankly I cling to the belief that Elizabeth fell accidentally, but there is a remote possibility that she was hunted down and killed as an act of revenge."

At this point we were interrupted.

"Your Grace's table is ready."

Damon smiled. "Thank you, John." The two men looked at each other briefly, as though exchanging a secret. John was old-school and Damon much preferred less formality but John was unbending.

We both extricated ourselves from our upholstered chairs and walked into the dining room, where we were seated at a very private corner table. Damon nodded and smiled at a number of members who were already eating.

I continued my explanation over a smallish lunch. Neither Damon nor I were very hungry. "I would never have brought this up had the whole sordid mess not exploded and now we have a killer after us. A killer who Lo Ban thinks may have murdered Elizabeth.

"Our contacts in Greece tell us that exhumation for purposes of a post-mortem, after all these years, won't fly. It's very unlikely that they would want to stir up something this old especially with really no hard evidence.

"So, that's why I am asking you to request that her remains be removed and brought home to England. That request coming from you would be granted."

"And then what?"

"I would like permission to have a post-mortem done."

"What would you expect to find after all these years?"

"I don't know. I would like to ask Sir Derek Denny-Green, at Oxford, to do the post. There's always the possibility that bones will reveal something. You know, there wasn't even a medical examination of her body. Everyone was so sure it was an accident. She had no enemies in the island community. If anything, she was a much-liked foreigner, surprising, given the insularity of the place."

"But Denny-Green is senile." I really wasn't surprised that Damon knew him.

"Not more than usual. I had lunch with him about a year ago. We ran into each other in the BM and went to that dreadful little French restaurant on Southampton Row for lunch. Part of a chain, you know, I think it's called Café Piaf. I gather Sir Derek actually knew the real Piaf—the little swallow—and this place stirs up memories of his youth. Not entirely misspent, it seems. Anyway, the food was rather all right that day and we made almost an afternoon of it. He was quite lucid, even after an enormous amount of midday wine. I think his seeming senility is an acquired habitual mode of behavior. It reminds me a lot of a pathologist I knew in Boston, who decided that all brilliant people were a bit crazy so he started acting a little bit crazy to simulate, he thought, brilliance. Soon he couldn't stop and wound up with people still thinking him not brilliant, but just a little bit crazy.

"Now Derek's really quite brilliant and certainly not gaga. Or if he is, then it's just a little bit it and doesn't interfere with his work.

"He's a pathologist, but not truly a forensic pathologist. Forensics is his hobby and he's first–rate at it. He consults on mummies and ancient bodies and determines how they died. Give him part of a femur with scratches on it and he'll tell you what made them and if they contributed to death. He was called in to look at some Indian burial material the American Museum had before they gave it back to the Indians. He decided the evidence was most consistent with death at the hands of other Indians, a conclusion today's Indians didn't appreciate.

"Anyway, if anybody can divine anything from Elizabeth's remains, it would be Derek."

"Have you spoken with him about it?"

"Certainly not. I'm here speaking to you alone and have not mentioned this to anyone else, other than, of course, my associates who also are being hunted by the same madman."

The Earl leaned back slightly, eyes partly closed. I took another bite of my cold salmon and a sip of nicely chilled Chablis. Under any other circumstances this would have been a most pleasant lunch.

"You've no evidence, just a hunch?"

"Correct. No evidence whatsoever."

"And you're proposing that she be interred here in England alongside her family?"

"I can't propose that. That's a family issue."

"That's how Elizabeth thought of you. She made that perfectly clear. And that's how we thought—still think of you."

"All right, then I'll propose it."

"Yes," smiled the Earl, "she will come back home. Frank, if there's even a slight chance that it was not an accident, the very slightest chance, and even the very slightest chance that it could be determined after all these years, then we owe it to her. I shall give my permission to remove her remains to England."

"Thank you. With your leave I shall find out precisely what the Greeks need at their end. There's bound to be a monstrous bureaucracy."

"Yes, please do that and send all the material to me. We will take care of the legal aspects at this end. Will you speak with Derek?"

"Yes I shall. I'll ring him later and ask if I may call on him tomorrow. If he's in Oxford now, of course. And who will be handling this for you?"

Damon pulled out a card and wrote the name of one of his secretaries on the back. "This fellow will. Feel free to speak openly with him about anything."

We finished the rest of the meal, largely silent. Much had been accomplished and we both felt a bit drained of energy. The Earl looked older and more haggard. I'm certain I did too.

We both walked out of the club. We shook hands and Damon walked away. I went back in and took a nap.

Later, I rang Sir Derek Denny-Green and fortunately was able to track him down. Yes, he would be in Oxford tomorrow, yes he would be most pleased to see me and suggested meeting in the SCR at Wadham College. "Better than my digs—they're a bit stinky, as you know."

I bought a day return ticket on the Oxford Tube, a bus that runs every half hour or so between London and Oxford. As usual, the bus was crowded and the seats were no more comfortable than the last time I used this service. I imagine they stole their legroom specs from Lufthansa. Nonetheless, the ride isn't too long and the bus is far more convenient than the train.

Gloucester Green bus terminus is but a short walk to the Oxford Union where I had a pleasant early lunch, then relaxed in their wonderful library and read a few newspapers.

Fifteen minutes before my appointment with Sir Derek Denny-Green I walked out into the pleasantly mild day and wandered over to Wadham College, walked past the Porter's Lodge and turned right at the Front Quad and entered the Senior Common Room where the pathologist was already waiting for me.

"Good to see you again, Frank." Derek stood up and we shook hands.

"And you, Derek. Thank you for agreeing to this visit on such short notice. It's most kind."

"Not at all. Have some coffee? I'm having a cup."

"Thanks, I will." I went over to the freshly brewed pot of coffee and poured a cup.

I think Derek could perceive my anxiety and wasted no time with small talk. He leaned back, spread his hands palms upwards inviting me to speak.

"Derek, I am here to ask your help in a difficult problem. It is partly personal but it involves others as well." I then filled him in on some of my activities, my relationship with Elizabeth, her death, our troubles with Morgagni, and now the proposed removal of Elizabeth's remains to England. "We need to know, if possible, whether or not she was murdered or if she died an accidental death. I am here to ask if you will help and do a post on her remains."

Sir Derek sat motionless for a moment. "If she was pushed, then there's probably no way of telling. If she was strangled first, or shot, or coshed, perhaps we can discern that even after all this time. But, of course, the probability is that I won't come up with anything."

"Does that mean you're willing to try?"

"Of course. Have her family get in touch with me. I knew her father...we used to shoot together...seem to recall that I vaguely know her brother. Hardworking fellow, as I recall. No, I don't think there will be any problem getting government approval to do the examination. I've helped enough people...I can call in a few favors and they'll pull strings for me every once in a while. Now, I must be terribly rude and throw you out. I have to demonstrate some congenital hearts. *Situs inversus.*" He gave me a conspiratorial wink.

We walked out together, around the Front Quad, through the heavy portal of Wadham College and out on to Parks Road. As we shook hands, Sir Derek looked at me directly. "I know how you feel, Frank. I lost an Elizabeth myself, many years ago. I, too, never forgot." His rheumy eyes cleared for an instant, we shook hands again and parted without further words.

Not wanting to visit old Oxford friends or old haunts, I walked quickly back to Gloucester Green for the return bus to London. A gloomy mood had settled upon me, a mood that was not altered one bit when I had to spend much of the trip back to London listening to a young woman talk loudly on her cell phone of her menstrual difficulties. I got off at Marble Arch and walked back to Pall Mall.

Dodging pedestrians on the crowded sidewalk was enough to occupy my mind while I pretended I was the frog in a video game.

Chapter 22

Elizabeth returns home

Damon's secretary cut through the red tape with amazing speed. He dispatched a Greek-speaking international lawyer to make the arrangements in Greece and in under a month permission was obtained to exhume Elizabeth and send her remains back to England. Damon decided to fly over and accompany his sister's remains back to England. He asked me to come along, and I did.

He and I sat quietly in the sun-dappled square under the vines that shielded us, just as they had Elizabeth and me, from the bright overhead sun. Elizabeth was being dug up, and Damon and I sipped our cassis, watching the spots of sunlight chase each other over the worn slabs of stone underfoot. There wasn't much to say.

An hour or so later, the village priest walked slowly over to us. I thought I detected a slight limp and he seemed to be acquiring the stoop of age. He told us the work was finished. The coffin, he said, had been in relatively good condition and had been placed in an aluminum transport container, the appropriate government seals affixed and all the papers signed. He had acted as the government's official representative at the exhumation and he now handed Damon an envelope with the necessary signatures and witness marks.

"Here are the documents you'll need." He shook Damon's hand. "I must leave now. I am glad she is going home. We still have the memory, and that we will not send away with you."

The priest and I looked at each other for some time, neither speaking. He and I, at some level, had become friends and now, with Elizabeth gone, we would never see each other again. We both knew it and didn't need to say so. We embraced silently and parted.

The flight home was uneventful and Damon and I, both relieved that this phase was now over, chatted about events of the past few years. He was particularly interested in the story of Morgagni.

"You know, we see similar things almost like that from time to time amongst the tenant farmers on our estates. At least my father and grandfather did. It's more unusual now. I hate to admit it, but their lives were sometimes quite brutish in those days. Much better now."

"You mean multiple torture and murders? I was intrigued.

"Sometimes. I think when things are very hard for very long, humanity leaks out of people. It doesn't leave just a void, it gets replaced by something. Most often evil. That's when slaughtering animals can become gratification. And then it sometimes becomes torture and the animals are slaughtered slowly, and then it sometimes makes the jump from livestock to people. Like a virus making a trans-species leap.

"I was quite young when a tenant farmer on a neighboring estate lost his wife to influenza. He had had several very bad years in a row, was facing eviction, and was quite convinced that the doctor had killed his wife."

"Why and how?"

"There was no why," the Earl continued, "but the 'how' is interesting. The doctor was a young fellow, just out of training. A city lad and not used to the ways of country folk. When the farmer wanted to hang herbs around his wife's neck as a folk remedy, the doctor pooh-poohed it and the farmer was too ashamed of his country ways to insist. Needless to say, when she died he blamed the doctor's reluctance to use the herbs.

"The doctor, oddly enough, also blamed himself. The herbs would have done no harm. He let his ego and his arrogance get in the way of treating his patient.

"Anyway, the farmer methodically killed everyone in the doctor's family, then the doctor, then everyone in his own family then he hanged himself. All his murders were decapitations and there was evidence he got gratification from each.

"But it isn't limited to just the downtrodden. There was a Fellow of Clare College, in Cambridge, many years ago with similar tendencies. He started out playing with Aleister Crowley and his group and it just got completely out of hand. He was also a decapitator. Practiced on animals. Maybe it was for ritualistic purposes, but he was doing sheep, pigs, dogs, in fact anything that he could get. Then two young women disappeared.

"Rumor of his activities had seeped out and the police went to his country house. There was nothing amiss, but they did find an altar of some sort, possibly bloodstained, in a cove behind the garden. It was built to look part of an elaborate Victorian folly, but clearly was a more recent addition. Several of the police refused to go back to it. They claimed they could detect "something" lurking, something they couldn't describe and they were terrified by it. One claimed to have glimpsed a dark, amorphous animal dodging about in the undergrowth.

"The police began to tear the place apart. Literally board by board. They started with the large barn, which was lucky. As soon as they ripped up the floor they found a set of elaborate underground chambers, including a small cell containing the two missing women. They were still alive."

"The Fellow was quite wealthy and was able to hush the affair to some extent. He paid a huge settlement to the two women, who then declined to press charges or cooperate with the Crown.

"Of course, the Fellow resigned from Clare. He then committed himself to an institution where he still resides. Rather comfortably, I'm told.

Damon stopped speaking for a moment.

"I'm certain," he continued, "that this kind of thing, the result of humanness leaking out to be replaced by evil, goes on far more than we imagine. They see the Beast, acknowledge the Beast, feed the Beast, and keep chasing it. They never can catch it but they keep feeding it. If only a fraction of them gets discovered then people like Morgagni must be really quite common, don't you think?"

I pondered that one. "Do you mean ritualistic murder or..." I stumbled for the word. "Binge murder?"

"Binge murder—yes, that's it precisely. Murder for profit, for love, or in the heat of an argument is one thing, but becoming habituated to murder is quite another. Death then infects the very core of a being, and becomes a ready, unremarkable ingredient of everyday life."

"Like lunch."

Damon leaned back. "I've often wondered about those two women in the barn. And I wonder about the feelings those policemen had—the ones who wouldn't return. They were senior cops and weren't people easily put off. If those two women had any contact with whatever bothered the cops they must have gone near-mad."

Damon seemed to drift off a bit. "I've been on moors at night, Frank, and have felt isolation—an isolation so profound that it almost removed me from the world. I couldn't feel the ground nor hear the wind. All I felt was total loneliness. And fear. Fear that was palpable. It was almost sticky.

"Frank, have you ever been terrified? Really, really terrified? Not of death or the kind of fear we all have before a conflict. But sheer terror. A tangible fear that shares your space with you and you feel you can grasp it with your fingers but you daren't."

I wondered about the question. "I think so. Yes, I have been terrified. And I still have nightmares about it."

"Can I ask about it?"

"I'll dig up those ghosts and share them, Damon. Maybe an airplane is a good place for ghost stories.

"Years ago, I owned several hundred acres in east-central Vermont and used it for hunting and shooting. I cleared areas and put in grouse cover, cut paths, and dredged a few ponds. I built a small hunting cabin that was blissfully isolated and I loved going there any time of the year for solitude if not shooting.

"One night I woke up around 2 a.m. The moon was just setting and there was yet a little light outside. I heard coyotes howling in the meadow and I could make out a few of the dog-like animals running about. I watched them for a while and then noticed that most of them ran in a strange way. It was a clumsy and ungainly manner. When one of them stood up, even though it hunched over, it had something of the appearance of a human. The animals ran around a bit, not very gracefully, and then lumbered into the brush and I saw no more of them that night.

"For some reason I didn't dwell on this apparition—I spent the next day doing some chores, stacked some firewood, and walked some of the trails looking for signs of deer or moose.

"That night I again woke up and again heard the coyotes and saw them in the meadow. The hulking man–dogs were more frantic than the previous night. I tried looking at them through binoculars but I could not seem to focus on them. Curiously, the silhouetted trees were in sharp focus but the animals were not.

"I had no light on in my cabin but they must have seen movement or perhaps the moonlight was strong enough to make me visible to their eyes. It was obvious they had seen me. They stood in the meadow, the man–dog on all fours, facing me. Then they disappeared. At least it seemed that they disappeared, in all probability they just walked into the surrounding bushes. But maybe they did actually disappear.

"I went back to bed, but had the feeling that I was being watched. Looking up I caught sight of an indistinct face at one of the windows. Backlit by moonlight. I could discern no features.

"Then I heard it. Scratching around the windowpanes, scratching by the door, and I heard the doorknob being turned gently, furtively. Fortunately the door was bolted but the near-silent attempt to open it continued.

"I got up and got to my guns. I had with me a few shotguns, a .38 revolver and my Heym .300 Win-mag rifle.

"The Heym is a formidable rifle but the magazine only holds two rounds. I loaded it and manually inserted a third round directly into the chamber. I also loaded my .38. I had a box of +Ps so there was a bit of advantage for my handgun. The loading-sounds made by my weapons were comforting.

"I have no doubt these sounds carried outside but whatever was there took no heed. The scratching continued and I heard creaking—the sort of sound that something pressing against the door might cause.

"I toyed with the idea of putting a round through the door or shouting or making some threatening move.

"But I stayed quiet, letting the scenario play itself out. Had the door given way I would have fired at whatever was there, but it held. After an hour or so the sounds went away. No more scratching, no more pressure on the door.

"In the morning I carefully went outside. Armed and expecting the worst, but not an animal was to be seen. The sills of some windows had been gnawed and scratched and the door bore deep gouges. A bit of grey fur was stuck to the jamb and the outer doorknob had mud on it.

"I walked out to the meadow where the animals had been and saw some trampled grass and some enormous paw prints in the damp earth near the meadow's edge.

"Then I saw the blood. And the dead sheep. It was a young lamb and its throat was torn out.

"I don't raise sheep. There were no sheep farms in the area. To this day I cannot understand where this lamb came from.

"And then I heard the sound that I shall never forget. From the dense undergrowth surrounding the meadow came a growling, gurgling sound. It was a low rumble as though a lot of air was expended producing it. Whatever made it was not alone and soon there was a spreading chorus. Some sounds seemed to emanate from below ground.

"Then the stench. The worst gangrenous, festering, pus-oozing wound did not smell this bad.

"At that moment, Damon, I was enveloped in fear. The fear was palpable, substantive. It was an entity coming from something in the bushes. I was armed but really didn't think that mattered. I thought of firing a round or two into the bushes but I had only 8 rounds total with me. Three in the Heym and five in my revolver. Better to save them.

"I didn't run. I think I wouldn't have been able. But I did manage to walk back to my cabin. The gurgle followed behind and when I got to the cabin there was more sound and the stench was wafting in.

"Damon, I put the manuscript I was working on into a duffle with my clothing, carried it and my guns into my van, locked the cabin's door, and drove off.

"I never went back. Put the place on the market the next day.

"My land had a reputation for good hunting and it sold quickly. And twice again in the next two years.

"About five years later a hunter was found with his throat torn out. He had been staying in the cabin and the police found the door had been pushed in. The hunter had managed to get two rounds through his .270 caliber rifle but there was no sign of anything having been hit. No bullet holes, no blood. A tuft of grey hair was found on the jamb and the report noted fresh gouging to the wood.

"There's an elemental nature to whatever was in my meadow. I'll never know but I think of it as the product of a demonic alchemical exercise gone wrong—instead of distilling the quintessence, the elixir of evil was produced and somehow bedded in my meadow. Dogs? Man–dogs? Probably not. But whatever it was, it was after me and manifested itself in some animal form.

"And that, Damon, is the most fear I've experienced and the fear is with me still and still I do not know what it is that I fear. I don't dare go back to the land to see if that essence is still there, I'm simply afraid. And I do not know if it is yet me that it's after."

"Hell of a story. Strange that these animal-forms seemed to morph and yet you couldn't focus on them. Tell me, Frank, would you consider these forms to be incomplete or complete? Do you think they were undifferentiated and not yet whole or fully differentiated but just malformed?"

"I suppose we would need to decide if evil is a transitional phase, sort of like an unsouled being or if it is fully souled but mal-souled."

"Or if it is just the soul, perhaps a malevolent soul, that is free of corporal restraint. Are soul and essence the same? Or does a soul require an essence of good for the final product to be noble? Or is it the loss of human goodness, leakage if you will?

"But there is not a doubt in my mind that you saw them. Whether or not they were there is another question." Damon said no more and we flew on in silence for a bit. We each had a whiskey-and-soda. I was glad to get away from that place, yet again.

Then Damon smiled.

"Frank, I have another story. This one from my grandfather's day.

"Seems a farmer, living with his wife and young son, went berserk one day and killed his wife. He had come in from the fields and discovered his young son dead near the fireplace. A fire had been lit and he saw the embers of what had been a log that he had stored in a corner. The farmer had had this log for longer than his wife and told her never to touch it or move it or burn it.

"Well, she had, in a momentary lapse, thrown the log into the fireplace. And now his son was dead.

"Enraged beyond control he stabbed his wife and sat there, cradling his dead son in his arms. That's how they found him the next day.

"He confessed to killing his wife but there was no body. There was absolutely no trace of her even though the farmer's knife was on the floor where he claimed to have stabbed her. There was not even a pile of dust.

"The cause of his son's death could not be determined but foul play was ruled out. The lad had just died without any known reason.

"The farmer was not charged and his son was buried in the churchyard."

"Good Lord. What happened to the farmer?"

"He stayed in his house. He pretty much gave up farming and spent much of the time wandering about in the woods as though searching for something.

"Clearly he was trespassing, mostly on Grandfather's lands, but after discussing it with his keepers Grandfather didn't do anything. The fellow was harmless and would only take the occasional piece of dry fallen wood for firewood. The keepers liked him and they often fed him and sent him home with a bit of food. The farmer wasn't a poacher and never took a single hare or pheasant, nor did he harm the land in any way. He was searching for something.

"My grandfather never disturbed the farmer.

"One day a keeper saw the farmer pull a waterlogged, moss-covered piece of wood from a marshy area and carry it away. He took it home and scrubbed it clean and let it dry in the sun.

"According to Grandfather, once the wood had dried the farmer brought it indoors and stood it in the corner.

"Mind you, this is now about a dozen years since his son died and his wife vanished. A few weeks later at the time of the village fete, a young man appeared in town. Plainly dressed, he was seen to walk purposefully through the village and out the lane to where the farmer lived. One of Grandfather's keepers was visiting the farmer when the lad, without knocking, opened the door and walked into the modest cottage. He hung up his hat and made himself a cup of tea. The farmer looked at him and smiled.

"Thereafter the young man lived with the farmer and nobody in the village questioned either of them."

"Are you saying that the lad was the return of his son? What about the grave in the churchyard?"

"Funny you should ask. The headstone hadn't weathered very well and somebody noticed that the inscription was no longer there. The entire surface of the stone had flaked off.

"Grandfather gave the farmer a small pension and took on the lad. I have a distant memory of him, he was a beater on the Caledonian Hunt, but he is, of course, now dead. When I was very little Grandfather seemed imposing and stern but I came to recognize an innate kindness in him. When he died, many of his keepers wept as they stood vigil and the town came and paid homage.

"And I never understood the whole thing about the farmer until many years later, looking through Grandfather's library, I came across his copy of Chapman's *Homer*. A page corner had been turned down, something Grandfather rarely did.

"I think Grandfather believed that the lad's life-force had been in that first piece of wood and his mother knowingly destroyed her son by burning it. Perhaps she hadn't been killed by her husband. Perhaps she simply returned to Olympus after inflicting pain on her husband; pain on the father of their son. But her husband went on his solitary quest for his son's life-force and finally recovered it. He thwarted the gods. And good people helped."

"Meleager's mother," I mused.

Damon looked at me but said nothing.

Only the murmurs of passengers and cabin attendants broke the steady hum of the jet engines. My mind wandered back and for some random reason I thought of an old friend and mentor, Graham Monroe.

I turned to Damon, who was idly leafing through a magazine.

"Graham Monroe, Damon. I have a story that tops all the evil we have been discussing."

Damon raised an eyebrow.

"Graham was a crusty New Yorker, his family one of the Four Hundred. Graham was in his late 50s when I knew him and both his parents were long-dead. He spoke often of his father who had been a partner in a New York white-shoe law firm.

"One day, Graham's father was approached by one of his clients, a wealthy man who had been seriously cheated in a business deal many years ago. He had averted ruin by a most narrow margin. And he was left with an abiding hatred for his former partner.

"Now, this client was dying. He had been diagnosed with a leukemia that would kill him in six to eight months and he had come up with a plan for the ultimate revenge.

"He wanted the lawyer, Graham's father, to draw up a codicil to his will leaving an annual sum of money to his former partner's only child, a son who was about 16 years old. The money was not to be a huge sum, but it would be enough to ruin the lad. He hoped that the youth would come to depend upon the stipend to generate an unrealistic lifestyle. The clincher was that the stipend would end when the boy reached the age of 25. Ten years of youthful, lavish living would have destroyed him as a man capable of standing on his own hind legs."

"Did the lawyer do it? Damned baroque form of revenge, if you ask me."

"No, Graham's father refused. His client died without exacting his revenge and the totally innocent boy grew up untouched by this perverse act of evil.

"I think it would have been understandable, in an oblique way, had the fellow simply murdered his ex-partner. He would have at least assumed the responsibility directly and he would have died anyway, either in a hospital awaiting sentencing or in a prison ward. He had a death sentence already.

"But he wanted to inflict a lifetime of anguish on the man he hated and his weapon of choice was a young boy, whose life would have been wasted, too.

"This brings to mind another friend, Red. Red has two children, both now grown. His ex-wife launched a demonic vendetta against him and successfully managed to poison his relationship with his son. She is long dead but his son still carries her hatred. The other child, a girl, who happens to be my god-daughter, was a bit older and perhaps less susceptible to this scheming and she's fine. But in effect Red has no son anymore, and the young man, Sam, has a father whom he despises for no reason other than his mother's hatred. Red did nothing to warrant Sam's behavior but Sam is fighting some old demons that possessed his mother and survived her death.

"I knew Sam's mother before she met Red. Sylvia was a charmer. But she was direct lineage to some sort of evil mojo that had infected her family. Suicide can become a familial infection, endemic violence another—these are passed from generation to generation like some existential congenital syphilis. Her own life had been trivialized by her parents and she was turned into a modern version of one of the Furies. I've never seen hatred in one individual as I did in her. Freud was right. About what, I'm not sure, but he had to have been right about something relating to this kind of fury. Red did the only thing possible – he took the kids and fled. But he wanted them to maintain contact with their mother, which was his big mistake. Poor Sam got the full dose. I've known Sam and his sister Annie since they were born. I had lunch with Sam a few years ago. Never told Red. I tried touching the edges of the topic of Sam's father and each time it elicited a near-anxiety attack. Sam is not rational about Red and even denies there's a family problem. But his hatred is palpable. It has a kind of religious fervor."

"What's Red doing about it?" Damon's question was perfectly reasonable.

"There never was anything he could do about it because he had no role in bringing it on and over the years as Sam's antagonism grew it became less and less possible for Red to even discuss their relationship. There is nothing Red can do and I think in order to retain his sanity he has written Sam off.

"Curiously, Red's airplane was found crashed in a field but Red was not. I think Red has either taken a "time-out" or is in deep cover. I can't prove it but I have good reason to believe he is alive. In fact, I was told that directly."

"Red's a spook?"

"I suppose so. My line of work, but he gets a salary and a pension."

Damon laughed. But he stopped quickly. "Implanting evil in a surrogate. Yes, Frank, that tops all others. There was evil in your meadow, but it trifles before that which uses a man's son as surrogate."

Damon's secretary met us at Heathrow. He had already made all the necessary arrangements to transport the coffin to Oxford, and the sealed boxes went through the entry formalities easily. It wasn't only because the Earl's secretary was very competent. The titled, even in this egalitarian age, still carry weight. Damon and I sat in the back of his Daimler as it followed the hearse that was carrying Elizabeth, now back in her ancestral country, to meet Denny-Green who would try to read her secrets.

Two days later I was flying home.

Chasing the sun over the Atlantic, I thought again about my hunting cabin and the coyotes and the lamb they killed, and an old, cold, fear visited me and sat next to me in my seat. Then I thought of my old friend Red and his no-longer son. I once again saw them as family, Sylvia and Red, with Annie and Sam walking along the path, Annie skipping and little Sam trying to. The old sadness came back. But the creeping fear from the dead lamb was now replaced by a brand new feeling, one of hatred. For the first time in my life I was certain I felt hatred. I had many times seen hatred, but never felt it from within, a hatred with my brand. I did not like it and I wanted it to go away but it circled me like some blood-starved mosquito and eventually I gave in.

I awoke from a fitful airplane-induced sleep, with a sudden realization about Sylvia. Accumulating hatred had been Sylvia's true goal, It was a lifelong ambition. The congenital syphilitic spirochete of evil that infected her soul thrived on her being the doyenne that consigned others to the dustheap. She wasn't a collector of people, she collected and treasured the animosity of those she harmed and then expelled. These were the trophies she pinned to her trophy corkboard; emotional scalps, each of which embedded more corruption in her inner self, and fed the need for even more.

"All right," I thought, "she can have mine but my old friend Red's isn't hers."

More important, Elizabeth was home.

Chapter 23

Merchants again

Lo Ban had made the necessary arrangements with the AAB Central Committee and we got space in the New York Book Fair. For a price, we got a well-located booth where we could look down the long aisle that led in from the entry. This was especially good, since Rodney Oufle had his booth partway down that aisle and we could monitor activity in his booth without being too obvious about it.

Amanda went down to New York with Lo Ban few days early in order to get, as Amanda put it, "our city fix." Maria and I welcomed the privacy and lazed about, relishing the languid Vermont mornings when the sun seemed slow to rise above the hills and the fog hid itself for dear life in the shallow valleys, holding tightly to the anchoring pines. This time together meant a lot to us, for we were going to war. I supposed this was what it was like for a soldier on his last leave before shipping out, except in our case we were both shipping. Maria and I had a history of lotus-eating, and we were doing it again. Years ago, much younger and perhaps less wiser, we wiled away the days before I left for Oxford to work on the biological warfare project. Now it seemed the intervening years had not intruded. We were back to that time and again we nestled happily in each others' arms, not caring what tomorrow would bring, and acting as though we still had all eternity before us. Nonetheless, early on Thursday morning we loaded my car with our collective inventory and drove south to New York City to meet Amanda and Lo Ban and exhibit at the book fair.

I looked forward to meeting fellow dealers again after my long absence from the fair circuit. The community of rare map dealers is quite small and we all know each other and get on. We compete in the business sense yet retain a reasonable degree of congeniality, and the degree of congeniality seems to run along lines of class and education. Map and book dealing is a trade and not a profession and there are no requirements for entry.

So we get people like Howie Knightly an old-school junk dealer who buys ephemera at local paper shows, writes good copy, and sells it at the AAB fair at obscene multiples. Howie used to wander into my booth when I had serious customers looking at rare, expensive maps and begin to explain that "he got out of the older material when it became ridiculously expensive." My clients would look at me and roll their eyes.

More pernicious was Cedric DeBrun. Cedric had parlayed a few thousand into a small fortune. Early in his business career he tried to cheat me and I never again bought anything from him despite his huge inventory.

I think I was the only major map dealer who never bought inventory from Cedric and it galled him enormously. From time to time he made discrete inquiries of other dealers but nobody bothered to tell him why I shunned him.

Cedric was tight with a major American map dealer and the two of them had it in for me. I remember one occasion when a private individual contacted me about an atlas he wished to sell and I made an appointment to see him. I didn't know that he had also contacted the American dealer who got there first. He didn't want to buy the atlas; it was an Ogilby atlas with a lot of European maps, and told the owner that I wouldn't be interested either, but that he should send it to Cedric.

What the owner never discovered was that the atlas contained an unrecorded state of one of Ogilby's America maps, an extremely valuable map. Cedric spotted it immediately and bought the atlas for a pittance.

Cedric had another nasty habit—he tried to steal my clients by telling them that "I bought all my inventory from him" so they might as well cut out the middle-man. The story got back to me but I couldn't, in fairness to my clients who told me this, file an ethics complaint with the ABA.

Bad guys often shoot themselves in their feet. Cedric was almost sent up for receiving stolen atlases, and his American friend was discovered possessing several very expensive stolen maps. Quite a coincidence.

Thursday was set-up day and the place was crowded and busy dealers carried, carted, or pushed their books onto the floor and into their allotted booth space. Lo Ban and Amanda had arrived early to guard our space from the otherwise inevitable encroachment of neighbors. They visited Oufle while he was setting up and previewed his inventory. Oufle had brought a sizeable number of books about death and executions. He also had, tucked away in a corner, a small group of books on torture.

"Special collection?" Lo Ban indicated the torture books.

"I've got a client who buys them." Oufle was being open about it. "He usually buys by mail, but said he's in New York and wants to visit the fair and wants to look at them. I've only met him once before. Strange guy. He pays quickly, though."

"We do meet some strange ones in this business," agreed Lo Ban. "What's your guy's story?"

"He buys early torture and killing books. Really, anything I get in. Sometimes asks me to hold them. But he always pays up front. If I have to hold them, they're his books. I just store them for him. Once I held books for him for years. Then he showed up and took them away. I wonder if he was locked up, or what."

Lo Ban said nothing. It appeared, at that moment, that our long shot had paid off. Oufle's customer could possibly be Morgagni.

Despite the heavy New York traffic, Maria and I made good time coming down the FDR Drive. Even crosstown traffic was in our favor and we quickly negotiated the few blocks west and finally turned onto Lexington Avenue to the fair's entrance. I hired one of the unionized laborers to dolly our books and maps in from the curb while Maria drove off and parked our car in a nearby garage.

Lo Ban waited for Maria to return from the garage before, exhibiting more than usual excitement, telling us about Oufle's customer.

"Suppose it is Morgagni," ventured Maria, "then what?"

That question was not dealt with, for at that moment Saperstein showed up. "Looks like you're cooking up some war plans, all huddled together. Planning for any more bodies? Ha-ha."

"You're in an unusually good mood, Saperstein. What gives?" Amanda smiled at him. No point in antagonizing him any more.

We had tormented him, with some good reason, in the past, and the bodies he referred to had been real ones.

"This is my last fair. I'm retiring. No more Saperstein to push around! No more Saperstein to beat up on. No more dead bodies! I think I'm even going to miss you guys."

"All in good fun, Saperstein. It comes with the turf when you run a book fair. But I promise we'll be nice to you this time."

Lo Ban walked over to him. "Good luck, Saperstein. Health and happiness." Lo Ban really meant it, and they shook hands. "Now, we've got to finish setting up."

It didn't take long for us to put our items on display. Not having a lot of inventory meant we had more booth space to use in other ways. We equipped a back corner with a small table and some chairs, creating a compact and private area for our inevitable low-voice conferences with colleagues, both from the book trade and from our other trade. We could also see Oufle's booth from that vantage point.

Every book fair passes through discrete phases. Like a set of Alken foxhunting prints, the stages can be described and pictured. First, during the early stages of setup when dealers are bringing their goods onto the floor there is apparent chaos. Electricians are wiring up lights, tables are being set up, and the drapery that defines each booth's limits is being installed. The aisles are filled with packing material and assorted debris.

Soon, though, a sense of order emerges. The drapes separating each booth are in place, lights are on, and tables assembled and arrayed in the booths. The aisles are beginning to be cleared of boxes and packing materials. And books, appearing on the shelves and tables, are on display. At this stage, although the fair is not open to the public, dealers are scouring each others' inventory for items they might want to buy. This "pre-fair buying" is an essential feature of book fairs and dealers will often exhibit at a fair just for the privilege of getting to look over, and buy from, other dealer's inventories before the public. Of course, this puts the public, collectors, and institutions, at a disadvantage because if there were any vastly underpriced items for sale before the fair opens it is likely that other dealers will have spotted them and snapped them up. Books may change hands several times before a fair opens, each time increasing in price. Indeed, some British antiques fairs have attempted to limit pre-fair buying, but with mixed success. Years ago, when I occasionally exhibited at fairs in London, I did so largely to buy at the pre-fair buying. My own sales were irrelevant to me and I would occasionally fly over to London without any inventory of my own and before the fair opened buy just enough cheap stock to be able to mount some sort of a decent display. It wouldn't do to exhibit with an empty booth! I know other dealers who actually borrow stock from local colleagues so that they can mount an exhibit. Again, the purpose of exhibiting for these dealers is to gain access to the other dealers' inventories at the pre-opening buying.

Finally the frenzy of setup and dealer buying diminishes, the physical installations are complete, the carpet is laid in the aisles and the fair is transformed into a scintillating showroom waiting for the public. This is the face the fair will present for the duration. Now, the dealers sit back and wait for the time to admit the public, who will rush in at opening, clutching wads of money. Hopefully. To complete the analogy with the Alken hunt prints, we might consider this phase to be "The Kill."

In this quiet time after the fair had been set up and before the doors opened, I wandered about a bit, poking through some of the dealers' stock driven more out of curiosity than by desire to buy. I passed the booth, a smallish one, of a dealer who specialized in travel books. He had a stack of not-very-old *National Geographic* magazines and I began to idly flip through them. An article in one of them caught my attention. I bought the magazine and took it back to our both.

I showed the article to Lo Ban. It was about Pasha Erlüp, a strange reclusive man living in the desert of Arabia. *An American brings sweet water to the desert.* The article was a typical *Geographic* story, but had a special appeal to me. Many years ago, Pasha Erlüp, then still known as Henry Boylston Dodge, had encountered some trouble in the Red Sea. I never found out what had happened, but quite by chance, I was on a tramp freighter visiting a few ports in the Red Sea when we saw a seemingly dead body, supported by an old-style Mae West, floating amidst some debris.

We pulled the floater up on deck and were surprised that he was still alive, although barely so. I got a faint pulse but the fellow was so dehydrated that he was mostly comatose and couldn't speak. Our ship, not nearly an ordinary tramp, was equipped with good medical supplies and we took him below to our sick bay. I needed to rehydrate him quickly and tried to set up an IV. It took me five tries to get a needle into him. I was about to do a cut-down but fortunately managed to avoid it. We got a bottle of fluid dripping into him and he made a remarkably rapid recovery. The next day we passed a British destroyer and they took him on board. We really didn't need him on board our vessel: we had no idea what problems we might run into and didn't want to be responsible for an unknown sick man.

I returned home some six months later, to find a nice letter from Dodge, thanking me and saying that he had decided to stay in Arabia. Years later I learned the rest of the story.

Henry Boylston Dodge had changed his name and was now known as Pasha Erlüp. A quixotic fellow, he had substantial family wealth and a very good knowledge of Arabic. He was sort of a Lawrence-type, but not quite with the same charisma or global impact. Erlüp moved into a remote part of the Arabian desert and occupied a ruined stone building next to a tiny part-time oasis. The little spring next to Erlüp's ruined house barely had enough water for him and a couple of donkeys. There was a larger water pool nearby but it had gone brackish and now the water in it was impossible to drink. It was too alkaline to support even plant life and slowly had become a scum-covered muddy marsh with a dry crust-like shore. When the larger pool had gone brackish, the community that depended upon it had moved away leaving behind dozens of mud-brick or stone houses, all slowly falling into ruin.

Erlüp got some equipment and sank a deep well. I learned that he claimed it was 5,000 feet deep. But it produced water, and lots of it. The well was artesian and the water came within 150 feet of the surface, making it easy to pump out.

Word of the ample fresh water spread and soon travelers and caravans were stopping again. Erlüp gave the water away free to anyone and their animals for three days. If they wanted to stay longer they had to work, and work meant help restoring the old abandoned stone and mud-brick buildings. Soon several of the ruins had been converted into usable buildings.

The water from the deep well seemed limitless. Erlüp used it to flush the alkaline marsh, making it sweet again. While the marsh water was still not very palatable, it could now support animals and agriculture, and its quality was improving as its own natural flow was encouraged. Erlüp let people occupy the restored houses if they stayed and planted dates or other suitable crops, or maintained small herds.

In this way Erlüp managed to attract, as permanent residents, about a dozen families and their animals. Travelers and caravans in increasing numbers stopped there, for the sweet water from the deep well and Erlüp's hospitality had become widely known. The small desert community was peaceful, pleasant and thriving. Green was spreading, trees thrived and gave shade. Children's voices joined those of the birds to acclaim the life that affirmed daily its decision to become part of the desert.

One day it all ended. Erlüp was killed. He was dragged out of his house, beheaded, and hanged upside down. The deep well was dynamited, never to yield again. Then the attackers dumped hundreds of pounds of copper sulfate into the larger pool, destroying it forever.

The action had all the precision of a military strike. It was never discovered who did it, but for some reason it was widely held that the Mossad had done it. To what end wasn't known, but otherwise normally rational groups pointed their fingers. Nothing came of this, however, probably for fear of retribution by the Mossad. Lo Ban would not even speculate on this, following his long-held principle of steering completely clear of Mossad.

Neither Lo Ban nor I had seen the *National Geographic* article before. The date on the magazine indicated that it had been written only a few years before Erlüp's death. I pointed to a large photograph showing Erlüp surrounded by a group of residents and visitors. In the far right was Morgagni.

Lo Ban arched an eyebrow. "Coincidence?"

"What are the probabilities of it being a coincidence?" To me, it seemed highly unlikely. "I think it more likely that there was a connection between Morgagni and Erlüp."

"And the Mossad? Someone killed Erlüp and it wasn't just him they wanted dead. It was the whole community. They wanted it out of there. Was Morgagni a friend of Erlüp? Or was Erlüp doing something that attracted Morgagni. Or, was it Morgagni who killed Erlüp?" Lo Ban had outlined the possibilities.

"But why the Mossad? Was Morgagni part of it? Simply a Mossad training exercise? Shooting Arabs for the sport of it?"

"Possibly" muttered Lo Ban.

I looked at the photograph some more. In the last row of figures was the unmistakable profile of Willow. She was turned to her neighbor and it appeared that he was in the process of turning toward her as the picture was taken. His features were slightly blurred but recognizable.

Holling C. Hollins. Career diplomat. American.

Maria, Amanda, and Lo Ban stared at the National Geographic picture.

"Erlüp's dead, his community destroyed; Morgagni, Willow and Hollins are visiting shortly before the whole thing turns to crap. What the hell was going on?" Lo Ban was frowning.

"Bad actors. Bad, bad actors."

A strange feeling ran over me and I continued to mumble "Bad…"

Chapter 24

Willow

In our business coincidences are red flags. If Morgagni's presence in this picture was truly an innocuous event, Willow's was simply too much to be also just coincidental. Hollins was the trifecta. Lots of red flags were flapping in the breeze. Our world is a small one, but not this small. There had to be a connection between Morgagni, Willow, Hollins, and Erlüp. Did it involve us? Who the hell knew. So many scenarios were playing at the same time that it was impossible to dissect them. Sometimes we just assume connections where there might not be any. Sometimes we are unwitting actors in several plays and not know it and just assume that it is all one production. Willow is one of the actors whose stage remains a mystery to me. I still cannot understand her relation to our Group, yet there has to be one.

Willow is a multilingual, brilliantly sarcastic ectomorph. I met her first many years ago during an unusually smooth Channel crossing. I was on the deck, leaning on the ferry's rail idly watching the water when I became aware of a new neighbor standing next to me. I had never seen this exotic woman before but was immediately a bit flattered that she should stand near me since most of the rail was free. A callow youth, I immediately assumed it was my handsome profile that attracted her.

An exchange of smiles and tentative chitchat. I was unable to learn much about her and couldn't get beyond a pleasant but superficial conversation. We left the ferry as acquaintances but Willow had adroitly dodged my attempts to arrange a sequel to our presumed accidental encounter.

I was quite surprised when I next saw Willow. She was on the arm of Colonel XX at one of his embassy's parties. Everyone knew what Colonel XX's real job was and I was startled to see Willow with him. Quite another coincidence. Willow had singled me out on the ferry and now she was with a foreign intelligence officer.

We chatted briefly and it didn't take too long to understand that Willow did not want to talk about that ferry ride. Oh well, I didn't think that I had revealed anything too interesting about myself. Still, had it been all innocent? I no longer thought so but couldn't figure out what was going on.

Osman Bey had once made a passing remark about Willow. I was startled but didn't inquire further. Here was another intersection between Willow and my life although I was not following her and had no interest in her activities. Whatever they might be. I had indeed told her I was a book dealer, but how on earth could she have traced me back to Osman Bey? Unless she didn't, and all this was my paranoia.

Still, Willow ran in background. I saw her every now and then in high-stakes circles. She certainly had some interesting friends and lovers.

"Manasek," sighed Lo Ban, "are you sure it isn't your Nordic blonde fantasy running amok?" I had tried to tell him about Willow and her curious associations and her somewhat peripheral interest in me. It was always prudent to keep an inventory of certain types of people and Willow was one of them.

"She's standing near Pasha Erlüp," noted Amanda "not near Morgagni. Could that mean that she's not associated with Morgagni but rather with Erlüp?"

"Could be. Maybe she's not associated with either one. She was there for a reason but this picture isn't going to help us learn what it was." Maria dashed some water on the speculation.

Willow's tied too closely to important international players to risk running with a pervert like Morgagni. Still, there's now a Willow nexus—Col. XX, Osman Bey, Morgagni, Hollins, and Pasha Erlüp."

"And you, Manasek." Lo Ban was serious. "Remember the Channel ferry?"

"There's a reason why Pasha Erlüp's desert demise was never really investigated. There had to be international pressure from somewhere. And the rumors of the Mossad never quite went away. Do we now think the Mossad is part of the Willow nexus?"

"Manasek, if the Mossad is involved at all, even peripherally, I'm not going to even talk about it. Something else was going down after this picture was taken, something that's not even beginning to be clear. We have no idea what Erlüp was really doing."

"Right. I agree. However someone is still trying to get at us, and so far it all points to Morgagni. I don't care whom he's hooked up with. I want the bastard dead. Then we can worry about who else will come along. We have not been involved in anything that remotely could have pissed off the Mossad."

Maria nodded assent.

"And that dirtbag Hollins is dead. He compromised a lot of people." Lo Ban was pensive. "You had a hand in that, Manasek."

It was a declarative. Lo Ban was fishing.

Chapter 25

Holling

The pheasants flew over, some solitary and some in small groups—high and fast with the wind against their tails and very visible against the pewter sky. The Taverton Shoot was late in the season and the birds were gun-wise and stayed high. Choosing my birds judiciously I managed to shoot decently. I more than held my own against the other Guns, many of who were wearing third-generation tweeds.

Although I hadn't shot driven birds in several years, a few hours with one of Holland & Holland's instructors got me back in form. It wouldn't have done to be rusty at the Taverton Shoot when Charley (Horse) Drakej had personally asked Lord Clough to invite me.

Charley Horse was about 20 years older than I and had the manner of speaking common in 1930s movies. He also looked like someone from a '30s movie—the distillate of all those guys who had charming manners, a touch of the rogue, and unexplained income. A Yale man, Charley Horse seemed to know most of the guys at State and on several occasions I saw him dining with men I knew, or suspected, to be clandestine operatives.

Ralphie de Gennaro was one of these operatives. Ralphie reveled in his Italian origins and whenever he was in New York or Providence he would go to the Italian districts and hang out with extended family, family that included, as he used to imply, "the family."

None of this slightly dark-side seemed to interfere with his business. Ralphie was in the fruit-and-vegetable business, but in a big way. He represented American organic growers worldwide and had been responsible for much of the growth of the overseas market for American organic produce. Especially skilled as a fearmonger, Ralphie exploited lawmakers' ignorance of anything technical or scientific to grant favor to growers who didn't use "artificial chemicals" on their crops.

"Toxins. The body makes toxins when you eat food grown with artificial chemicals." Ralphie seemed to know about this stuff. "Your constituents would be upset if they couldn't get wholesome food that didn't give them toxins."

Gregarious and a good listener, Ralphie was welcome wherever fruits and vegetables were grown. Lo Ban and I had also noticed, independent of each other, that Ralphie seemed to be well-connected in the diplomatic community. This could, of course, be explained easily by his job and his need to be connected to policy-makers if he was to promote American exports of organic produce.

But Lo Ban and I had other explanations.

Especially when Ralphie was found floating in the Rhine.

Shortly after Ralphie was removed from the river, Charley Horse was conveniently invited to deliver a foreign policy lecture at Dartmouth College. This gave him good cover to be in the Hanover, New Hampshire, area and since he was up here already on a legitimate lecture gig, the two of us dining at the Hanover Inn aroused no suspicion. Since I live in Norwich, Vermont, just across the river from Hanover I dine often at the Inn.

The Daniel Webster Room at the Hanover Inn is a splendid formal dining room reminiscent of those of hotels of another era. The service is impeccable and the food mediocre, but food is not the reason why many of us dine there. Regulars at the Daniel Webster Room are afforded a privacy and grace of service not readily found elsewhere in the region. Waiters such as Alex are invisible and provide nonintrusive and professional service and most of all, nothing they might overhear ever escapes the room. Unless, of course, Lo Ban or I want to hear it. Over the years the Daniel Webster Room has provided us with invaluable information. Who could ever suspect that this college inn, in rural New Hampshire, is not a perfectly safe place to discuss sensitive issues? And Ivy League Dartmouth College provides a perfect excuse to invite visitors who have sensitive information to discuss.

"Manasek," said Charley Horse, "we have a problem."

I nodded.

"You know Ralphie."

It was a statement not a question and I simply nodded.

"He's dead. We know who did it and we know why."

"I assume I'll need to know the 'who' but do I need to know why?"

"Theoretically, no. Practically, yes. Manasek, it's clear to all of us that you were on to Ralphie—you knew what he was doing. And you were friends. Ralphie's dead because he was fingered by a mole. We know who the son-of-a-bitch is. He is one of us and pretty high up and trusted. And we don't need anything more from the guy so he can be removed. Want a job?" Charley Horse didn't waste words.

My somewhat -under -three-cartridges per bird was a lot better than most of the other Guns' ratios and I was about even with Sir Fester LaVage, Bart., my neighbor at the peg to the right. LaVage prided himself on his shooting form and he was indeed as elegant a shot as he was good.

LaVage shot at a rather high bird that changed course and headed my way. I had just dispatched neatly a low-flyer with my right barrel when LaVage's wounded bird entered my area. My left barrel brought it down cleanly.

I thought I noticed LaVage's slight disapproval. However, he smiled. "Nice shot," he mouthed.

I nodded and mouthed a "Your bird." We continued shooting.

The wind was picking up and the temperature dropping and each successive drive had been harsher. Lunch was a welcome break. The next drive, Upsan Downs, was notoriously difficult with very high, fast birds.

"Hello, Holling." I smiled as I approached one of the other guns. It was Holling C. Hollins. Holling was a career diplomat, most recently ambassador to Italy. "We'll be at adjacent pegs. And you've got the guinea peg."

Holling smiled back at me. "Manasek! Good to see you! Haven't seen you in donkey's years. You look well!"

"Good to see you too, old man. Let's play catch-up after the shoot. We've more than a bit of catching-up to do!"

Holling smiled as he picked up his Boss. He seemed genuinely pleased to see me.

I was genuinely pleased to see him.

The sky had become darker, the wind was blowing a bit harder and I was glad for my heavy tweeds. Looking over toward Holling's guinea peg I realized that we were spaced closer on this drive than on earlier ones. "Good and bad," I thought.

Holling opened his cartridge case, opened his Boss and inserted two shells. He put the open Boss down on the cartridge case and began to look around.

I wandered over. "Getting colder," I said. "And windier."

"Gotta spring a leak." Holling was looking around. I pointed to some nearby bushes and off he went.

While his back was turned I slipped the 12-gauge cartridge from the top barrel of his Boss, dropped in a 20-gauge shell and replaced the 12-gauge. It needed a slight tap to seat fully. Then I dropped two more of the bright yellow 20 gauge shells into his cartridge case, put my hands into my pockets and stood looking up at the sky. Neither of us had loaders, otherwise this wouldn't have worked.

Holling returned and we barely had a few moments to begin a conversation before the whistle signaling the start of the drive blew.

"Good shooting!" I said as I returned to my peg.

The birds were sparse, high and fast. And not near us. Finally I had a shot and downed a particularly high one—a pheasant so high I wouldn't have tried except that I really felt I had to do something. The inactivity was nerve-wracking. A few more birds appeared but too far off and I left them for the Gun to my left.

This wasn't turning out to be a good drive. My concern was deepening when a group of four birds appeared, heading straight overhead.

I shot at and hit the left-most bird. The others veered toward my right, over to Holling.

His first shot took the leading pheasant. The bird spiraled earthward. His second shot blew off most of his left hand, his right eye and half his face and brain.

At the inquiry the barrel explosion was ruled an accident. Holling was an experienced shot and had used the same shotgun, a 50-year-old Boss over/under, for the past 20 years. The 12-gauge Boss was in proof, having been re-proofed some ten years ago after the barrels were honed at the Boss shops. Holling's cartridge case held two boxes of 12-gauge shells, but the police also found two bright yellow 20 gauge shells mixed in. One of Holling's barrels had exploded when he pulled the trigger—that barrel had a 20-gauge shell lodged deep in front of the 12-gauge cartridge in the chamber. This was a not-too-common accident known as a "20-12." It is mostly self-inflicted when a shooter carelessly drops a smaller 20-gauge round down a 12-gauge chamber. The smaller cartridge drops through the chamber and gets stuck in the barrel. Unless this is noticed the shooter may carelessly insert a 12-gauge shell on top of the 20 and when he fires the barrel the metal just beyond the chamber gives and the barrel explodes. The two 20-gauge shells found in his case suggested that Holling had simply been careless.

I was able to visit Holling in hospital a few weeks after the inquiry. Holling had less than half his mandible remaining and despite the bandages it was clear that much of his face was but a cavity. He could not speak and his one eye only afforded him defective vision. Holling was not going to make it.

I held his hand. "Holling, you can hear me. If you understand, just squeeze my hand."

A weak but unmistakable hand-squeeze.

"Holling, you motherfucker, Ralphie was my friend.

"And when you get to hell, tell them 'Charley Horse sent me'."

Chapter 26

The fair opens

Opening night at major book fairs can be an elegant event and tickets to the opening are often quite expensive. There usually is a good crowd waiting to get first dibs on scarce or unusual items and these opening-night visitors, many of whom are repeat customers, will often spring for expensive items. This night was no different. I sold a nice Bordone *Isolario* and a not-so-nice Waldseemüller *Ptolemy*.

The usual tire-kickers also came by and either fingered the stock without knowing what it was or asked inane questions. Looking numbly at our maps and atlases, they would query, "Do you have autographs?" or "Any Ernest Hemingway?"

During all this, one of us always kept an eye on Oufle's booth. He did a brisk trade but the one client we were looking for did not show up. From that standpoint, opening night was a bust.

Just before closing, I saw a tall, slender woman walk across the aisle a few booths away from us. "Lo Ban!" I hissed. "It's Willow! Here at the fair!"

"Unreal." Lo Ban didn't say more.

The next day was busy. The fair was well attended and we had to deal with throngs of visitors. Fortunately there were four of us in attendance and we were, working together, able to cope with the crush in our booth. As the day wore on, it became clear we had not brought enough stock and toward the end of that first day, all of our better items had sold. Our shelves were looking edentulous.

And still no Morgagni. I don't know if we were discouraged or relieved. It wasn't clear what we would do if Morgagni did show up. I think we were most likely to confront him, but after that, what?

"Manasek!" I turned around at the sound of the familiar voice.

"Crummy!" I responded.

Ted "Crummy" Martin smiled broadly as he came over to our booth. "Hoping to see you here. Here on book business or are you up to some of your old tricks? How've you been?"

"Never better, Crummy. And you?" I walked Crummy into the booth to introduce him to Maria and Amanda. Lo Ban, whom he knew well, was out of the booth at the moment. Crummy's genuine, infectious smile charmed both Amanda and Maria. He wore his age and his well-tailored suits well. With only a hint of slowness, he eased his frame into a chair, but I noticed that he seemed to need the rest.

I first met Crummy years ago at a dinner party in Oxford. Americans, Crummy and his wife, Bo, were visiting England and having great fun driving around in their newly bought right-hand drive Triumph TR-3. We struck up a friendship that lasted some 30 years. Crummy and Bo were older than I, but we had much the same sense of humor and over the years shared many of the same friends. We saw each other several times a year, generally over a dinner in some foreign city. Crummy and Bo traveled a lot and our paths often intersected. Seeing them for short periods of time over several decades had the effect of a time-lapse motion picture or a sped-up video, with age on the fast track. Bo had died a few years earlier and Crummy took it very hard. They'd had a great life together and now Crummy was alone.

"Finding any good books?" Crummy was not carrying any purchases, but it was also possible that he had bought some items and left them with the various dealers to be collected later or shipped to him directly after the fair.

"And what do you collect?" asked Amanda.

"Military stuff. Books about cannons, artillery, early rangefinding instruments, books by the early mathematical practitioners. Sometimes I even manage to buy something from these guys," pointing to me, but clearly meaning to include the absent Lo Ban, "but their prices are too steep for me. Ha-ha. But I already got a few choice items at this fair. I just bought a *De Re Metallica* from Jeffery Mancevice. And this—he pulled a small folder from his pocket—'a spotter guide.'"

Crummy was more of an eclectic collector than he liked to admit.

Crummy withdrew a small chart from the folder and showed it to us. The chart contained several small black silhouettes of WWII-period Japanese airplanes. It was used to identify airplane type. Each airplane has its own characteristic performance and in air-to-air combat it is helpful to know what aircraft one is up against. That way one can plan, at least to some extent, tactics.

Crummy pointed to the silhouette of a Japanese Zeke. "Haven't seen that outline since Pearl Harbor. It's as fresh in my memory as though it was yesterday."

"Pearl Harbor?" Maria asked the leading question.

"Turning point. Turning points are wild cards that disrupt existing order and forever change things. Pearl Harbor and the years following the war were turning points for me and my life and all my friends and their lives as well. And it started in a bizarre way." Crummy was settling in to one of his famous stories.

"My old pal Billy McAllister, my wife, Bo, and Billy's wife, Lee, and I were in Hawaii in '41. We were there to play. Of course there was already war in Europe, but we could still play.

"Billy was a specialty steel guy—he manufactured special alloys—and I was involved with a lot of other stuff at the time. Billy's family maintained an apartment in Honolulu and we all took the Clipper to spend some time playing. The apartment was a nice one—a penthouse with a very nice roof garden, all terraced, with big planters filled with attractive plants. We were all looking forward to a nice time.

"All the men in Billy's family were avid sportsmen. Especially shooters. His father, Wills, had gone on safari many times and was known to be fearless facing dangerous game. He had the fiercest Cape Buffalo I've ever seen on his library wall. Wills had shot it with a .375—a real "pop-gun" when it comes to these beasts. You can put a slug right into their engine-room—it won't stop them unless you're lucky and using at least a .416 or .450. Anyway, the old bull was off into the bush and Wills reloads his H&H double rifle and goes in after it before his WH catches up. The bull ambushes Wills who goes down but while he's falling put both barrels into the buffalo's head. Bull and Wills wind up in a heap, Wills slightly gored but smiling like an idiot. They needed two lads to pull the bull off him.

"The Honolulu apartment had a large gun cabinet with several fine London double barrel 12 gauge shotguns, a couple of .410s and some rifles, including a Sauer double rifle—.416 Rigby I believe. We had planned to use the shotguns when we went shooting later in the week.

"Anyway, it was that fateful Sunday morning. We were out on the terrace having Bloody Marys when it started. At first none of us knew what the hell was going on, but we soon saw the markings on the Japanese Zekes. As they made their runs on the harbor, they passed, in single file, at low altitude, quite close to our terrace. They were following sort of a flight pattern. We were, of course, stunned because we realized quite quickly what was going on. Suddenly Billy leaped up and shouted, "Let's get 'em." He ran inside and opened the gun cabinet. He grabbed the Sauer .416, a handful of shells, and ran back outside. The Zekes were still coming by.

"Billy, as I said was a sportsman. He had a great natural body action. His swing in golf was awesome, sort of classic Ben Hogan. His shooting was very fluid also. Everything was part of a single motion. I remember standing in awe of him as he stood on the rooftop terrace and started firing at the Zeke. It was as though he was birding. But he had the double rifle. Fine stance. Bam! Bam! A smooth reload and he took a lead on the next Zeke. Bam! And the pattern repeated.

"It was a futile gesture, but it was also noble. The rest of us ran inside and took out some 12-gauge shotguns. I passed around boxes of slugs and we too went outside. By now the harbor was ablaze and our apartment seemed to be the turning point for more Japanese planes making their runs on the ships sitting in the bay.

"Then there was this one pilot. He sees us. He probably can't believe what he sees, but he's flying slow and close, and one of Billy's bullets must have hit him. The guy breaks out of his pattern, does a hammerhead and comes at us. We actually get strafed! Planters go flying, we hide behind a terrace wall. Real Smilin' Jack stuff. The pilot must be really pissed because he decides to hit us again. I wonder what his superiors would have done to him had he made it back. At the end of his first run he does another hammerhead to set himself up for another run on us. Sort of like a crop duster at the end of a row of cotton.

"But he's vulnerable for a moment when he's hanging almost stationary in the hammerhead. We collect our senses and the guy sucks up six barrels of shotgun slugs and a couple of rounds from Billy. Bye-bye Zeke. No smoky trail, no spiral or spin in, the guy just stops flying and falls.

"For the next 10 or so minutes we're out there, as though we're on the fantail of a cruise ship shooting clay pigeons. No more Zekes to our credit, but a lot of shells used up. Shooting slugs out of a London Best makes me cringe, even today, but none of us thought about it at the time. And remarkably none of the shotguns got ruined.

"After it's over, we go inside and the apartment is a mess. Broken windows, glass all over, bullet holes in the walls. We put away the guns and refill the Bloody Marys.

"Of course all is chaos after the attack. We spend the next few days boarding up the apartment and arranging travel back to the mainland. Billy goes to the naval base and tells them about our adventure. They haven't really got the time to spend on it but they know Billy, or know of his steel company, and they do send a young lieutenant over. We show him the apartment and the shot-up terrace and he sees all the empty shells still out there. I think he believed us but nothing ever came of it. Can't say I blame them.

"But that was our last adventure together. And it was the end of our salad days forever. In a couple of weeks we get space on a ship back to the mainland. Billy goes to Ohio where he manufactures special steel and jumps full-bore into the war effort. The military needs it real bad. His firm does better than ever and at war's end he has enormous wealth, much more than before.

Then, shortly after the war is over, tragedy hits them. Lee dies of leukemia. Completely untreatable in those days.

"A year or so later, Billy makes a really bad decision. He marries one of the Henle women, gal by the name of Angela, but better known as Loopie. Tall and thin, she's a couple of years, maybe three, older than Billy. She's a real pisser. Loopie and Bo never did get along and I didn't care for her company either. Our friendship with Billy gradually dies. No single reason. It just does. I think the fact that the whole world changing so quickly was as much a reason as Loopie. Billy couldn't cope with all the changes and he suicided. Possibly Loopie helped him with that decision. I don't know. I never saw her again after the memorial service.

"But the suicide always bothered me. I still can see him standing on the terrace, in perfect shooting style, throwing shots at the Japs. That's my forever image of Billy. His son, by Lee, moved to South America. Bolivia. Married a tin heiress. Drank himself to death after they nationalized the tin mines. She had also had some affair with some German guy—I don't know his name—maybe a Nazi. Who knew?

"As I say, the world just became different."

Lo Ban had returned, did not interrupt, but stood smiling as Crummy reminisced. Crummy noticed Lo Ban and the two shook hands wordlessly, both smiling. Crummy did not get up for the handshake. Clearly he was feeling his age a bit.

We had all been engrossed in Crummy's tale and neglected to keep our watch on Oufle's booth.

Crummy was the first to notice.

"Say, Manasek, that chappie over there,"—he pointed toward's Oufle's booth—"I'd say he's a strange one. Keeps looking at his book and then over this way. Is he a lad you're looking for? Or is he a lad looking for you?"

It was Morgagni.

Chapter 27

We meet at last

Maria chambered a round in her .25, Amanda did likewise in her .22 and I in my .32. That sound was to me then, and always was and always will be, a most satisfying one. It is not just a sound, but a sound-action-mechanical-psychological process all tied together. Sometimes, with a promise of things to come. One can feel the sound as well as hear it. It can bring death, resolution, mayhem. Victory or defeat. It indeed is a promise of future events, but doesn't even give the slightest glimpse of a forecast. I welcomed it like an old friend. And that was a bit scary.

Crummy saw what we were doing and did not seem surprised or alarmed. "Thought so," he said.

Saperstein, who was standing near our booth, had heard the sound also. He looked at us, then fled down a corridor.

Lo Ban, Maria, Amanda, and I walked slowly over to Oufle's booth. We looked at displays along the way, hoping that we didn't stand out too much and that we passed for just another group of tire-kickers.

Morgagni was leaning against a column. Clearly he needed the column for support as he perused one of Oufle's volumes.

He looked up at us. "I assume you are the people who are looking for me." He was a cool character.

"And you for us." Amanda smiled her words but there was little amusement in her smile.

"We will have coffee together now. All of us." Lo Ban spoke very softly. He again used the tone of voice that made the hairs rise on people's necks. Oufle shuddered and backed away. Morgagni put down the book and stood back from the column. He swayed slightly.

"Very well. You will not shoot me."

"Not here." Lo Ban's voice had not changed.

Oufle's face played a panoply of emotions as we all walked away. He thought he was about to lose a customer. But he didn't want to be involved with any violence. Lo Ban's reputation was the subject of much fantasy within the rare book world.

We went over to the café section of the fair. It was crowded and all the tables were taken. I spotted Lope de Nada sitting alone at a table. He was drinking a Coke and eating potato chips. He had managed to spill half his Coke and the table was a mess.

"You will certainly let us sit here, won't you?"

Lope de Nada looked up, displaying the bits of chips and spittle in his moustache. "Oh, hi." His calf–like eyes searched our group for approval. Was this an invitation for him to join us?

"Thank you." In answer to his unspoken query, I added, "And, would you please fetch some napkins and clean up your spill before you leave?"

We sat down. Amanda was directly opposite Morgagni and made a point of letting him see her semiautomatic. I was next to her and Morgagni saw mine as well. The same with Lo Ban and the same with Maria. Maria had backed her chair away from the table a bit and was effectively, from a line of fire perspective, behind him. Much of this was, of course, for psychological reasons. We clearly didn't want a gunfight here at the book fair and Morgagni had to see that he had no chance if he started one.

Morgagni tried to seize the initiative. "Well, what do you fellows want? You've spent a lot of time tracking me down and now you've found me. So?"

Lo Ban drummed his fingers on the table. "You're a dead man, Morgagni. I don't know when or where, but you are dead. You fucked with us and you fucked with our friends. Don't forget, we know about Luther. And that's it."

Morgagni smiled. "I don't think you know what you're doing, but I advise you not to try some of your hard–ball with me. I have good people working for me and it is you who are now in trouble. All of you." He gestured dramatically and I noticed he was wearing a Yale class ring. His suit wasn't shiny.

"Sorry to rain on your parade, Morgagni, but this discussion isn't yours. We now tell you again. You are fucking dead. And we don't care about your 'people'. They're dead also." I was pissed. And yet there was something strange in Morgagni. He was breathing in a curious way—exhaling as though against resistance—sort of like trying to inflate a balloon. I looked at his eyes and saw a yellow hue.

I took a piece of notepaper and scribbled a few word on it. "Here, read this." I handed it to Morgagni but, deliberately, I didn't bring it close enough. Morgagni had to extend his arm to reach for it. I withdrew slightly and Morgagni instinctively extended his reach. I noted a slight up-down motion of his extended hand. A slight flapping-like movement.

"Well, Morgagni, I guess we won't need to shoot you after all. Something much better is doing the honors for us." I stared at him and smiled broadly. "And it isn't fast." I blew him a kiss, and signaling to my comrades the four of us walked away.

"Fuck you." Morgagni mouthed the words silently. Uncertainty and fear played over his face. He struggled to stand up and supported himself with both hands on the tabletop. Sweat was beading on his forehead. "Fuck you!" This time he shouted. "Fuck you!"

The cafe emptied out. In typical New York manner nobody wanted to know from nuttin' and it was deemed best to disappear and not become a witness to whatever was going on. The dealers in their booths, however, all stared and several came from other aisles and peered at the cafe area.

Morgagni straightened up, lifted his hands from the table and walked slowly away. Three men fell in behind him and one of them moved up next to him. Morgagni leaned on him as he shuffled away. I saw Willow following a bit behind them. She exchanged a few words with one of Morgagni's men, nodded, and walked briskly away.

Back in our booth we were the recipients of quite a few strange looks from the other exhibitors. But nobody queried us.

"What did you mean when you told Morgagni about something being much better?" Amanda was curious.

"Scleral icterus, liver flap, emphysema, maybe some more things I didn't pick up just by looking at him. His liver's shot. Lungs, too. He's not going to be walking around very much longer. Then the long slow death. If he's lucky he might have a massive hemorrhage and die in his sleep but he most likely will die gasping for breath. If the liver disease doesn't get him first. And he knows it and he knows that I know it. Hence the 'Fuck you'."

"So let's not shoot him. This is better." Amanda's face was grim. We were all silent for a while. "But I still would like to know where he lives. Just in case."

"I think we need to think this over. It might be prudent to cause him to be gone. More certain than letting nature take him. We need to be sure." Maria was pressing hard for the kill. "Let's plan how to do it as soon as possible."

"Morgagni is walking dead, Maria. I'm concerned now about Willow. It isn't making sense. Willow runs in important circles and Morgagni is a pervert. Of course, that's not to say that no important people are perverts but generally not in the style of Morgagni."

"Willow is up to something. And here she comes."

Willow strode towards us but when she saw me rise she turned quickly and headed down another aisle.

"Shit!" Maria had seen her also. "What's that all about?"

I sprang up. "This one's on me." Ducking behind the wall of drapery, I ran around the perimeter of the fair to the exit leading out to Park Avenue. Willow was just walking past the security guard.

I walked out behind her. She didn't see me. At least until she felt my .32 in her side.

"This way, Willow." I steered her down a darkened corridor, down to the side of the old Armory, the old campaign flags hanging lifelessly above us in the gloom. There was a door partly open. I pushed it open all the way and saw a small conference room. A quick shove and Willow was inside, against the wall. I was next to her, one foot on top of her left shoe and my gun now in her throat. I could send her sprawling or I could kill her. "OK, Willow." I tried to be as calm as I could. "What the hell's going on?"

The gloom of the unlit conference room did not obscure her beauty—she was as exotic as ever. And cool.

"Hello, Frank."

"Sorry, Willow. No friendly chit-chat. An answer. What's coming down?"

"You always were a cocky bastard, Frank. You know what, Frank? I am not your enemy and never have been. I am not your enemy and Rodney isn't either. You and your gang don't get it."

"I don't have a 'gang,' Willow. And right now I'm very sensitive about being followed or stalked or whatever."

"Put your stupid gun away, Frank. This isn't about you. At least not any more. Morgagni's garbage, we both know that. Why, he'd go so far as to kill someone's dog."

"What the hell are you saying, Willow?" I lowered my gun.

Willow started to speak. "Morgagni is your man, Frank, he's the one but he's not the head honcho. We know about your dog and we know about Red."

"What about Red?"

"He's been losing men, Frank. Morgagni isn't doing it but he's part of the whole damn mess. This is much bigger than your group can imagine. And, by the way, Red is alive and well."

At that moment the door opened. It was security.

Willow quickly put her arm around me and leaned into me.

"This area is closed. What are you doing here?"

Willow snuggled close and I leaned over. The guard smiled but told us to clear out. "Not here, you two. Go to a hotel."

We walked hand-in-hand back along the corridor. I was impressed by how quickly Willow had covered.

The armory corridor had several dark oak benches lining one wall. Dim torchieres on the wall made the yellow-brown walls appear darker than they were and barely cast shadows from the faded, tattered battle flags that punctuated the long wall. Willow drew me to a bench and we sat down.

"Frank, you've been a good soldier and everyone knows and supports wht you've done over the years. I think most people believe that none other than you and your group could have helped our cause as brilliantly. And I'm not just saying that."

"Willow, to put it mildly, who the fuck are you?"

Willow smiled a friendly smile. "I'm really your friend and I suppose you just have to believe me on that one. Despite your activity over the years you really only know a very circumscribed part of what's going on. And keeping it that way was deliberate. You stood a good chance of getting killed or caught and it was a lot better if your group was an isolated cell with no tangents to any others."

I nodded, It made sense and we always knew that we were only part of the picture.

Willow stretched her legs and continued. "Frank, it's huge. It involves Khmer Rouge groups that have survived and have never lost their ideology, it involves perverts like Morgagni, and it involves several foreign governments that need to keep the background churning. We've known how you tracked down Morgagni and the FBI doesn't even know we know. That was good, Frank. A very good piece of work.

"I began to tell you about Red. He needed help and we approved his request to see you. Advice? I don't think you should buy into this one, Frank. There's a time to hang it up and in our work loyalties sometimes get stretched over the years."

"What are you saying, Willow? We have loyalty problems?"

Willow looked at me for a few moments and didn't say anything. I heard anyway and let it go. She wasn't going to tell me more anyway. And I didn't want to hear an outsider sowing discord.

"Red, as I said, is alive. And it was Morgagni who had you tailed and had your dog shot. We know that. Morgagni's usefulness to the other side is largely over; there's only so long a defective like he can be managed. We'll leave him to you."

"Thanks," I thought.

"Frank, lay low. Take a holiday. Istanbul is safe for you. Or go shooting in Scotland. Get domesticated again, Frank, and leave this behind."

196

We stood up. Willow hugged me and gave me a sort of sisterly kiss on my cheek.

"I wish we had been able to get to know each other better."

I nodded agreement as we approached the armory's exit to Park Avenue and paused.

"Watch out for yourself, Frank." With that she let go of my hand and ducked outside.

My exhibitor's badge let me go back into the fair without waiting on line, and I walked pensively back to our booth. A customer was browsing Lo Ban's inventory and Maria and Amanda were quietly talking. They paid no attention as I entered the booth and sat down.

Lo Ban's browser soon left, not buying anything.

Amanda turned to me. "Did you find out what she wanted?"

"Nope. But she knows about my dog and also about Red's problems." I was going to add "and I copped a feel," but thought better of it.

"At least Willow told me she knew about my dog. That was Morgagni's doing, too. The guy must have gotten very close to us and we didn't even know it. Or maybe it was Red he was getting close to."

The other stuff Willow told me was going to have to wait.

We were interrupted. Saperstein stopped by our booth. "Are you guys alone?

"Please, don't do anything to ruin my last fair. C'mon, guys. Please. This is it—my last fair. Ever. No more promoting goddamn book fairs that guys like you turn into the Biograph."

"Let's do a deal. Saperstein, you got a list of everyone who bought a ticket to this fair?"

"Yes."

"Well, we want to see it. I assume the entries were made as received and I want to look at the list in chronological order of receipt. I promise we won't 'ruin' your fair, Saperstein."

"Deal."

We went into his office and I sat down at his computer. If Morgagni had bought a bunch of tickets for his associates, as well as for himself, they would probably have been bought all at once, and would appear close together in Saperstein's database. Unfortunately, there was no ticket listed in Morgagni's name. I tried variants such as "Norgagni" and other spellings that were minor enough to ensure postal delivery of tickets, but enough different to be able to hide in a computer database. No luck.

Reluctantly, Lo Ban and I decided to ask Oufle for Morgagni's address. It would have been easier if we could leave Rodney out of this, but we had no choice. We found Oufle in his booth, looking at his receipt book, and approached him gingerly. I hoped his receipts had been good so that his humor would be also. He looked up at us and smiled. Evidently his sales were meeting expectations.

"Please don't tell me what's going on. If I don't know, nobody can make me tell. I don't want to be caught up in some wild scheme of yours." Oufle was being very up-front about it. He clearly was not involved in any of Morgagni's activities, but knew something big was underway. I had always been a bit leery of Oufle—his travels overlapped mine to an extent that should not have been chance alone. His recent appearance in Istanbul and then in Nierenstein were the two latest examples. Whatever he was up to, I'd like to know, but it probably didn't involve our present operation and we were too far into that to get diverted.

"Morgagni. What's his address?" No point in beating around the bush. Rodney already knew that.

"I thought that was it. Kinda suspected that was what you wanted." Oufle slid a 3x5 index card across the counter. I glanced at it briefly and put it into my pocket.

We packed up our booth quickly when the fair ended. The last straggling customers had not yet cleared the exits and we were ready to go. It was easy for us to pack up the few books and maps and hand-carry the cases out to the van. When we were in front of our hotel, we reversed the process, and had the bellboy take the cases inside and the parking valet take the van.

Lo Ban and Amanda, and Maria and I had adjacent suites and we had been able to have the connecting door opened. We engaged in the usual end-of-fair post-mortems. Lo Ban had brought along a small bottle of Johnnie Walker and we sat back, feet up, and sipped that delicious liquid. It was worth falling off the wagon.

"Not a bad take for three days work." Lo Ban leafed through his sales receipts. My own sales were in the mid six figures, not a record, but a pretty good fair. I was pleased.

And then there was the business of Willow. I filled in Lo Ban, telling him what Willow had told me.

"I still don't know. Have no idea what Willow was up to—for that matter I still have no idea what she's been up to for the past decades. She's really an insider in the covert world, that is certain. She knows about Morgagni and Blaser and tells me she knows about Red's problem.

"And Willow was not low on the totem pole. Why would she be doing fieldwork herself?"

"Damned if I know. Was it her whim? I don't think we ever did an operation that involved her in any way. Unless maybe this one. But I still don't even know what this one is really about. Morgagni, Mehmet, Willow…are they connected? And Rodney…" The whole thing was puzzling. And very disturbing. "Lo Ban, I stuck a gun to Willow. Because she happened to be there. I feel like I'm chasing the dragon.

"And Willow was telling me that we needed to retire. And implied a problem within our group. And she's right in a way. There is only so much that one can take over a long period without burning out. Or changing within ourselves."

"What you mean is what has happened to us all…or to you…? This whole thing, beginning with Amanda and Hong Kong is doing a job on all of us. We need to resolve it or…"

"It could spiral out of control?" I was pensive. "I have a feeling that there is another layer to all this—it isn't just Morgagni. Too much weird stuff. Too many loose ends. Willow told me as much. Khmer Rouge," for example. I think I want out, Lo Ban."

Lo Ban didn't acknowledge my last statement but simply said, "Loose ends, such as Elizabeth."

As soon as Lo Ban said this, it was clear he had second thoughts. We all let it pass. But I felt my stress level ratchet up a notch or two. Lo Ban was looking at Maria.

"And then, there's the big enchilada." Maria said slowly, bringing us back. "We tracked him down, finally."

"I'm not sure if we tracked him down or if we just stumbled on him." Amanda wore a puzzled look. "I think it was more luck than great planning."

"Come on, Amanda, don't beat yourself up. We needed a win and one finally came our way. I don't care if it was luck or our genius. I'd like to believe it was the latter—don't forget we exhibited at this fair hoping to find him. We now know where the bastard is. We're better off than we were a month ago. Besides, Willow seems to have followed our progress and she didn't think it was simply fortuitous."

"What we have is an address from Oufle. We don't yet really know where Morgagni is. He might be in the Beinecke, hiding in the air conditioning ducts." Lo Ban sounded testy. "Let's figure out how we check this out and what we do next."

Oufle's address did indeed check out. Amanda rented a car and parked it down the street from the address Oufle had given us. The building was a large, well-restored brownstone on West 81st St. Gentrification had turned his block into a quiet street of beautifully restored houses, debris-free sidewalks and shade trees that were no longer scarred¬-bark saplings growing in scruffy patches of earth punctating the sidewalks.

Amanda had put on a wig, lots of bright red lipstick, and she now sat in her car filing away at the fake long red nails she had glued on earlier that morning. Even if Morgagni spotted her, it was unlikely that she would arouse his suspicions. She did, though, arouse the interests of several male passersby, one of whom tapped lightly at her window. He was quickly dissuaded from expressing further interest.

The wait was a long one, but successful. Late in the afternoon Amanda spotted Morgagni slowly emerging from the front door. He had two men with him and it was soon evident what their function was. They had to help Morgagni down the stairs to the sidewalk. Once on level ground he was steady enough to walk, but he seemed either too weak or unstable on his feet to negotiate the stairs. Even on level ground, he walked slowly and had a curious posture, as though walking into the wind. He lifted each leg in a choppy manner as though he was beginning a goose-step. His two helpers fell back and followed him at a discreet distance. They were bodyguards as well.

Amanda started her engine and pulled out of her parking space. One of the bodyguards looked at her briefly but she made no eye contact and the connection remained casual. It was evident that Morgagni had not put his troops on high alert. Which was curious, because he surely knew that by now we would have gotten his address and would probably be coming for him.

The small group, led by Morgagni, walked slowly down the sidewalk. It had a processional, a near-ecclesiastical appearance, a slow, almost dignified line of men, in hierarchical order, led by an elderly man who rolled a bit as he walked. Lucifer and his host. Amanda watched intently as it neared the museum. Turning north, it continued for a block, crossed 80th Street, and entered Rudley's, a small luncheonette on the northwest corner of 80th and Central Park West. Rudley's appeared to be a typical small neighborhood lunch counter with a few booths. Amanda continued her stakeout and in about an hour Morgagni and his group emerged, and began retracing their steps, heading home.

When they were about half a block away, Amanda left her car and went into Rudley's, sat down at the counter and ordered coffee. The counterman ogled her and gave her, what he thought, a sly glance. He was about to proposition her.

She smiled at him. "The gentleman who was just in here with his friends—the older man—the guy who walks funny—is he a regular?"

"Yeah." The counterman tried to look important. "Comes in almost every day, same time, sits in the same place." He pointed to a booth. "Eats the same thing. Soup, burger, fries. Salts hell out of everything. Never talks, just eats. He leaves a nice tip, but someone else pays the tab. Then they go. Know who he is?"

"No," said Amanda, "do you?"

"Naah. I thought maybe he might be mob, with all the goons he brings with him, but he ain't Eye–tie. Maybe some fruit?"

That, of course, would clarify everything.

Amanda returned to the hotel and waited for us. Dressed as she was, she received some curious looks from the front desk.

"Very strange," commented Lo Ban after Amanda had briefed us on her stakeout. "A sick man who hobbles out to the corner greasy spoon each day. Now, that's weird behavior. Make anything of it, Manasek?"

"It makes no sense on the surface. Presumably he still has money. At least enough to buy Oufle's books, and that has to be a lot of money going into discretionary purchases. He's a physical wreck—wonder if he's also drugging. Wouldn't be surprised. Might be syphilitic.

"Then again, he might really be collapsing from within. His debauchery, if you can even call it that, probably feeds upon itself. It cannot be satisfied no matter how much or how far he goes, and it only increases his hunger. He's a profoundly evil being, and he moves among the rest of the world freely. That contrast has to have an effect on him, or at least at some point in his life it did. Whatever moral fiber he might have had is gone—perhaps he never had any—no place to fall really, he was born fallen. Anyway, he's in a moral swamp, and although he walks among humans, he is not. I don't think he can have normal human intercourse—he communes only with his demons. There's no way for him out of his moral swamp and the Morgagni we see is truly rotted inside. First morally and second physically. But why the greasy spoon? Who knows? And I don't care.

"Just what are we really seeing when we see Morgagni? He has a human form, but just what is he? Not who, but 'what.' He's crepuscular and occupies some metaphorical part of space. Sunlight doesn't reach him.

"The other big question is what do we do? We can watch him spiral down until he implodes into a small pile of shit, or we can remove him."

There was an uncomfortable silence. No quick answers were offered.

"You sound like a bit of a theologian." Lo Ban took another sip of whiskey. "That was a Western view."

Somehow, I didn't think my last comment was particularly theological. "Then, give us the Eastern one."

Lo Ban didn't answer me.

"Let's go back home," suggested Maria. "I don't think we'll lose him. Then we can decide how to disappear him."

Maria's reference to my house as "home" made me fell good inside. But that feeling was countered just a bit. I think we had just tacitly agreed to ice Morgagni.

Amanda caught it, too. "I can see the argument for just letting him die of disease. It won't be long according to Frank. However, I would feel better if he died knowing he was being killed intentionally. Not quite sure why, but maybe it really is a form of justice I want—that it really isn't bloodlust. I hope to hell we haven't gone down that way. Killing might have gotten easier but that doesn't mean we should look forward to it. Are we really chasing a dragon, Frank?"

"I dunno," was all I could think to say. I thought about pressing my gun into Willow. And that was before I knew she had known about Red and Blaser.

But then, I *had* copped a feel.

Chapter 28

Home fires burning

A stack of mail was waiting for us when we returned to Vermont. Some for Lo Ban and Amanda had been sent on from Hong Kong. Maria had a few envelopes from Madrid, and my pile was divided about equally between business and personal. In the latter subset I found a letter from Charlotte.

I had, with some success, been trying not to think of her. Now a letter. Charlotte wrote that she was coming stateside for a while to work on a project with a colleague at Harvard. "Could (or should) we connect?" She hoped this letter would get to me in time. After finishing her work at Harvard, she planned to go to London for a longer stay, doing research at the University of London.

Charlotte's letter made me feel a bit wobbly and I put it down, not knowing how, or if, to respond. "I'll figure it out later," I rationalized as I slipped it back into the pile. I was glad, again, that I still belonged to the letter generation and that we didn't do everything by email. There is a measured pace by which human interactions go best, and email doesn't have the right beat.

"You look bothered—bad news?" Maria came up to me and put her arm around me. "Everything OK, Paco?"

"Oh, yeah." I hoped I sounded better to her than I did to me.

Maria gave me a quick hug and left me to my thoughts. I returned to my stack of mail.

After every book fair there is a flurry of after-fair business. Collectors who suffered fair-fright or sticker-shock while at the exhibit wondered if we still had the item they hadn't bought (generally not); offers to sell; orders changed. It took Lo Ban and me a week to sort it all out. In one sense, this was good—it gave us time to let the Morgagni issue percolate. Perhaps a solution would brew.

Evenings, we all discussed Morgagni and what to do about him. We had, essentially, two options only. First: do nothing and just check on him once in a while and sort of watch him die. Second option: kill him.

It would be easy enough to kill him. The technical side of assassinating the man would be straightforward. We had done it many times and this would be a cakewalk.

"Should we kill Morgagni? Even if he's a medical mess?"

"The Israelis kill aged, decrepit Nazis. Guys who would die naturally in a few years." Amanda had a point.

We sat and mused. Had he been in robust health and likely to inflict more torture on innocents I think there would have been no discussion other than "how." But Morgagni was now a pathetic creature. For some reason, that made a difference. So now, instead of acting, we punted. Even Maria, who earlier had wanted to kill him, was now silent on the matter.

She seemed preoccupied with some project. Maria had each day for the past few days borrowed my car to go to Dartmouth Medical School to use Dana Library. She didn't volunteer why, nor did we pry, but she returned each day with a determined look and an air of success. Once she asked me to confirm the identity of some mushrooms she had gathered.

Life had returned to its normal, slow pace. I wondered about Charlotte and we continued to try to decide about Morgagni. We had never been able to deal with Red's death. If, indeed he was dead. Willow had told me he was alive. But Red's Cessna was found nose-down at the end of an abandoned pasture near Gettysburg. He had been fishing and was returning home and never arrived at his home airport. The weather was fine; Red had not filed a flight plan and it was a few days before he was missed. And then a few more days before his plane was found. The crash had the appearance of an attempt to abort an emergency landing, but could not be explained by physical evidence. Investigators found fuel in the engine, the magnetos were working and Red was a safe, experienced pilot. He would not have botched a pasture landing in his 180. I remembered Red saying that the people he was losing had died in seemingly explainable ways, like a skydiving accident. But was Red dead? Or was Willow right? I fervently hoped the latter.

There was no body in the airplane. His daughter, Annie, had sounded upset but I wasn't convinced that she wasn't being theatrical. Maybe she knew something and was playing along. Sam about hung up on me when I telephoned him. "Fuck him" was his only coherent response. Something inside of Sam had gotten badly twisted and for a fleeting moment I hoped fervently that my old friend was indeed dead and rid of such an incredibly rotten offspring. But then I thought of Annie and I took it all back. Red had something to live for and I was going to suppose he had disappeared for a reason. And I silently thanked Willow for her news.

Lo Ban and I had to put Red's disappearance, on the back burner. This was a matter for another time.

But perhaps it was time again to check up on Morgagni and Maria volunteered to go to New York and do some reconnaissance. To make certain our man was still around and hadn't fled nor died.

"Give me a few days. I'll check him out and I also want to pamper myself and go hog wild in Bloomingdale's."

"Like me to come along? I can ogle you at Bloomie's."

"Paco," Maria pressed herself against me and hugged. "Paco, girl's night out. I need some downtime and do girl stuff."

I kissed her and, although I understood what she was saying, I didn't believe her.

For the next few days Maria seemed to be engrossed in her project that she still didn't share with me, or anyone else. Then she left for New York.

Maria decided to take Amtrak to the city and I drove her down to the train station in White River Junction. Surprisingly, the train arrived on time and we didn't have much chance to chat. A quick kiss and she jumped lightly onto the train. A backward glance, a silently mouthed "I love you," and Maria was gone.

Amanda, Lo Ban and I didn't have much of a dinner conversation that night. We all felt something was amiss, but none of us wanted to confront it. So we said nothing. The evening had turned a bit nippy and we lighted a small fire in the living room fireplace. The wood was nice and dry and the fire burned brightly, cheering us immeasurably.

We heard from Maria three days later. She had spotted Morgagni, he seemed no worse than the last time we saw him and, if anything, walked more strongly than before. He still went to Rudley's for a meal at the same time each day, which made it easy for Maria to keep tabs on him. Maria had, for the past two days, gotten a booth directly across the aisle from his regular place at Rudley's. She ordered, each time, coffee and a grilled cheese sandwich, ate slowly and read a New York Times to prolong the meal. Maria blended in, ignored Morgagni and was, in turn, ignored by him and his guards. She was just another customer.

"I'm having a nice time, Paco." Maria told me. "I miss you but I'm doing some serious damage at the shops to compensate! I'll be back in a couple of days and I'll ring you before I leave New York. Will you pick me up in White River?"

"Of course. Looking forward!"

The days passed slowly and I didn't mope about even though I certainly felt incomplete without Maria. I was also feeling guilty about ignoring Charlotte's note and I was also feeling guilty about Charlotte herself. I couldn't bring myself to write, knowing my note would pain her. In an attempt to delay the inevitable, I found all sorts of tasks, and dragged them out. I did my banking in town, then came home and then went back to Norwich to pick up my mail. One trip became two and that delayed for, another bit, writing Charlotte.

"A fax just came in for you," said Lo Ban.

"It's from Denny-Green," he added softly, as I took the curly sheet.

"Dear Frank. I've finished the P-M and I think it best if we speak in person. Can you possibly arrange to come here? I will move my schedule around to accommodate yours. Sincerely, Derek."

"Sounds ominous, doesn't it?"

Lo Ban nodded agreement. "Amanda and I will stay here and we can pick up Maria when she arrives. Denny-Green sounds as though you ought to get there ASAP. We'll also try to find out more about what, if anything Maria was up to with the mushroom stuff. She never before went out collecting by herself."

One quick fax to Derek filled him in on the situation and another one to the Oxford Club that would hopefully hold me a room.

On the bus to Boston, I penned a hasty note to Charlotte explaining that I was off to Oxford on urgent business. Perhaps she could fax me when she got to London and we could connect for a drink. I didn't know how long I'd be in Oxford, so I asked her to fax me in care of Linacre College. My old college was always willing to hold a fax or letter for me. Besides, if for some reason I had to remain in Oxford overnight, and the Parsonage didn't have space for me I would probably be staying in one of Linacre's guest rooms. I posted the note at Logan Airport and boarded the non-stop flight to London.

A wave of fatigue hit me when I landed in London and I fortunately had a place at the Club. I slept for 18 uninterrupted hours and felt quite refreshed when I went down to a large English breakfast at 8:00 the next morning.

Derek Denny-Green was not in when I telephoned his office later in the morning, but his secretary told me she was supposed to create a two–hour appointment with me for whenever I could get there. We settled for 10:00 a.m. the next day.

Thinking of Maria made me uncomfortable. "What the hell was she up to?" was the thought I could not shake. That, and my general anxiety regarding Denny-Green and Elizabeth made the day a somewhat miserable one. I frittered it away, took in the Turners at the Tate and looked at the new Islamic exhibit at the BM until closing time, then wandered about Bloomsbury a bit. Had the bar at the Montague been the least bit competent, I would have broken down and had a martini. But past experience taught me that no matter who the bartender, it was impossible to get a good martin at the Montague. Without directions I would get a glass of crap; with directions I got a hostile barman and a glass of crap. Instead, I slowly walked back to the club, down Charing Cross to Pall Mall and then just a few more blocks. Sleep was welcome.

The trip to Oxford was measured in unusually long hours and I was glad when the bus finally turned onto the High. I got off at Queen Street and walked north, through the winding way, to Wadham College and Sir Derek Denny-Green.

The small office he had commandeered for the meeting was sparsely furnished. A small table, a few lamps and two hardback chairs. Derek opened the door and showed me in. We sat down at opposite sides of the table and the old pathologist began.

"Glad you could come, Frank. I think this is important to deal with face-to-face and I wanted you to know first. Before Elizabeth's family. To put it bluntly, she was murdered."

I had expected this since getting Derek's fax. But still, the words hit me like missiles and I could barely speak. "How...?" I was croaking.

Derek raised a hand. "All in time. I examined the skeleton very carefully. There were several fractures consistent with her fall. I cannot say whether she was dead or alive at the time of impact, but she had been shot. Almost certainly before the fall."

"Shot?"

"I found a single, small-caliber bullet in the base of her skull. It had entered from behind and did not exit. Typical of small-caliber rounds. That's why they are favorites of assassins. Large-caliber rounds make a mess—they can explode the skull...ragged exit-wounds..."

Denny-Green stopped. "I'm sorry, Frank. I digress and there are places I shouldn't take this.

"In any event, the bullet came from behind and probably made her pitch forward, over the cliff."

"And her death definitely was not an accident.

"I weighed the bullet. It was deformed and badly oxidized. After all this time we can say very little about it, but we know approximately how much weight it should gain for each year buried. By subtraction, I can guess at the original size. I don't think it was a .22—I think it was a tad heavier."

"Point three–eight or three–two?"

"No, smaller. By quite a bit."

"But what about the odd-weight .22—such as those made by Aguilla?"

"Those fifty-grain bullets weren't being made then."

We talked a bit more about the evidence and Sir Derek showed me photographs and a good lateral skull X-ray. The former documented the visible damage to the skull and the latter, taken before the bullet was removed, showed it in situ. The entrance hole was obvious, as was the massive damage that resulted from the fall.

"Any chance you can determine the angle of entry and get some idea of the shooter's size?"

"Very difficult. I can only guess. I think, however, it would be consistent with the entry wound to suggest a shooter shorter than the victim. But don't forget, Elizabeth was a tall woman."

I sighed. I had heard enough.

"Her family...they need to know."

"Yes, Frank," said the pathologist, "her brother is out of the country and I have made an appointment for him to see me when he returns." That's why I hadn't gotten an answer to my fax.

"And, by the way, this is it." Derek took a pasteboard pillbox out of his side pocket and slid it open.

Nestled on a bed of cotton lay a small, corroded lump of lead.

Lo Ban had been right. And I, by refusing to accept the possibility that my Elizabeth had been murdered, had probably made it possible for her killer to escape forever. I was glad the truth was known, but profoundly sad that it was learned so late, and a dull, numbing ache entered me.

Sir Derek put his gnarled hand on mine and gently said, "Perhaps whoever did this will never be found out, but, at least Frank, it is good to know."

From Wadham to Linacre is a short walk and I ambled along, moving slowly behind a group of undergraduates who, secure in their immortality, were talking of their career plans. Indeed, life does go on.

Linacre's main building abuts a cricket field and a practice was going on. I stopped for a moment to look at that pastoral scene, so typically English, the England to which Elizabeth belonged and which belonged also to her and which she had lost to a little lump of lead that now sat in a pasteboard pillbox.

I checked with the porter's lodge and indeed a fax was waiting for me. I took it into the common room where the general hubbub was welcoming and I sat down in a well–worn, but comfortable, chair to read my message.

Charlotte had gotten my note the day before she left Harvard and she was now in London and would like to have a drink with me or maybe we could have lunch together. She appended a list of contact numbers.

The third number on her list worked and I was connected with Charlotte.

"Something's wrong, isn't it?" Charlotte sounded concerned.

"Yes, no, maybe, who knows? But stuff seems to be moving very fast. On all fronts. I'm glad we connected. I need to get back to the States as soon as possible. Are you free tomorrow?"

"Lunch OK? My treat?"

We agreed to meet at Virginia Woolf's, a café just a short walk from the University of London.

Charlotte had arranged for a secluded corner table and was there, waiting for me when I arrived. She smiled when she saw me, but it was a sad smile. It made me feel terrible all the more. Surely, she knew.

I have no memory of the food, other than it tasted like ashes. My mouth was dry and I was not hungry.

"You look like your puppy just got run over. Are you in trouble?" Charlotte tried to make light of it, but lightness failed and she backed off. "There really is trouble, isn't there?"

"Beyond my wildest nightmare. I'm flying back tomorrow morning, for whatever good that might do."

I then told Charlotte what I had just learned about Elizabeth's death. She listened raptly, pale, and a tear formed in each eye.

"I'm so sorry. It's horrible."

"And to make matters worse, we might have a rogue amongst us." Referring to Maria as a "rogue" tore at my insides. My pain increased.

"But," countered Charlotte, "your group is so small. How can that have happened? Don't you know each other too well for something like that? A rogue doesn't sound too good for someone in your business."

I sighed. I was unloading and I might as well go all the way. I filled Charlotte in on the events since we were in Istanbul. Including Maria.

"Maria and I go back a long time."

For a fleeting second, Charlotte looked stunned. "It's nice when something from long ago comes back again." There was pain in Charlotte's eyes.

"I've said something terrible. You and I go back much, much longer. I'm truly sorry." I put my hand on hers. Hers was cold and remained motionless.

"I know. Sometimes things go crazy and change so fast we can't keep up.

"Would you mind terribly if I stayed in touch with you? You sound as though you need a pal." Charlotte was struggling and there was a slight tremor to her voice, as well as to her lower lip.

It was my turn to sound tremulous. "I think I do and I'm glad it's you."

The absurd rhyme made us both smile, but, I'm certain my smile was as sad as hers.

"I'll send you my schedule—I'll be moving around the next few months—when you get back. Stay in touch. I'm a good listener." She pushed back from the table and we left Virginia Woolff's.

My good-bye hug from Charlotte was genuine, but sisterly. We walked away in opposite directions—she north to the University of London, and I to catch a taxi. I turned to look back at her and, at the same moment she turned to look back at me. She was just far enough away that I couldn't be certain, but I thought I saw tears running down her cheeks.

I spent part of the afternoon penning a note to Damon. Although I would ring him when he returned, I wanted to have my note waiting for him. Sir Derek would, of course, also telephone him.

But I thought it important that Damon learn from me that his sister had been murdered.

Chapter 29

La fin, le début

Maria was waiting for me when the bus from Logan Airport pulled up in front of the Hanover Inn.

She kissed me and said, quietly, "Paco, I'm so glad you're back." She sounded relieved.

I squeezed her hand. "This was a very, very tough trip."

She pulled into traffic and swung around the Green. We were heading home. "What did your pathologist friend say?"

"Let's get home. I'm very tired. Need a shower. Need a drink. There's a hell of a lot we need to go over."

Tired as I was, I noticed a dark green Toyota pull out of an angle-parking slot in front of Hopkins Center, pull an illegal U–turn and fall in behind us

"Is that a tail?" I asked Maria, "the green car behind us."

She looked into the mirror. "Shit! I saw it earlier but hoped I was wrong. Who the hell is it?" Maria was angry and was practically shouting. "Is this all starting up again?" She pounded the steering wheel in fury. "I want to get away from all this!"

"Probably can't anymore," I thought. I didn't ask more about the tail or the green Toyota. I also wanted an end to all this.

My grey house with the blue shutters waiting at the end of the driveway welcomed me. I felt I needed its refuge as never before.

Lo Ban and Amanda were out of sight and Maria and I went upstairs. As I leaned over to unpack my suitcase, I felt her arms around my waist, gently probing. I turned around and our embrace was hungry, almost harsh. Our lovemaking hard, and we sought each other out not to give but to take away.

Afterwards, we lay there silently, looking at each other. Crushing fatigue rolled over me and I closed my eyes and slept.

I tried not to think about the green Toyota when I drove into Norwich the next day to pick up my mail. Picking up mail at the post office is a daily social event in many small American towns. Taking trash to the dump is a social event also but not a daily one. The dump's only open two days a week.

I got into the short queue at the P.O. to trade the yellow notice I found in my post box for a package. Jorge Malcolm came up behind me.

"Hola, Francisco."

"Hola, Jorge. Qué pasa?"

"Nada."

We smiled at our ritual—we had greeted each other this way for the past 20 years. Jorge was a freelance chemist with a small but impressive basement laboratory. He did contract synthesis of small amounts of esoteric organic compounds for scientists or industry. Since he worked alone he wasn't subject to OSHA regulations and could use synthesis procedures that would give OSHA fits if done in a conventional industrial lab.

"I'm not going to ask why you wanted it, but I hope it was pure enough. It's a simple extraction and precipitation to get it to this stage but a bitch to get it much purer. Anyway, glad to do it for you."

I had no idea what Jorge was talking about.

Jorge looked puzzled. "The alpha-amanitin—Maria your girlfriend—she came over to my lab with a sackful of *Amanita verna*. Asked if I could do the prep for her. She had photocopied the procedure—it didn't take me but a couple of hours. Glad to do the favor."

The postal clerk handed me my package but I was too dazed to respond to her friendly banter.

I turned to leave and thought it best if I covered for Maria. Whatever she was up to needn't become a public issue. "Thanks, Jorge. Sorry for my confusion. Lots going on right now. I'll get back to you but I gotta run."

Jorge stood there, still with a puzzled look.

Fleeing the post office, I got home as fast as possible. Fortunately Lo Ban and Amanda were there.

"Listen to this—Maria had a supply of alpha-amanitin with her in New York."

"What the hell's alpha-amanitin?" Amanda frowned.

"It's a protein found in the mushroom *Amanita verna*. They grow like crazy around here. The protein is extremely toxic. Very nasty stuff. It blocks RNA synthesis and if you ingest it you die in a couple of weeks or so when you run out of RNA. There is no antidote. Horrible miserable death.

"Maria harvested a sack of them and had a friend of mine, an organic chemist, extract and partially purify the toxin. It's a fairly simple procedure and he was pleased to help. I've asked for his help with weird organics many times in the past and he didn't pry. Maria evidently read up on the procedure at the Med School library."

"I hope she didn't do what I think she did." Lo Ban was speaking very softly. We all sat down. Lo Ban shook his head slowly.

We were still sitting quietly when Maria came in.

A profound change had occurred in our group. We used to be very comfortable and easy with each other, the ease of decades of friendship, the ease of decades of trust, anticipating what others would say and laughing together about it. We could also act together as a well-disciplined team, sharing danger and its rewards. Now a sullen shadow was overhead, and spontaneity was gone. I think we all felt it and I wondered what was causing it. My friendly living room now held an ominous presence.

Struggling with myself, I forced the end of the silence. "Maria, Jorge told me you have alpha-amanitin. Why?"

Maria was defiant. "This isn't a court, Paco." Her voice was raspy and hostile.

"No, it isn't. But we are a team and we have been one for decades. Our lives have depended upon us acting as a team." Now it was Lo Ban's turn to sound hostile.

216

The teakettle whistled in the kitchen. Amanda, glad for the interruption, sprang up and tended to it, returning with a tray bearing four cups and a pot of hot tea, still steeping.

"Jorge is my friend and believed I wanted the protein for some reason." I tried to sound offended as I waited for my tea to cool.

"Maria, did you use it to kill Morgagni?" Lo Ban barely whispered the question.

Defiant Maria. "You're goddamn right I did. I was in the booth across from his in the diner in New York and asked to use his salt shaker. I had taken the one from my table, dumped out some of the salt and replaced it with Jorge's alpha-amanitin.

"Can I use your salt, please?" That's all I said. One of Morgagni's goons put his shaker on my table and ignored me. I salted my sandwich and returned the one laced with alpha-amanitin to his table.

"'Thanks,' I said.

"I then outwaited Morgagni's group. Lots of coffee, two desserts, re-read the Times, etc. Morgagni finally left and I re-switched shakers. I took the poisoned one away with me.

"Nobody else was hurt. A perfect hit."

Maria's eyes flashed anger and triumph. She exuded confidence and power.

I had never seen her like this. There was a ferocity that I could not suspect in her. Maria—my Maria—kind, sweet and gentle—my lover and friend. Baffled and uncertain I stayed quiet.

"We don't do individual hits." Amanda sounded very sad.

"Bullshit! What about Hollis?" Maria sounded ferocious—she spat out the words. "Disappear the bastard and the world's a better place."

"So Morgagni's dead now?" Lo Ban's question seemed to stop, for a moment, Maria's descent to another level.

"Probably not." I ticked off the days. "He's probably really sick now but won't die for another few days. It's unlikely that he'll be diagnosed, and even if they do figure it out, nothing can be done to reverse the poison. It's all over for him."

"No apologies." Maria was adamant.

Lo Ban and Amanda looked fatigued. I certainly was drained.

"Tell us about Elizabeth." It was a statement, but Lo Ban made it sound as though a response was optional.

"Derek found the bullet. She was murdered." I said no more. But I felt worse than before and the whole mood in the room darkened.

Amanda shuddered. "Who?" She mouthed silently, "Why?"

"It must have been Morgagni, don't you think?" Maria made the point emphatically. "Or one of his goons?"

"Any way to identify the bullet?"

"No, Lo Ban, it was too badly oxidized. Just a misshapen piece of oxidized lead. Derek was able to determine caliber—or at least bracket it. It was small caliber—bigger than .22 and smaller than .38."

"Nine millimeter?"

"No, closer to .22 caliber."

"Point two-five?" Lo Ban honed in.

"Possibly, but Sir Derek can't be certain."

"Do you believe him? I heard he might be senile."

"If that's senility, then I look forward to it."

"But who killed her and why? How do we find out? Obviously our Group needs to deal with this—this cannot be allowed to happen to one of ours." Amanda spoke with finality. "But what do we do?"

"Do? What the hell is there to do?" Maria, seeming to be on the verge of exploding got up, took her purse and walked out. She turned as she left the living room. "I love you, Paco."

Somehow, it didn't sound right.

We heard the outside door open and then close. Maria was gone.

Lo Ban took command.

"Amanda, why don't you and Manasek go into the office? I'll deal with Maria. I think I should."

Lo Ban left the room.

I was still sitting there—stuck to the chair in a stupor. Amanda took my hand and as though I was her child, helped me stand up and led me outside and into my little office building.

"Amanda...Amanda...you don't think Maria..." I couldn't finish the sentence. I had always thought of myself as tough. A hard-core guy. Now I was trembling.

"She loves you, Frank. I see it. I see it as a woman can see it. She loves you, but I think too much."

Just then the fax machine rang and answered. The curling sheet of paper began to emerge. It had a red stripe down the left side. "Gotta change the roll, " I thought as the text began to appear. Anything to delay thinking about what was happening.

The fax was from Charlotte. She was sending me her schedule along with contact phone numbers. A short handwritten message was appended. "Hello from Osman Bey. He wishes you well. Keep in touch. Remember, I'm a good listener and have big (well, sort of) shoulders. And, I'm your pal."

"For you?" asked Amanda.

I was choking up. Not trusting my speech, I simply nodded.

At that moment, Amanda and I heard a faint sound. Faint, but unmistakable. We both had heard enough sounds like this one to know it was a shot. I wanted to go outside, but Amanda held me back.

"Wait." that was all she said, but she kept my arm tightly in her grip.

A few minutes later, Lo Ban came in.

"Why don't you, " he said to Amanda, "take Manasek into town. A good whiskey is in order." He followed this with a short burst of Chinese. I was startled. In all the years I've known Lo Ban he never, in front of me, spoke Chinese to an English-speaking person. Now, for some reason, he made the exception.

Lo Ban turned to me. "Please go with Amanda. It's all over and I will take care of things here. The police will come and you needn't be here."

Lo Ban. My friend. My comrade. But most of all, my friend.

I trusted him.

I left with Amanda.

But, before I left, I tore off Charlotte's fax and stuffed it into my pocket.

I needed my pal.

Nina B Jaffe was the copy-editor.

The text was set in Adobe Caslon type.

Cover design: Carrie Fradkin